IT'S HELL TO CHOOSE

The Kurtherian Gambit 09

MICHAEL ANDERLE

COPYRIGHT

DEDICATION

To Stephen Russell
May you recuperate
quickly and
not lose
your mind as you
get better!

GET WELL SOON

**It's Hell to Choose - The Kurtherian Gambit 09
Street Team**

*Bree Buras
Tom Dickerson
Dorene Johnson
Lisa Mitchell
Heather Paul
Scott Paul
Diane Velasquez*

Editor

Ellen Campbell

**Thank you to the following Special Consultants
for It's Hell to Choose**

**Jeff Morris - Asst Professor Cyber-Warfare
Stephen Russell - Ideas & Suggestions**

CHAPTER ONE

PARIS, FRANCE

If they don't stop aiming cameras at me, I'm not going to be responsible for the damages." Bethany Anne murmured to Michael under her breath.

The two of them were walking along Avenue de Champs-Elysees after taking a stroll through Bethany Anne's Mecca—the Christian Louboutin St Honore' store on Rue du Faubourg Saint-Honore'. They were standing in the line waiting to enter the store like everyone else when a few of those waiting realized who she was. A couple of covert phone camera pictures were taken and then the social sphere got busy. A couple of camera 'journalists' from the gossip magazines came in and started taking pictures, some annoyingly so.

Michael noticed that a few were taking shots from an incredible distance using very long telephoto lenses. He pulled out his phone and typed a note to Tabitha and put it away.

He would have a report from her within the next few

hours he suspected, certainly by tomorrow. If there was something to hack and delete, he felt comfortable it would be gone.

If not, he would know more.

Within a few minutes, the manager of the store came around the corner and up to them. He discreetly tried to ask Bethany Anne to step ahead of everyone and come inside.

She absolutely refused, which frustrated the store's manager. Finally, security got involved and explained to Bethany Anne she was causing a security issue with the traffic and unexpected paparazzi taking pictures outside on the sidewalk.

Waving the manager closer, she pursed her lips and whispered into his ear. The manager nodded once and then walked away to disappear into the store for a minute.

Michael smiled to himself as he continued his visual scan. Eric and John were each half a block away, also keeping their eyes out, but knew that Michael would die before allowing anyone to get to Bethany Anne.

That was good enough for them.

A moment later, the manager stepped out of the store and started handing unique cards that were each signed by him to every one of the people in the line. He bypassed Bethany Anne and continued down the line. When he returned, he nodded to Bethany Anne and the two were taken inside.

Once this step was accomplished, the manager stepped back outside and explained to each of the customers these cards were good for the purchase of a pair of Christian Louboutin shoes. This was in appreciation for allowing Bethany Anne to step ahead of them, or they could surrender the cards for a $3,000 gift to three charities that helped the families of those hurt or killed in the recent terrorist attacks.

Michael didn't need any special abilities to hear the

raucous cheering going on when those in line found out they held a card for a pair of shoes in their hands.

He watched Bethany Anne, and the only reaction she had was a slight blush and ducking her head.

He knew at that moment that not only was she the right choice to help clean up the UnknownWorld, but she was also the right woman for him.

If he could just woo her.

———

SEATTLE, WASHINGTON, USA

"Are you telling me," a gruff voice shouted from the phone. "That we have unexplainable tech that can lift stuff up to the moon and God only knows what else and you brains over in R&D can't even tell me HOW?"

The five men flinched when they heard the slam of a hand on a desk erupt from the conference room speaker.

He continued berating them. "I just had an awful—no let me change that—a *scathing* conversation with a senior senator in charge of military appropriations. It becomes a pretty one-sided conversation when the CEO of a company the size of ours is not only caught unaware of new technology, but our radar emplacements and security satellites can't even spot the sons of bitches!"

"But sir!" Jeovanni "Jeo" Deteusche spoke up, "How are we supposed to detect a revolutionary new drive system or even detect these containers when they have a coating on them that reduces their radar signature to something the size…" Jeo had been ignoring his bosses' vigorous head shaking. Having been with the company for a little over a year, Jeo was fed up with the politics, the bullshit R&D priorities, and the snide comments from people who had been in the system for over a decade.

This company, he had decided, wasn't about protecting his country. It was about fleecing the people of the country out of their tax money to keep the conglomerate going. They used the constant threat of the Russians or Chinese coming up with new technology in order to maintain the influx of hand over fist budget money.

Jeo could imagine just how upset the senator had been when he had figured out, that despite the ludicrous amount of funding, their tech was officially second-class.

By a large margin.

Jeo had been sitting in this room with these other four scientists for the last half hour and had been fuming. He hadn't wanted to go into defense in the first place, but R&D positions in his specialty in advanced metals use and theoretical metal production in low gravity weren't something that too many companies were looking for.

Unfortunately, that meant that he had only a few job options despite coming out of one of the highest rated engineering universities. He could have stayed in academia and moved up the professorial track, but he wanted to apply the technology. Not just develop the concepts, sell the licensing, and move on.

He wanted to be a part of a team that was building the next stage of space exploration.

Two minutes ago, before he started what he knew would be his last conversation as an employee of this company, he placed a short phrase on his Twitter account. One that wasn't directly connected to him, so he had no idea how they had figured it out.

He shrugged mentally; it wasn't his to wonder why, but to just type out the twelve characters and then start the last hoo-rah he would accomplish as a member of the R&D team. He looked at his social account and smiled at the phrase. It said:

#WEWILLBUILD.

MOON BASE ONE

"Penn, do we have room up there for a few more containers?" a voice from the wall caught Michael Penn's attention.

Penn looked at the monitor where he saw Bobcat looking back. A grinning William and Marcus were peering over Bob-cat's shoulder into the video camera from over 200,000 miles away.

Damn. He was doomed. There could only be one reason those three individuals were grinning at him like three Cheshire Cats from their lair back on earth.

They were about to set him up.

Penn took a moment to compose his thoughts and finally replied, "Is it too late to resign?" Their raucous laughter and glee traveled through the Etheric link and out his speakers, echoing down the length of his container and clearly audible to everyone in the next container.

Coach stuck his head through the opening, and the move-ment caught Penn's attention. When he looked over, Coach asked, "What shit are we about to receive?" then finished his question with a grin. Penn noticed that ReaLea and Bree had their heads stuck out from behind Coach and were also smiling.

Penn rolled his eyes and turned back to Bobcat on screen. "I take it that's a no?"

"Well," Bobcat replied, "I suppose I could ask Coach to grab your stuff from your cubicle and show you the door."

Penn heard the snickers from his team. Penn retorted, "Damned difficult to walk back to Earth, you arse!" Bobcat smiled at him. "So, lay it on me. How many are we talking?" he asked.

"Oh, only about ten," Bobcat started, and Penn felt his tension begin to ease slightly, "… to the second power," Bobcat finished.

Even the Coach's crew didn't have a response to that. "You want us," Penn pointed to himself and the off screen group. "To pull together a hundred new containers up here?" Penn was trying to sound calm and collected and NOT allow the squeak that was threatening to call his manhood into question into his voice.

Bobcat looked over his shoulder as Marcus chimed in, "I was for sending up a hundred and thirty, but the General wants thirty for a base in Australia." Bobcat nodded as he turned back to the screen.

Penn answered, "Marcus, you are off my Christmas list this year." Marcus made a hurt face. "So, is there a reason we need to hide a hundred containers up here?"

This time, it was William who spoke. "Yeah, we need to get some of this off Earth. We should have enough people to help out. Well, twenty or so to put up there and ADAM is picking up chatter that we have some potential sticky-finger suggestions going on. Like major power players wanting to see what's up. Easier to move the candy jar than teaching the child he or she shouldn't get grabby."

Penn could feel three of his team come up behind him and the three faces on his screen turned to those people over his shoulder. "Hey guys!" Bobcat said, "Want some company?"

Bree responded, "Will you bring more coffee in one of them?"

"Coffee?" Marcus answered. "We just sent you twenty kilograms in a pod a couple of days ago."

"She's a hoarder of the stuff," Coach quipped. "She stores half and then eyes everyone who looks like they're putting too much into the pot."

Bree slugged Coach. "I'm not hoarding, you poor excuse for a coffee snob. I'm making sure that the coffee is kept fresh!"

The three men on the video watched the two verbally spar. Coach turned slightly towards the barista. "Those are vacuum sealed containers that you are keeping, might I add, in vacuum!"

Bree sniffed. "No rats."

ReaLea was smiling at them, a glint in her eye.

"How the hell," Coach began. "Are rats going to get up here?"

"Is it completely impossible, one hundred percent, that there are no rats in any of these containers?" she asked magnanimously.

Coach's mouth turned down into a slight frown. "It approaches it!"

"But, it ISN'T one hundred percent!" Her eyes stretched wide. "And where am I going to be if the precious stash of coffee is ruined? It isn't like there's a Starbucks around the corner out here!"

"It isn't like we can't send up another pod," Marcus began only to have Bree turn to the monitor and stick a finger out at him.

"If I wanted your take on how to help me with my post-apocalyptic coffee plan, I would have told you what to say."

She turned back to Coach ready to start again.

William leaned towards Marcus. "That lady needs her caffeine, I think."

Marcus nodded, too shocked to say anything.

Bobcat was beginning to understand how Jeffrey felt when the three of them wouldn't calm down. He looked at Penn, who shrugged in response.

ReaLea piped up from behind Penn, "Why don't we put them together up at L2?"

"What?" asked Bree, momentarily distracted from her coffee conversation with Coach.

"That's a good suggestion," agreed Marcus. "We can use the mitigated gravity situation at L2 and start creating a temporary space station with the containers."

"That's not a small moon," Bobcat quipped.

"It's a hundred cargo containers all jacked together," finished William. "I think we need to consider how best to connect them, using the existing brackets. Jeffrey wants them gone posthaste."

"Do they all have to be connected right now?" asked Penn.

"No," answered Bobcat. "But as soon as we have everything, we're delivering the first eighty to you. The following twenty will be along soon."

"When should we expect the first eighty?" Penn asked.

Bobcat looked over his shoulder to Marcus and raised an eyebrow. Marcus grimaced. "Like you don't already know the answer." Marcus looked at the screen and smiled. "In about half an hour or so."

That caused all four of the Moon Base One team listening in to stare at the screen like prospective parents who had just been told they were expecting quintuplets.

Bree whispered into the silence, "I'll get the coffee."

NEW YORK CITY, NY, USA

"I'm telling you, they have technology that they unquestionably need to provide to the world!" Johann Pecora spoke to the men and women in a sub-assembly for the Advancement of the Human Race. While it was a very auspicious sounding name, it held a group of individuals who focused on the advancement of a select group of companies—their members.

"This group, this TQB Enterprises, must have even more technologies if they can move shipping containers to the moon!" Johann continued.

There were sixteen people present. This room was in the basement of the Waldorf-Astoria. They used it whenever they needed to step away from the United Nations and meet offsite. It wouldn't be odd for any of them to have a meeting here individually, the choice of location was not something that would raise any red flags.

Sixteen nations were represented in the committee. These representatives were connected to some of the most powerful, or most influential, countries in the world. None of these people had direct personal power, but acted as behind the scenes movers and shakers focused on the interests of their respective countries.

"And how," Ms. Stephanie Lee asked, "do you intend to encourage them to supply what technologies they have?"

Johann considered the question. "What leverage do we hold?" he asked. "It isn't like this is the first time we've come up against an entity that wasn't already a member."

"That," Eugene Guarran said, "Might be true. However, we have never tried to go against this group."

Johann waved that away. "So what? We represent the combined might of twenty-two percent of the gross national product of the sixteen top countries in the world and their allies." He took a breath but Eugene cut him off.

"Did you do research on TQB?" he asked. "Just curious."

Johann shrugged. "I'll admit I did not. I've had to settle down three congressmen and one highly upset senator this weekend. I know that part of our ability to stay relevant in the short term for two of our requested projects is going to be dependent on our ability to, um, acquire access to this technology," he finished lamely.

Anna Elisabeth Hauser interjected, "I will provide some information, but only this much." All heads turned to the representative of the most secretive member of the committee. "Because it will be on pain of death if I am ever found to have spoken this truth. Is this understood?"

The light-skinned lady with the long blond hair looked into each face to make sure she got an acknowledgement. She didn't expect any of them to listen to her, but she had to try. In her country, there were whispers about a shadowy group in the highest reaches of power. She had a glimpse of the elusive leader of TQB Enterprises and hadn't been able to shake the feeling she had seen the lady before.

At three o'clock this morning, she had bolted up in bed and hurried to put on a housecoat. She made a special, secure request to confirm the facts of an incident that had happened in her country some time earlier.

Anna Elisabeth had sought information on a bank heist. Not a successful one, but a crime where the criminals had been captured, but nobody knew how it had been stopped. The bank videotapes had mysteriously been erased. No one had ever been brought up on charges for failing to supply the police with the evidence.

She had seen a picture of a woman leaving with a hat shading her face. It was the jawline that she remembered. Poised. It was confident, it was determined.

Her name had been on the list of those interviewed.

There could only be one answer to this question, and it scared Anna Elisabeth beyond reason. She had discounted the rumors ever since she had heard them. She had risen to this level of responsibility because she didn't scare easily. Oh, she knew the power and strength of respect for those more influential than her, and those more desperate. But these were all aspects of the great game.

Now this made her blood feel like it was turning to ice. It had taken her eighteen years to get to this position, and she was about to throw it away in a futile gesture to warn fifteen others she had worked with secretly. This conversation was going to be debated for weeks and months, or perhaps, years. If the former, then these idiots were going to ignore her. If the latter, then they would have learned enough to use caution.

Because with some entities, a bigger stick isn't the answer.

With all eyes on her, she started what she considered her farewell speech.

"There is a group known in our country for over a thousand years. A group that is never addressed. It has been said that those in power will kill those underneath them if necessary to keep this secret."

Now she had their attention. When you're known for your secrets, it doesn't take much to get attention when you admit you're spilling one.

"While I have never heard of such a killing myself, I would not be surprised if it had happened in centuries past.

This group has much influence and holds incredible wealth across many countries throughout the world. Individually, they hold controlling interests in the economies in my nation and many of yours."

"Surely you spin a great tale." Johann interrupted. "If there were still such a secret society, we would know about it!"

Anna Elisabeth stared at Johann. Not only because he was an arrogant prick, but because he compounded that attitude with rudeness. Johann felt the power of those he represented defined his own authority, never understanding his position as a simple figurehead. Anna Elisabeth had always recognized her similar position and had sought to be the best representative that she could be.

Until now.

She had been able to piece together what had happened at that bank and knew that the rumors, the stories, the whispers were true.

"Sorry," he finally mumbled.

"I cannot tell you much, but I can tell you that if you choose to do something drastic, then expect severe consequences. This group makes the Israelis' eye for an eye attitude seem plebian." She looked around the table. "I share this because if TQB Enterprises is in an alliance with these people, then your directors are not safe. Your people are not safe, and I dare say your countries are not safe."

At this Johann and two others around the table chuckled.

Well, that was the best she could do and still keep her head. "As is my right, rarely employed by my country, I ask for a table vote on whether you intend to acquire TQB Enterprise technology through whatever means necessary?"

"Whatever means," Stephanie said. "Doesn't always mean force, Anna."

Anna turned to Stephanie Lee and smiled. "You will not get the technology any other way. I require a vote right now whether you will approve using force to acquire this technology."

In her country, Ms. Lee would be more circumspect about the question. But she had learned in this group, her country's long history was little understood and even less appreciated. She raised her hand while staring at Anna. "All the way to force."

Fourteen other hands rose around her. Anna Elisabeth shrugged and moved her chair back. "Then I wish you the best of luck on your peaceful negotiations." She picked up her notebook and tablet and pushed her chair back under the table.

"Can you give us any other hints?" Johann asked. She looked at his face, he was smirking as if she was the little girl at school running from a scary story.

Fuck them all, she thought. She started for the door. "Yes. Don't screw with the Archangel."

She opened the door and stepped through. They could hear the click-clack of her steps on the stone floors as she walked away.

MOON BASE ONE

The base had grown from the original seven containers to fifteen. Six of them were double stacks that had been welded together on Earth before transport to the moon. Now they had twice the space in the three forty foot long and sixteen foot wide rooms.

IT'S HELL TO CHOOSE

They helped for get togethers like this.

"What I'm saying, boss," Coach stated as he stood up in front of everyone who was watching him try to manipulate two forks. "Is that we plan on connecting everything for five containers long, then one at the side to angle up ninety degrees. Then we use another one positioned at the end, attached to the side. With that second container, we go back the way we came. The middle container of the five has a side as well to allow us to connect across at will. BUT, that assumes we have a new type of connector. One that just plugs in and locks through force, no screwing in or twisting to finish. We won't have the ability to make that turning motion."

"Pretty much a one way connection," William said from the monitor on the wall.

"I can have you the design in the next half-hour, William," Adarsh said. "I've been working on something similar for the last couple of weeks too. But it has a special release from both sides; it isn't permanent."

"That would be fantastic!" Bobcat said. "If we built a small chamber with two of these, we could do some sort of universal connector that helps with ship-to-ship transfer through the atmosphere. Have a ship connect, pipe in the air, a person steps through, suck the air back out and disengage."

Penn thought about it. "It would be easier than these little screw actions we're doing right now."

Adarsh had been feverishly working on his tablet. "Okay, William. I sent you what I have so far. As soon as this meeting is over, maybe the two of us can talk it out?"

"Works for me," William agreed.

After further discussion, the teams broke up to figure out how to best handle another one hundred plus containers.

It would be, Penn mused, the World's Ugliest Space

Station. But considering it was only the third in existence, there would be plenty of opportunity for something uglier to come along and knock it off of its podium.

CHAPTER TWO

UNIVERSITY JUST OUTSIDE OF PHILADELPHIA, PA

'm telling you, James, this shit is getting real!" Nick looked at his computer screen scrolling through the messages in the chat room. "TxSatan99 is saying that he knows of three verified takedowns in France outside of Paris. One of the guys over there says he was told by a cop he knows that MyNam3isADAM started printing shit out on the cops' own printers!"

Nick looked over the rim of his laptop screen at his friend who was staring at his own laptop display. "God, can you imagine? This guy not only finds the dirt, but he also hacked the cops own network to print the proof."

Nick shook his head and looked back down. "Woo! Satan says there's a reward for anyone who can figure out who My-Nam3isADAM is. The reward just got upped to 30 bitcoin."

"Shit," James replied. "That's only like fifteen thousand dollars right now. There's no way I'd turn in ADAM for any money. Besides, what kind of name is 'Satan' anyway?"

Nick shrugged. "I asked him, and he said Texas is hot as hell in the summer, so it seemed appropriate." Nick kept reading the messages. "I'm not saying I want him caught. I'm saying that there's a bounty on him."

Nick looked up from his screen and reached over to snap his fingers in front of his friend's face. James looked up, annoyed. "What the hell?"

"Do you think he wants help?" Nick asked.

"Who?" James replied.

"Adam!" He pointed at his screen. "This is bullshit."

James scrunched up his face. "What the hell are you talking about? Is this another drop the shit on me and then run around the block thing for you?"

"No. Look, that was back in high school! You should let it go, I did," Nick said.

James leaned back in his chair. "That's because you weren't left holding the evidence when the cops came charging in. You know how hard it was to explain all of our computer equipment wasn't hacking stuff?"

Nick grinned. "Yes, you've given me the play by play at least forty-two times in the last four years." He spread his arms. "Besides, you got out of it! I would have been stuttering and busted."

"You shouldn't have been trying to co-opt the school's wireless to change your fucking grades," James told him.

"Whatever. So, answer my question," Nick said.

James gawked at his friend. "You want to know if one of the preeminent hackers on the planet right now, who has a price on his head, wants you to help him?"

"Well, say it that way and it seems a little far-fetched." Nick turned back to his screen. "Fuck it."

IT'S HELL TO CHOOSE

"Wait, what 'fuck it?'" James began to get worried as Nick continued typing and didn't answer him. He stood up and walked around the little card table in the dorm room they shared to look over his friend's shoulder.

"Oh, that 'fuck it.'"

———

TQB BASE, CO, USA

>> **Bethany Anne?**<<
Yes?

Bethany Anne was grabbing her suit coat and slipping on her Christian Louboutins. John was outside the door of her suite, and it was nearing the time she needed to be at the meeting with the lawyers.

>>**I've run across a situation I wasn't prepared for.**<<
Really? Like what?

>> **My hacker persona is getting requests from people asking if they can help me.** <<

Bethany Anne dropped a shoe. *What?*

>>**I have been receiving more and more requests from people on the dark web to see if they can help me.**<<

She finished putting on her shoes and stood up. She moved around and pushed a chair under a table. It had a pair of Michael's pants neatly folded and hanging across the back. The man was so neat it was like he came from a Neiman Marcus magazine—'Perfect Male. Wise in years, Young Body, Cleans Up After Himself.'

He had left over an hour ago to mind read and give her his impression of the new teams before she went into her meeting with the sharks.

How many?

>> Sixteen at this time.<<

You have sixteen hackers who are seeking you out to see if you need help?

>>Yes. They want to join in the ADAM Revolution. <<

Wait! What Revolution? You and TOM haven't started anything have you?

>>No. This was not part of my plan. I can see where they could be useful as I am dealing with more than I counted on with the stock market. But I don't know your expectations and whether having additional help is a good solution.<<

Did you want me to help ADAM start a Revolution?

Hell-to-the-no, TOM! You two did enough with China. Lord almighty! If it ever came out that an AI and alien-backed dark web-enhanced hacker group was trying to affect society… Oh, I shudder to think about the PR debacle from that.

Bethany Anne stopped for a moment and added before opening her door, *And the crap Cheryl Lynn would give me for allowing you two to do it!*

But, it's OKAY for just ADAM to play?

Bethany Anne nodded to John and finished her thought. *I cannot believe I'm saying this, but yes. ADAM—keep me up to date on what's going on with the people, but you can communicate.*

———

The lawyers from Mill, Sethy, and Brimer followed Cheryl Lynn down the hall. All of them passed a sharply dressed man lounging in the hallway. Their guide said, "Michael." He nodded to her as the men stepped around him. Mr. Mill and Sethy returned the nod, while Brimer ignored him altogether.

They were a couple of minutes behind the team from Thuresson and Guaran, and they had noticed Jakob Yadav pulling up in his older silver Mercedes Benz E350 behind them.

Like them, Yadav had come personally. Thuresson and Guaran were rumored to have sent a pinch-hit team.

Apparently, Thuresson and Guaran hadn't done their homework.

This account could easily add tens of millions to the coffers of their practice, and among the three firms, they had over one hundred and twenty years of legal experience. They felt pretty confident that there wasn't anything this group could throw at them that they wouldn't be able to handle.

This was it, the final round that had started quickly in the last two weeks.

The men were shown into the large meeting room, and all of them were surprised at the display of sophistication. The room was actually a small amphitheater with four levels of desks and screens and a large conference table at the bottom.

Thuresson and Guaran had five people already seated down at the first level of desks on the left. Mill, Sethy, and Brimer were shown the chairs to the right on the first level.

Brimer smiled, that meant Yadav would probably get a second row seat.

When she got back to the entrance, Cheryl Lynn found Jakob Yadav waiting for her. He was dressed in a simple three-piece suit and had a fashionable gold pocket watch and chain. Cheryl Lynn found it cute. The man had already taken his hat off, and he was bald and had a rather large nose. He reminded her of the legendary NY Yankee manager Yogi Berra.

"Hello." He reached out to shake her hand. "Pleased to

meet you. I'm Jakob Yadav. I was asked to attend, but I have to be honest. I wasn't planning on taking any customers." He shrugged, pointed to his bare head and smiled. "Brain is good, but some cold mornings it takes more than one cup of coffee to get going!"

"Well," Cheryl Lynn said. "As far as I know, they want you for your mind, not your body." The twinkle in his eye assured Cheryl Lynn that Mr. Yadav had not lost any of his sense of humor.

"If you would follow me?" He grabbed his yellow pad and a pen and started to follow her down the hall. She nodded to Michael again, but was caught by surprise when Mr. Yadav called out from behind her.

"You are Mr. Michael, are you not?"

Cheryl Lynn turned to see the two men shaking hands and Michael replying, "I am."

"Good to meet you, my name is Jakob Yadav. Those hooligans getting snapshots of you and Ms. Bethany Anne when you have been on your dates have to be a right pain. If I were younger, I think I might risk getting thrown in the pokey after taking a swing at those bastards." Mr. Yadav released Michael's hand and then leaned forward to poke him gently in the chest and leaned back again. "If you happen to punch one, call me. I'll consider it a public service and I'll represent you for free."

Michael smiled at the much younger man whose body was rapidly getting away from him.

"I'll tell you what," Michael answered. "Next chance I get I'll deck one of them. But it isn't with the police I'll need your intercession, but rather my girlfriend." He winked at Jakob. "She tends to frown at unnecessary violence."

"Hmph," he replied. "They are rude. They are taking

pictures when you are having a private dinner and it is certainly a justification for violence. At least in my day it was."

Michael smiled and turned towards Cheryl Lynn, a gleam in his eye. "My day as well. Jakob, why don't we go sit down together and hear what the group is going to say?"

Jakob turned to walk with Michael. The two of them stepped around the stupefied Cheryl Lynn in the hallway.

She turned her head and watched as they disappeared through the doors leading into the conference room. Looking back towards where her work waited for her, she shrugged her shoulders and turned to follow them.

Michael wasn't expected to be a part of the meeting. That he invited himself along was an indication that exciting times might lay ahead, and Cheryl Lynn would need to know the details for when Giannini grilled her later!

NEW YORK, NY, USA

"Sir, Nathan and Ecaterina are here to see you," Gerry's secretary informed him. He punched the speaker button. "Thank you, Ashley. Please send them in."

Gerry finished the email he was working on and stood up as the door to his office opened and Nathan stepped in, followed by his mate Ecaterina. Both smiled at him, and they met in the middle of his large office. He shook Nathan's hand and hugged Ecaterina briefly. "Couch or desk?" he asked.

"I am thinking the couch," she replied, pulling on Nathan's arm and changing his direction. "These shoes are beautiful, but they are not comfortable." She rubbed

Nathan's back in passing and Gerry tried to keep the smirk off of his face.

Whipped.

He sighed inwardly, he was happy for Nathan. He was getting up in age, he shouldn't be jealous of Nathan's happiness. Now that the politics had been reduced substantially by Bethany Anne he might have the time to look around one last time for a significant other. Probably a human woman as a Were lady would outlive him.

The couple sat down on his couch and Gerry asked if they wanted anything. Nathan accepted a Scotch, but Ecaterina demurred. Gerry raised an eyebrow to Nathan, who shook his head and shrugged a shoulder.

That was interesting, Gerry thought. "Perhaps water with lemon?" She agreed and Gerry made their drinks and handed them out. He made a gin and tonic for himself and sat down.

"So," Gerry started. "How did the recruiting run go?"

"Too well, perhaps," Nathan replied.

Gerry was surprised. "What? That's kind of shocking. I figured with the fallout from the last council meeting, there would be a lot of bullshit cock-blocking of the recruiting effort."

"Oh, they tried that in the beginning." Ecaterina agreed. "But it didn't work very well."

Gerry looked back over at Nathan for an answer.

"You really didn't hear any news?" Nathan asked, and then was surprised when Gerry grinned. "Who would have thought you would take so well to not being the top guy?" Nathan mused.

Gerry shrugged. "I was mostly taking the responsibility to keep a lid on anything Michael might do. That massacre made an impression on me. Since Bethany Anne is heading things, I feel comfortable relaxing on this. Plus, you're my contact. If they have a problem with you, well shit—they can just complain to you!"

"You sneaky bastard, you turned off your phone!" Nathan accused.

"Not true," he replied quickly. "I shunted anything but a couple of people off to voice mail." He took a sip of his drink. "So, back to how you got them to get in line."

Ecaterina cut in. "He grew furry and picked both of the alphas up and growled right in their faces. It was an exciting moment for many, I assure you." She grinned. "The younger crowd got so excited about seeing a Pricolici that anything the alphas said went right out their ears." She made a gesture with her hand. "Poof!"

Gerry chuckled. "Discussion through intimidation? I thought Bethany Anne was a kinder, gentler influence on you."

Nathan smiled. "That was Ecaterina, who told me to 'get this dick-beating over with, it bores me.'"

Ecaterina blushed when the men leaned towards each other and high-fived as they laughed loudly. She interrupted their howling with, "I just asked myself what Bethany Anne would say…" That didn't help at all, now they were practically rolling out of their chairs. Finally, she stood up. "I think I will go talk to Ashley for a moment while you two boys get this out of your system."

Nathan reached under to push her up more quickly and she popped his hand, then winked at him. "Promises, promises!" She stepped out of the room, and the two men turned back to each other.

"So," Gerry asked. "Turn into a Pricolici and everything is good?"

Nathan grimaced. "Not quite that easy. Having to fight the rage that occurs when I'm in that form is a challenge. It isn't an option you want to provide to just any idiot with the raw ability. I'm a little surprised that Peter handles it so well."

"Peter?" Gerry asked.

"Yes, John started calling him Peter and said that Pete was his old, younger name. It kind of caught on. Occasionally we call him Pete, especially if we're trying to tease him. But outside, and now more often inside the group, he's Peter."

"He's grown up, huh?" Gerry asked before taking another sip.

Nathan looked around the office for a minute. Gerry could almost see his mind replaying the incident with Peter's dad and Nathan in this very office that decided Peter's fate. "You know Gerry, for Wechselbalg, he is basically our chosen child," Nathan said soberly. "He was the child sacrificed to the vampires and has risen up to become the leader of our next generation."

Gerry was taken back to that moment. A moment which at the time had felt a lot less momentous and much more spur of the moment decision making. "Who would have thought? Now we have three that can turn into Pricolici and we're tied at the hip with one of the most powerful vampires ever to have existed."

"The," Nathan said.

"What?" Gerry asked, "Do you mean she's stronger than Michael?"

"Oh, maybe not in sheer physical violence. I imagine he can still take her on in a one on one display. He has a thousand years of practice she doesn't yet. No, I'm talking about her organization and what she heads up. Bethany Anne has built our group, and we're on the Moon, Gerry." He took a sip of his own drink. "The damned Moon!"

Nathan turned to look around the room before coming back to Gerry. "We have over two hundred Wechselbalg volunteers right now, and that's the first wave. I expect by the time we finish with the U.S. and Canada, we'll have close to a battalion of Wechselbalg eager to sign up." He sighed. "I don't know if they're signing up because of me, because they need change, or because they understand who Bethany Anne is."

"Well," Gerry said. "My experience suggests no matter the original reason, Bethany Anne will focus their attention where it needs to be."

Nathan saluted Gerry with his whiskey and downed his drink.

CHAPTER THREE

TQB BASE, CO, USA

Bethany Anne and John walked over to the main offices and through where Cheryl Lynn should have been, but wasn't. Then she passed where Michael should have been and wasn't. John reached ahead of her and put out a hand.

She stopped. She could hear everything in the room ahead, and there was no indication of trouble, but she had learned it was easier to be obedient to the hand than to give him too much lip. Besides, she was saving up all of these little indignities for a time when she could get him back.

Your time is coming, Mr. Grimes, she thought, oh yes, your time is coming.

Satisfied that everything was safe inside the room, John stood back, and his posture told Bethany Anne she could walk ahead. Bethany Anne stepped around the corner to find her two missing people. Cheryl Lynn was blushing furiously in the back row, and she saw Michael sitting next to one of the lawyers. From his profile, he would be Jakob Yadav. She walked down the steps and up to the conference table in front of all of the chairs. She turned around and leaned against the table with her arms crossed.

"Welcome," she started. "I understand from the people who vetted you before you arrived that your firms met all of our specific requirements." She turned to the group from Thuresson and Guaran. "Unfortunately, I don't recognize any of you. I will presume that Misters Thuresson and Guaran have justification for missing this meeting?"

The people at the table looked at each other before the person in the chair closest to the aisle spoke. "Hello, Ms. Bethany Anne."

Bethany Anne put up a hand. "It's just Bethany Anne. No honorific necessary." She nodded for him to continue.

"Certainly. My name is Will Sethi, and I'm here on behalf of the firm. Misters Thuresson and Guaran were called away on urgent business for a senator and respectfully ask your pardon." Bethany Anne caught Michael's slightly negative shaking of his head out of the corner of her eye.

She pursed her lips.

ADAM, can you tell me where Misters Thuresson and Guaran are presently?

>>**One moment, Bethany Anne.**<<

"Will," she said. "Would you introduce me to the team?"

Before Will finished, ADAM came back to her.

>>**Both Thuresson and Guaran are presently at a hunting lodge in Western Canada with two clients and a significant number of single ladies.**<<

How the hell do you know this? I'm not doubting you, I'm just curious.

>>**Mr. Guaran has the location on his personal itinerary with two client names and their employers. I found one of his clients is presently sending pictures to a password protected social board of the events for a group of men to view.**<<

"Thank you for your introductions Will, but unfortunately, I was premature when asking for them. I don't believe in wasting time, nor do I believe in falsehoods as a good way to start a relationship. It breeds distrust. As Thuresson and Guaran are presently not on the East Coast of the United States, but rather up in Canada enjoying themselves, I can only surmise that either you don't know, which means they lied to you. Or, you do know, which means that you lied to me."

She looked up at John, who started walking down the steps to stand on the floor with her. "Mr. Grimes here will make sure you get to the front gate." John was talking on his little mic, calling Eric to come in from outside to help them.

Will looked like he wanted to argue the point, but then grabbed his laptop and started shoving his books, writing pad and mouse into his bag.

"Michael," she said very quietly.

Yes? he replied in her mind.

Would you check out the third lady from their group? Bethany Anne saw Michael purse his lips and look like he was studying the whole group.

She is upset. She had hoped to help win this account so she could work, at least tangentially, with this team, because Jennifer loves what she has seen and learned to date. Hmmm, it looks like she has a crush on you.

What?

She has a professional crush. She's researched everything

that is known about you. My, did you know how many websites have sprung up about you?

God, yes! It's like the more I try to hide, the more they dig. I've had ADAM go through and leave behind some fake crumbs at times and delete stuff occasionally. He's found over seventy-two websites and four Facebook groups.

Hmm, Michael sent.

What?

It seems she has a crush on me as well, he replied.

How could she have a crush on you? What business information is out there on you?

Not that kind of crush.

It was a second before Bethany Anne came back to him.

I will rip your dick off.

Michael pressed his lips together trying to keep his mirth in check. Bethany Anne had become more and more jealous sounding in her remarks to him in the last three to four weeks. She never showed anything externally, but occasionally she would make comments like this one to him personally.

She had apparently decided he was off the market.

This was all right with him; he had already decided he would focus all of his attention on Bethany Anne. *Should I be jealous of all the men that find you attractive?*

Don't play Mr. Logical with me. I'll just go illogical on your ass. I'm not the one reading all the minds finding out just how bad these ladies want you.

I thought we had this conversation already? Tabitha was a fast-track course in not reading minds unless needed.

This time, it was Bethany Anne's turn to press her lips together. When Michael finally came clean about all of the ways Tabitha had burned him when she believed he was reading her mind, Bethany Anne couldn't stop laughing. What should have taken him at most fifteen minutes to tell took him over an hour because she would start laughing again.

God, she sent to him, *don't you dare say a word about Tabitha!* It wasn't that her mind reading and sending wasn't considerably stronger since working with Michael so closely, it was that she didn't use it often, for philosophical reasons.

If you can get past your jealousy, what do you want to do about this lady?

I'm not jealous! Ok, I can't sell that. I'm only a little jealous and to be fair, you're my first long term boyfriend in years. You are hunky, rich, powerful, and you've got a nice ass. So yeah, you're all mine.

He caught her eyes, and she quickly flashed a little red in them.

Just how fast can we get this over with? Michael asked.

Why? She asked.

I want you. Michael answered directly.

Oh. She paused then asked, *Give me your rundown.*

Jakob here is ethical, smart and he has honor.

And?

The two dill-weeds, as you are fond of saying, in front of me are thinking how much money they can fleece from the company. The other one here on the right of me is fronting another client as a spy on this trip. He is hoping for a short trip around the premises so he can drop another three listening devices around the base. There is already a bug planted in the first secretary's room up front.

Boy, wouldn't he be surprised to learn that room is not occupied? she quipped. She turned to look at John who tweaked just a little when ADAM came over his earpiece asking him to find a bug planted in the front office.

He took off up the stairs at a steady pace, two steps at a time. Everyone was startled at his sudden disappearance around the corner and Eric's appearance right as he left to escort the group out. Jennifer Tehgen was surprised when her personal phone beeped with a text. She mumbled an apology, as she was confident she had told everyone not to communicate with her while in this meeting unless it was an emergency. She looked at the phone and then did a double-take.

You are invited to apply personally for a position as in-house counsel with TQB Enterprises.

The text provided Cheryl Lynn's contact information. She dropped the phone into her purse and turned to stare back at Bethany Anne, who winked at her.

She left the room more confused than ever. How the hell had they just pulled this off?

Jennifer passed by the man of muscle in the hall who was marching back towards the meeting room.

John stepped into the room and walked down the steps where he turned and leaned on the table across from Mr. Brimer. Mr. Brimer tried to look affronted, with an expression perfected in front of judges from California to Maine. Those men of the bench had honed Brimer's ability to stand stern in the face of adversity.

But he was sweating looking at someone extremely pissed with him who looked like breaking his back was the least painful thing he wanted to do.

"What is the meaning of this?" Marcus Mills asked. "This isn't how you treat invited representatives from a firm as prestigious as ours!" He turned towards Bethany Anne, who was walking towards John with her hand outstretched. He didn't look at her, but he did drop something into her left hand. She caught the little item and then stepped over in front of Mills.

She placed the bug on the desk between the two men. "I will treat spies like I treat vermin, Mr. Mills." Bethany Anne replied. "I have a very, very short fuse when it comes to shit like this."

Mills was caught by surprise and he turned towards his partner. "Bill? What's the meaning of this?" He reached towards the bug, but his hand landed on Bethany Anne's.

"No, no touching the evidence again, Mr. Mills," she said. "We can take genetic swabs and prove who's touched it. If you do so, we will be forced to bring you up on charges as well."

"Bullshit!" Brimer said. "There isn't any way that you have…"

"You fucking idiot." Sethy interrupted him. "They're on the Moon right now, and you want to argue whether they might have some other forms of advanced technology?" He stared at Bethany Anne's hand before turning to his partner. "How many more do you have on you?"

"I don't know what—" he started.

This time, it was John who interrupted him. "You can answer truthfully, or I will take pleasure out of strip searching your ass right here," he growled.

Brimer started to splutter. "I will sue you so badly you will…"

He wasn't having any luck at all completing a sentence. "Oh, I'll be more than happy to represent him in court, Martin." Jakob Yadav spoke from behind him, "So please, please sue him so I can make it four out of four wins against your useless ass!" Bethany Anne looked up to see Jakob's face alight with open glee at the idea of being able to go to court against Martin.

I like this guy! she sent to Michael.

Why do you think I'm sitting next to him?

He probably told you to kill someone, she replied. Michael failed to respond in time, so she added, *Please, tell me he didn't suggest you kill someone!*

No, he didn't tell me to kill anyone. Like I'm the problem child here. Which one of us has a problem with her anger?

Oh, shut up. You're getting me riled up, and every time you do that before sex, blood ends up everywhere.

Like that's a problem?

No, I guess it hasn't been with you. It just drives me nuts and then I wake up, and it just seems so... so...

Stephen King?

No, more Clive Barker.

Haven't read him.

Don't worry about it. ADAM supplied the response for me.

That's cheating!

That's using my assets.

Those are some very attractive assets.

My mind is up here, mister!

You keep telling me to catch up to the present generation and to stop being so stodgy with my actions.

Need I remind you we are in the middle of getting rid of a nationally known and respected law firm?

Who brought up sex first?

Instead of answering, she spoke. "So you have two options. Admit to how many you have or you will be forcefully searched by Mr. Grimes here."

"Three," he said, his shoulders slumping a little.

"You chicken shit!" Mills started before Bethany Anne put up a hand.

"Eric will be here shortly to escort the three of you back to your vehicle. Mr. Brimer here will be relieved of his bugs and he will provide the name of the company who employed him to accomplish this, you may all go once that is complete."

It took another five minutes to get through Brimer's final attempt to get out of it. By the time they left, they were yelling at each other. Eric was careful to make sure nothing else was left behind.

Bethany Anne watched them exit the room. She turned to Jakob. "And then there was one." She smiled at him, and he looked back.

"I don't suppose you want me for my body?" he asked with a slow smile and all five of the people left in the room cracked up.

Cheryl Lynn walked down from the top. "That was well worth the price of admission!" she exclaimed, and sat in the chair just vacated by Mills.

"I'd ask what suggested something might be going on, but I already know the answer to that." Bethany Anne said. "So, Jakob, what brings a horned unicorn to TQB Enterprises?"

"A horned unicorn?" he asked, perplexed.

"Yes, I figured I would meet an ethical lawyer about the time I met a horned unicorn." she said.

"Well, I'm not sure I know what to say to that," he replied. "But before we go further, I have to tell you I don't know how many days I have left. I explained to Mr. Michael here that I mainly wanted to see the fireworks happen."

"And offer to represent me if I punched out a paparazzi." Michael smiled at Bethany Anne.

"That doesn't sound very ethical to me, Mr. Yadav," Bethany Anne said.

"On the contrary, my dear. It is an effort to teach the

young hooligans the fine art of minding their own damned business!" He grinned up at her, and she had the hardest time not smiling back. This man's good humor was contagious.

"And if you were healthy enough to do this yourself?" she continued.

"Well, you know that the first rule of lawyers is to never represent yourself. So, since it looks like Michael here is in great shape, and I have the mind for it, and you carry the interest of half the world, we have a real shot at teaching a lot of young hooligans!"

At this, Bethany Anne gave in and started laughing. First, she snorted, then put her hand up to her mouth and shook herself before the chuckles became outright laughter. It took a moment for her and Cheryl Lynn to quiet down.

At this point, the two men were looking at her as if she was the mom, and the two of them were guilty of something, but both looked so damn cute, you just told them to go play outside again.

She sighed out loud. "Mr. Yadav, how much would it cost me to hire you so we have client confidentiality?"

"Well," he started. "While I would do it for free, let's say a dollar so we have financial consideration in place."

Bethany Anne looked at Michael, who rolled his eyes and started reaching for his pocket. "I told you in London that carrying cash wasn't a bad idea." He pulled his wallet out and reached over to give her an American dollar. She thanked him and moved her hand a few inches to deliver it to the chuckling Yadav.

"So, what is it that needs my confidentiality?" he asked while pulling out his wallet to place the dollar inside.

"Well, let me introduce you to the General. You might

notice something about him that would encourage you to listen to the pitch for you to start up my in-house counsel…"

With that, the five of them stood up and left to go find her father.

CHAPTER FOUR

THE DARK WEB

MyNam3isADAM - Welcome.

>>B33dyRed - Hello.

>>Ih8tuGeorge - Hello.

>>ki55mia55 - Hello.

>>luckyu11 - Hi.

>> MyNam3isADAM - Hello. My understanding is that you would like to help me?

>>B33dyRed - Yes! Dude, you've got the whole dark web talking. How the hell do you do these things?

>>MyNam3isADAM - Why would I explain that?

>>B33dyRed - Sorry - good point.

>>B33dyRed has been dropped.

>>MyNam3isADAM - And then there were three.

>>luckyu11 - I'm not questioning how, just wondering why you don't think he will come back on?

>>MyNam3isADAM - Because we aren't where you think we are.

>>luckyu11 - Ok. I'll assume you have us re-routed somewhere and leave it at that.

>>MyNam3isADAM - Safe assumption. How is it that you want to help?

>>luckyu11 - Not sure. I can't speak for everyone, but the three of us each represent a hacking group that would like to take on some of the crap we see happening.

>>MyNam3isADAM - And you other two?

>>ki55mia55 - That is the same for my group. There are five of us.

>>Ih8tuGeorge - There are eight of us, but two are just newbies with a lot of server access.

>>MyNam3isADAM - And you want to come in on my side against those I'm fighting?

>>luckyu11 - Yes.

>>ki55mia55 - yes

>>Ih8tuGeorge - y.

>>MyNam3isADAM - Do you realize that I'm taking on nation-states? This isn't just one hacker group against another, but major players. I can't, and won't, promise you safety. If I am ever figured out, I will be physically attacked.

>>luckyu11 - Yeah, the countries like to do unto others without us doing it back unto them.

>>ki55mia55 - fuck 'em.

>>Ih8tuGeorge - Yeah, we all talked about it already.

>>MyNam3isADAM - Ok, then two of the major challenges are handling the different ways China and Russia go about cyber-warfare. The Chinese are like vacuums, they attack everywhere and steal as much as they can and as a result, they are drowning in stolen data. The Russians, on the other hand, are very persistent and very targeted. They will take months, even years, going after the same target. They are

stealthy and try to be as quiet as they can, but they are technically much better than the Chinese. I would ask for your teams to help conduct reverse DDoS attacks against Russian cyber experts. Russia is using cyber criminals and unaligned hackers to carry out operations on their behalf from Estonia, Georgia and Ukraine as cutouts. I need you to take on these hackers to free up some cycles to go after other targets.

>>ki55mia55 - Us against them? Russia is sending these pricks against you, and you need help defending to free up time so you can attack?

>>MyNam3isADAM - Yes.

>>luckyu11 - One second, let me confirm.

>>ki55mia55 - We're in.

>>Ih8tuGeorge – Vote's done, we are in.

>>luckyu11 - 100% on yes. We're in. We are bringing 32 of us from across Europe. When a couple of others find out who we are going after, I bet it grows.

>>MyNam3isADAM - Then welcome to ADAM's Revolution.

———

WEST COAST, USA

"Right now, I have responsibility for almost 200,000 people on my payroll." CEO Sean Truitt spoke across the table from his head of Aerospace, Javier Fernandez. The two men were in an exclusive area of the cafeteria that was soundproof and actually a Faraday cage, blocking all communications in and out.

"So tell me again," Sean went on as he cut into his steak. "Why the four billion in R&D we spent last fiscal year was inadequate to even understand their technology, much less copy it?" He put the piece of steak in his mouth.

Javier was annoyed. His 'best and brightest' didn't have anything for him. In fact, one of the little pricks quit before he could fire him. If it weren't for the HR benefits he would have had to pay, he would have told Jeovanni you can't resign from a job you had been fired from.

"I don't have an answer to that." Javier replied. "I've been on their asses for two weeks, and we still have nothing to go on. One guy has been sacked." No need to be too exact on sacked or quit. "And the others live at the job right now. Still, for all of that we have nothing," he finished.

A few choices went through Sean's mind. He could fire Javier right now, but that wouldn't get him anything, and the company was doing well. It wasn't like this same discussion wasn't happening all over the world with other bosses. If there was any consolation, it was in the rumor mill. No one knew how TQB was doing what they were doing.

The industry reports had all sorts of guesses from high-level theoreticians spouting a variety of ideas. The best yet was from a quack using quantum theory to pass through another dimension siphoning energy.

Idiot.

Sean leaned forward, looking into Javier's face and lowered his voice. "I don't care what you have to do to figure it out. I don't care if you hire more, fire more, hack it, attack it, or steal it. But you need to make sure we are the ones who have that technology. Is this clear?"

Javier paused, then came to a decision and nodded.

"Good," Sean said. "Make it happen. Let's get off of that subject for a few minutes. It makes me nauseous." He picked up his tea and took a swallow before asking, "So, how are Helen and the kids?"

IT'S HELL TO CHOOSE

MOON BASE ONE, MOON

"All right, Gott Verdammt!" Kris noticed a slight twitch from container number 54. "John get your shit together! I swear to God if this has anything to do with the scotch last night, I will personally do a spacewalk over there and kick your ass." Laughter was heard through the line. Everyone understood John never let his occasional drink get in the way of business.

So far, the team had been able to connect seventy-two of the containers. The rather square design that they had figured out was working fairly well. They had seven cameras taking video of the whole project. Unfortunately for the world, they were not presently streaming the video back. No one wanted to screw up something this large on TV.

Adarsh was quickly showing himself to be the best at manipulating the finer controls, and Penn had put him in charge of the particularly difficult tweaks. Although the computers did most of the work, there was always a human to make sure something unexpected didn't cause a permanent problem.

Penn spoke. "People, let's focus. We got another hour and a half of this to go. So far, so good, and I'm sure we'll all be happy with the new facilities these containers bring us."

"Hell yeah!" Bree said. "Bobcat promised me at least a year and a half's worth of coffee on one of those containers. Although the wicked little bastard wouldn't tell me which one it was."

A few chuckles were elicited from that. ReaLea broke in again. "I'm looking forward to the Jacuzzi container."

"Workout container," John said.

"Lounge with video games container," said Coach.

"That's going to be one of William's favorite places," Kris said.

"Which is why I think it says 'Williams' on the outside," Adarsh pointed out.

"Really?" ReaLea said. A moment later she followed up with, "Wow, could he possibly have painted those letters any larger?"

"Not without wrapping them over the top." John said.

"Okay, I can see where this is going. Everybody pause and let's take ten before we continue. We are almost three-quarters of the way done, and it won't hurt us at all to relax. In fact, let's make it more like thirty minutes."

Everybody gave him a thumbs up on the monitor. Things were going to plan. So far, there had only been four minor hitches and Penn was feeling okay with the results. He knew that Bobcat, William, Marcus, and Jeffrey were watching from Earth, but they never jiggled his elbow in these situations. Penn was the man on the spot, and they left it to him to get the job done. It felt good knowing he had their support, and he sure as hell didn't want to make a mess of things.

He took one last look at the video feed from outside, watching as the containers held position, waiting for his crew to start connecting them again.

Space Station One was taking shape.

CHAPTER FIVE

Cheryl Lynn nodded at Eric, who was standing by the door warming up. She walked over to where Bethany Anne was going through a kata and took position near her to slowly mimic the same actions.

"So I have a question," Cheryl Lynn started. "And it has some far-reaching consequences." She gently brought her arm around in an arc as she stepped forward on her left foot.

"I figured as much. It isn't often you schedule the time to work out with me just because you're looking for a reason to get sweaty." Bethany Anne pivoted on her left foot a hundred and eighty degrees and both women now faced the opposite wall. "This time give me the negative part first and what you're suggesting we do about it second."

Both women took one step forward and rapidly punched the air with their right fists while pulling their left elbow back against them. "We have a large faction of people around the world screaming for us to share the space technology. I'm working with seven agencies on that problem. I'd like to consider other options outside of forbidden technology where we could at least refocus their attention if possible." Each woman had taken three steps forward and now blocked with her left arm, then kicked with their right.

Bethany Anne nodded. "Okay, I've seen a lot of the news reports and ADAM has provided me a very detailed update. Which technologies are you interested in?"

Both ladies twisted their heads behind them once again and blocked with their right arm following up with snap kicks, leaving them with their weight balanced on the right foot.

Cheryl Lynn continued, "Is there any way we can use the medical technologies we have available to us to both support people who have given up part of their physical bodies for their countries, and what we're doing in space at the same time?" Both ladies stopped with their feet together and bowed forward slightly. Then both broke and started stretching out a little, sitting on the mat to talk while they stretched. "I really wish I had warmed up more before joining you on this kata. I'm going to feel this later," Cheryl Lynn complained.

"I suggest four ibuprofen, it's the same as taking one of those 800 mg pills, or at least that's what the pharmacist told me one time." Bethany Anne said.

Cheryl Lynn groaned as she stretched her calves. "I thought TOM took care of that for you."

"Oh you did, did you? And which little birdie is telling you that?" Bethany Anne inquired.

Cheryl Lynn blushed. "Um, a really tall one?"

Bethany Anne smirked. "TOM doesn't do that as often as John thinks he does. I have been known to ask TOM to alter my emotions or pain level occasionally. But if I do it too much I'm concerned that not only would reduced pain levels possibly become habit forming, but would lower my situational awareness."

"So, you actually feel a lot of the pain when you go out on operations?" Cheryl Lynn asked for confirmation.

"Oh yes. I'll tell Tom to adjust the pain if I can't focus on the problem at hand. But as soon as we're out of danger he will bring it back up so I feel it. Except for that time when half my chest was blown out. I didn't want to deal with that shit at all. Occasionally, I still wake up from a nightmare where I'm reliving that moment. If I could bring Petre back from the dead, I would do it just so I could kill him all over again." Cheryl Lynn noticed that Bethany Anne had subconsciously started rubbing her chest.

Cheryl Lynn was starting to understand just how much Bethany Anne had suffered in the last few years.

When she first arrived at the base, it seemed to Cheryl Lynn that nothing affected Bethany Anne. The longer she was around the woman though, the more apparent it became that each little problem was another tiny rock on her shoulders. Fortunately, it seemed that her relationship with Michael was slowly starting to take rocks away. Perhaps, one day, he would be able to get to the rock that was the situation with Petre and lift it off for her.

"So you're thinking something like military personnel?" Bethany Anne asked. "Or are you talking more like first responders?"

"I'll admit I was thinking more of military personnel. But first responders or frankly anyone that's done something amazing would be good. Plus, if they already had citations or other awards for what they sacrificed, it would allow us to quickly filter who gets into the program," Cheryl Lynn said.

"Okay, I'm good with where you're going so far. Now tell me more." Bethany Anne started reaching toward her right leg, bending so her head touched the ground.

Bethany Anne's hair was blocking her eyes so Cheryl Lynn stuck her tongue out at the woman for her display of athleticism. Cheryl Lynn turned to her left leg and reached over to grab her foot. The pain in her hamstrings intensified.

One of these days she would be able to touch the floor with her head. "So, I thought we would look and offer to any individual who sacrificed a lot for an altruistic reason. While I was thinking military, I see your point. We could filter first on firemen, policemen, or frankly anyone that helped someone else and lost limbs or were substantially physically disabled as a result."

Both women switched legs and started stretching again.

"I thought that the second filter would have to be something related to a willingness to go up into space with us." Cheryl Lynn grunted when one of her muscles twitched. "Son of a bitch, that hurt!"

"Pain is just weakness leaving the body." Bethany Anne mumbled from underneath her hair.

"Don't you believe that crap," Eric snorted from across the room. "Well, not just that. It *is* weakness leaving the body, but the pain is a total bitch when she leaves!"

Bethany Anne's voice erupted from underneath her hair. "Eric, you wrinkled bunghole sniffer! Stop bitching and keep working out. If you interrupt my work to make Cheryl Lynn all she can be by telling her the truth again, I'll let Ashur use you for a chew toy!"

Eric chuckled, but he didn't say anything.

"How are you going to deal with the massive amount of

people signing up for the program?" Bethany Anne asked.

Cheryl Lynn sat back with her arms behind her. "I think we have Frank and Barb do research to look for the best recipients. Somehow, they'll have to figure out if those recipients are willing to go into space. Personally, I'm not sure how to do that, but I figure it's worth a try. Maybe we could find news clippings or other info about their heroism." She bit her lip for a few seconds before continuing, "But I have to admit that I don't have a clue what to do about getting overrun. I've spoken with Kevin about the base, and he agrees it's pretty secure, but he would prefer not to have five thousand people camped out in front of the gates all of the time."

Bethany Anne sat up and looked at Cheryl Lynn. "No, it would be preferable not to have that. I would suggest a ship."

Cheryl Lynn looked at her for a moment trying to figure out where she was going. "Don't we have enough ships?"

"Actually, I'm thinking something like a medium sized cruise liner. Have it retrofitted as quickly as possible and invite the people who are going to be changed. They would be rotated through the Ad Aeternitatem so that we can inject them with nanite blood. Put them to sleep first, shoot them with the infusion, let them rest a few hours and wake them up in a room full of machinery and then wheel them out." She rotated her head around her shoulders. "That way, everyone has a memory of a sophisticated medical room with lots of equipment."

"Red herring," Eric commented. "You think that if the ships go out to sea, not as many people can surround them?" he asked.

Bethany Anne turned her head toward Eric. "Yes, not too many people can walk on water these days. I'm sure we're going to get enough rich folks who have boats that will try to track them, so we need to come up with another solution in case it gets too busy right around the ships."

"What about a method for leaving quickly? Something like a superior propulsion system?" he asked.

"I think I may have a good idea about that. Is it okay to get with Marcus first?" Cheryl Lynn interrupted.

Bethany Anne turned back to Cheryl Lynn. "Sure, I don't mind. If Bobcat and Jeffrey give the idea a thumbs up, go ahead and implement it. I'm sure whatever they agree to will be satisfactory."

Cheryl Lynn smirked. She had just been given a blank check from Bethany Anne.

LONDON, ENGLAND

Stephanie Lee exited the armored Mercedes and stepped inside the open door. This hotel had a special back entrance so that the elite could enter and exit without worrying about paparazzi or the many CCTV cameras that filled the city.

Rank hath its privileges.

She nodded to the gentleman who held the door open for her. She pulled off her gloves as she walked down the hallway to the private elevators. She hit the open button, and after a few seconds stepped inside, turned around and hit the button for the penthouse.

When she arrived at the top floor, the doors opened, and she nodded to the two men on either side who were standing and verifying everyone who came through.

The elevator opened into a circular room approximately twelve feet in diameter with a door on the far side that was immediately opened by a third individual. She walked through that door, and it was closed behind her.

She kept the look of disgust off of her face. She was not fond of Johann Pecora, but he did represent many incredibly powerful companies.

"Stephanie." Johann nodded in her direction.

"Johann," she replied and then stepped over to the bar. She picked up water and turned back to the small group. Beside Johann stood Beatrice Silvers, who represented a large contingent of companies from both Ireland and the United Kingdom, and Terrance Burrens, representing companies in France, Spain, and Germany.

Together, the four of them made up over fifty-eight percent of the number of enterprises and over seventy-two percent of the financial muscle of the 'Sub-Assembly for the Advancement of the Human Race.' With Anna Elisabeth stepping out, twenty-five percent of the money and twelve percent of the companies had also left.

She had represented a large portion of the group, but when the current plan proved fruitful, it would strengthen the four of them, and Switzerland would lose a significant amount of face.

"I appreciate the three of you joining me here so quickly. I have had conversations with those I represent back in China. Let me be frank, is there any type of coercion your members will not accept?" She took a swallow of water while waiting for their answers.

Johan spoke first. "No. But it would be preferable if diplomatic efforts were tried first."

Beatrice waved that off. "That has already been tried. We have used forty-two different avenues to implore TQB Enterprises to work with others regarding their space technology.

None of them have proved fruitful. In fact, their responses are annoyingly succinct. They say, "We apologize. This technology is not available to the general public at this time. We will keep your information and should this decision be changed, we will get back with you."

"Fourteen ourselves," Terrance added.

Stephanie Lee looked over at Johann, who looked disgusted. "One hundred and seventy-two" he admitted.

She wanted to slap the man! "And why are you asking for diplomatic methods?"

He shrugged. "We thought perhaps it had something to do with American companies. She seems to have connections all over the world."

Beatrice asked for clarification, "But she has a base sitting in the middle of your country. Most of her top personnel seem to be Americans."

Johann said, "We're still trying to get a handle on that. It could be that most of her relationships evolved around America, and now she's branching out. But all of our answers seem to be aligned with your results as well. Short, succinct, annoyingly trite." He sniffed. "We've made a few runs on her publicly held companies. Not only were stock acquisitions blocked, but her bankers, whoever they are, were able to take a superior position during the stock manipulation attempts. We have learned that they have some excellent options people."

He took a swallow of his amber drink. "When it looks like we're going to run up the price for a stock drop, they made money on option calls and before we could drop the price, puts are already in place to earn money on the drop. Anytime there is significant activity and volatility, there are butterfly spreads. Our people have looked, and whenever we attack a company without options, we find activity in sympathetic verticals that react to our efforts. We've been able to keep our losses to between sixty-five and seventy-five million at the moment, but we're pretty sure they have acquired the majority interest in four additional companies and have realized a surplus of close to sixty million."

"That speaks to some significant smarts." Terrance considered. "And a fund manager that knows the industry incredibly well. They must have an enormous amount of computer power. What is being done on that front?"

"What isn't?" Johann asked. "We have over twenty-five hundred attack vectors focused on their Colorado base, trying to get in."

"What are the results so far?" Beatrice asked.

"About the same as yours, I imagine." Johann snapped. "Don't try to tell me none of your companies aren't trying desperately to be the first company to crack their security?"

"Oh, we are." Terrance said. "And I would agree we have had no success. It has become a challenge more than a project to many of our best and brightest."

Terrence turned to Stephanie. "We have noticed a significant drop in attacks on our companies. Would you care to provide any insight?"

Stephanie smiled. "I can neither confirm nor deny that the Chinese government and corporations have decided that acquiring TQB Enterprises technology is a superior goal at this time." She took a sip of her water. "Personally, I believe that whoever is able to crack the data first is going to make a killing. Either through sharing the technology or learning what to do and then bringing it to market."

Johann said, "If we don't share the technology, and TQB Enterprises has the opportunity, I'm sure they'll sue the hell out of anyone who makes themselves a target."

Stephanie nodded. "Speaking of targets, we have to discuss any physical attacks."

Terrence smiled. "I was wondering when you would get to that point. It does seem that you guys are a little more impatient than usual."

Stephanie wanted to lash out at the man, even if he was correct. It was just rude to mention it in polite company. "We believe that an attack on their ships, the Polaris and Ad Aeternitatem, are our best options. Presently, they are off the coast of France and are eventually going to enter international waters."

Johann asked, "Do you need support? Or are you asking us to create a diversion?"

Stephanie knew that all of them would want to limit their risk, but would certainly want to be there when they cracked open the treasure chests. "No, the military aspect is not a joint operation. You are welcome to try this on your own."

Beatrice looked disgusted. "Not from us. The Swiss have totally fouled up anyone's courage in that regard. I don't know why our people listen to them at all, but it's like everyone has lost their balls or something."

Terrence just raised his drink in Beatrice's direction.

The Cabal was simply one more relationship the Chinese used and, to date, they had honored all commitments and kept everything as honest as any of the members. Then the upper government had stepped in and, over the angry voices of many of the top business leaders, the rules had changed.

"It would be a legal thing for us," Johann said. "Since they are so tied in with us in America, they could make it pretty damned hot for us from both a legal and PR perspective. If they find any Americans in a raid and could provide proof, I shudder at the problems that would bring."

Such a shame, Stephanie thought, because mercenary groups with Americans involved were integral to her plans.

CHAPTER SIX

COSTA RICA

What we want, Mr. Simmons," the female voice said from the speakerphone. "Is for your experienced direction and a team to work with ours to infiltrate and deliver packages to the base in Colorado."

It wasn't odd for Phillip Simmons to work with external contacts. Due to his long involvement in South American black ops, he had made multiple weird relationships work in the past.

Although this would be one of the oddest yet.

He had spent a couple of days up in Washington with Terry, who was spending time in a military hospital. His brain had been fried and couldn't recognize his own boss and one of his best friends.

Well, at least Terry's own boss.

The look of fear on Terry DeLeon's face when Phillip went to see him was telling. Phillip didn't know what could have caused it, but he knew it wasn't right for Terry to be acting this way. Something was going on on that base and Phillip wanted to know what it was. While he doubted it was good for America, at this point it had become an obsession for him to get back at that group.

Phillip had lost the chance to grab the analyst in Washington DC, but he had found enough information to confirm his suspicions so far.

These people had shot his men, stopped his operations, and mind wiped Terry. Further, he was now able to associate the CEO's partner with some substantial goings on down here in South America. It seemed that Michael, no last name that he could find, had been secretly working with someone to repatriate money or, in his estimation, probably using the money for bribes. Either way, he was attempting to affect three different countries here in South America.

This group was too dominant in his opinion. They needed to be knocked down at least a couple of pegs, if not more, and he was personally going to be responsible for helping to accomplish that.

Unfortunately, it would have to be completely off the books. There was no way he could be associated with anything going back to an action inside the United States.

"Unfortunately, Ms. Lee, I will not be able to provide any physical resources to accomplish anything inside of the United States. Having said that, I am open to personally reviewing and helping plan to both create a diversionary attack that would then allow a primary attack on the base. My expectation is that we could insert devices for data acquisition as well as infrastructure destruction."

"And what would you require in exchange for the support?" Ms. Lee asked.

"I want the data to be shared. Understand, I am aware that you will desire to renege on this agreement. I will have insurance in place should that occur."

"Of course. It is good that we understand each other," she said. "From our satellite pictures, it seems that the base is substantially defended with what looks like armed emplacements. Unfortunately, we cannot ascertain the type of defensive armament."

"We were trying to learn that ourselves when my asset was neutralized," Phillip said. "We've tried using long-range telephoto lenses and have seen enough to believe they are barreled weapons of some sort. They're not manned, and if I didn't know better, I would say they are a type of railgun technology."

"Why do you say 'if you didn't know better?'" she asked.

"Because the minimum specifications for railguns at that size would require dams near a hydroelectric facility the size of the Hoover Dam. So, they have not dug up the countryside enough to power such devices, nor have they a suitable power generation unit," he said.

"What about those two containers up on the hill?" she asked.

Phillip considered his response to that question. "Honestly, we're not sure. It could be surveillance and sophisticated radar assets, or it could be a type of power unit that's superior to ours and is set off from the base for safety purposes."

"So, either way, we need to destroy that target?" she asked.

"Not positive. It could very well be a ruse, one that was a pain to put in place… No, I guess it wasn't a pain for them, was it."

"No, it would not have been. They seem to have been pretty circumspect so far. While I would not put it past their military advisors to plant a decoy up there, I also suspect it has value as well," she said.

"The best we will have available might be helicopter access. Planes are going to be too easy to defend against. Or, we could do some sort of backpack or RPG options. I suspect you're right about it having value. You have to make the cheese smell delicious, don't you?" Phillip quipped.

The lady's voice came across the phone. "Yes, you do."

―――――

TQB BASE, CO, USA

The Learjet was approaching from a mile out. Gabrielle was on this flight with fifteen vampires from Japan.

Gabrielle had brought the Queen a new clan, sort of.

When the team took out Kamiko Kana, it was acceptable for Kamiko's followers to either die or change allegiance.

Three of the remaining vampires decided to 'accept death by attacking humans.' It was an excellent demonstration that the four men in front were not merely human any longer.

Their quick deaths provided Gabrielle a chance to explain the situation with Bethany Anne, the changes to the Queen's Own, and why they were here to implement the justice required by Bethany Anne. The next thing Gabrielle knew, she was accepting the oath of allegiance from fifteen vampires as Bethany Anne's representative.

She hesitated before making her first phone call to Bethany Anne. How does one go about calling your boss and telling her, "You know that request for more vampires? Got you covered." Or, "Hey boss, I have fifteen vampires that are going to follow me home, can we keep them?"

John had made it easy and just dialed Bethany Anne and said, "Tell Dan we have fifteen members for the QB Elite team."

When he got off the phone, he winked at Gabrielle and told her, "You were overthinking it. Make it seem like a win and send the problem to Dan. You're golden."

She wanted to both smack him and also give him a hug because she wasn't sure what Bethany Anne wanted to do with fifteen vampires that had just attacked her team.

In the end, she should have just gone with her gut. Gabrielle's overanalysis of the situation brought about 'analysis paralysis' and nothing got accomplished. She went to John and whispered, "Thanks." He didn't look at her, he just replied, "We got your back."

The sudden overwhelming emotions threatened to break her exterior facade. Gabrielle stepped over to a window to peek out and give herself a few moments to compose her face. If she had to die in order to protect any one of these four men, it would be a payment she would be willing to make and consider it an honor at the same time.

Fuck the back door exit, no Queen's Own was ever going to be left behind when she was around.

She turned around with a renewed sense of purpose and caught John watching her. That damnable man was too smart by half. He just nodded and continued to grab papers, asking one of the vampires to translate the content so he could decide which ones to take. They only had a few hours to gather intelligence, make plans, and schedule a date to pick them up.

They all agreed to meet back in Japan for pickup. Now, Gabrielle was bringing them to the base.

The schedule had been planned to coincide with the

arrival of the first Wechselbalg group of one hundred volunteers accompanied by Nathan and Ecaterina.

The goal was to get the two groups together, lay down the law and provide a demonstration why upsetting the apple cart would be a bad idea. Dan was coming in via Pod himself in an hour.

The teams knew that all of the major superpowers had to be constantly tweaking their satellite and radar to capture the comings and goings of the Pods. That made their team, fronted by TOM, who found the idea of a technology race against the humans to be a fun challenge. TOM would work with ADAM to see what was happening and what chatter about the supposed radar returns could be intercepted.

Occasionally, there was a significant amount of chatter that TOM knew wasn't anything of theirs. On two occasions, TOM was so involved he was trying to figure out if radar signatures were other aliens. In one of the two instances, he butted into a meeting Bethany Anne was having to explain he wanted to chase a UFO in a Pod in case it was truly not of Earth.

Bethany Anne excused herself from the meeting to jump in a Pod. Her present conversation wasn't a subject that needed her input, and it was rare for TOM to ask for anything, so why not?

She was excited to find out that the radar pings had been consistent until they came over the horizon on a straight shot towards the anomaly. The UFO had vacated the area suddenly, twenty-two seconds before they came blistering through the upper atmosphere in chase.

She could see the planes below try to track the Pod's entrance into the area by the visible streak they were making across the sky. Bethany Anne had TOM keep the Pod disturbing the upper atmosphere enough so they could be visually detected by the jets.

Unfortunately, the UFO was gone and not even their existing technology focused down towards Earth was adequate.

Which caused the two of them to disappear back up into space and ponder the issue.

She sent a note for Marcus to start working with TOM to increase the effectiveness of their spying on Earth by an order of magnitude. They had been so focused on outer space that Marcus' wisdom about the best place to look for aliens would be on Earth had been wasted.

So, whenever the superpowers on Earth were able to successfully tweak their abilities to better trace a Pod, TOM normally had an upgrade figured out within twenty-four hours. With ADAM and Marcus' help, they had modifications to bring to the Pods within forty-eight hours to further minimize the radar signature.

So far, most of the changes were to the composite paint-like substance that made them so damned hard for radar systems to detect in the first place. The updated composite was quickly used to repaint the Pods each time.

Once, TOM had to request a slight tweak to the gravitic engines because the humans started looking for changes in the airstream. Now, depending on the flight plan for the Pod, the engine would start disrupting the air with a tiny pinprick a hundred feet ahead of each pod. These modifications allowed the air cavitation protection to stream around them and recede gently back behind them.

The tweaks to the engines for rapid maneuvers weren't up to the same level of sophistication yet. If a Pod needed to do a lot of rapid directional changes, then their chance of being spotted on the upgraded radar feeds went up.

So far, TOM had been working a week to overcome that.

Dan descended straight down from above, with a detailed flight plan that allowed the Pod to minimize his air turbulence.

The team was convinced they had eyes and ears on their base and the darkness, plus the new protection to hide the comings and goings of Pods made it damned difficult for visual identification.

He saw the plane with the vampires touching down as he came streaking in from above.

Dan sighed. It had been so much easier to sneak around before the moon base went in. Now, everyone and everything was ramping up. It felt like something momentous was just over the horizon, and he hoped it was good news.

He could see the bright lights of the jet that carried the Wechselbalg. Dan's Pod slipped behind huge curtains surrounding the landing zone that allowed Pods some distance to slow down without anything registering his arrival.

Tonight was going to be a party, that was for sure.

———

Nathan wasn't concerned with the Wechselbalg he had on the plane with him. They had all been through an introduction video that he had requested from Dan. It included the original film the Queen's Bitches had used to introduce the Navy personnel so long ago and then to the Wechselbalg who became the core of the Queen's Guardians.

Both groups were damned near considered the elite now. Nathan made sure that John, Eric, Darryl and Scott's faces were recognized. Once he got that out of the way, he brought up Gabrielle's photo and mentioned she was the captain. He allowed the wolf-whistles and comments to continue for about four seconds before he played a video that showed her in action against the Wechselbalg Guardians.

The display of her martial prowess put a damper on their jubilation. When Peter switched to his Pricolici form and tried to get inside her defenses, the respect for her fighting prowess increased significantly.

"I show you these videos," he cautioned them. "Because as Weres, you will have a problem with submission to someone you haven't fought, or who hasn't beaten someone who has beaten you. You are programmed this way, and it takes an effort to think past that programming."

He walked down the aisle. "Once we exit this plane, our first stop will be a demonstration match where you can consider who the top dogs are in this organization in one of two ways." He turned to walk back towards the front, knowing that every person on the plane could hear him just fine. "The first option is by using your intelligence. I tell you right now don't fuck with the Queen's Own, they will kick your ass."

He stopped to look around before walking forward again. "The second is to raise your hand at the level you want to try and take a chance beating one of them. I told you earlier we have a group of vampires from Asia joining us." Nathan was surprised to hear a feminine 'cool' come from three rows behind him.

He turned and raised an eyebrow at the young dark haired, blue-eyed female. "Jennifer is it?" She nodded. "You approve?"

She shrugged. "I've liked vampires since Twilight." That got her some catcalls from a few guys around her, and she blushed. "I know it isn't the same, but from what you've said we are all modified humans, right?" He nodded. "So, it isn't like this is the Montagues vs. the Capulets?"

"Who?" came from four rows back. Nathan looked back. "Jason, is it?" He nodded. "Shakespeare. You should have paid more attention in English." He got a few chuckles from that. "She has a point, though. This meeting isn't some sort of us versus them match. These particular vampires are now considered the Queen's Elite. They owe their honor to Bethany Anne…"

Nathan was interrupted from halfway to the front. Once he allowed one interruption, others worked up the courage to ask questions. "Why? Did she save them or something?"

He turned back towards the front. "Well, in a way," he said. "The Queen's Own allowed them the option of changing allegiance or not." He put up a hand. "Before you ask, they would have had the option of leaving peacefully, but the only way they could leave with honor would be to fight for it, and three died. Leave it at that, okay?"

He resumed walking. "So, you're signing up. The only difference between the Queen's Elite and everyone on this plane is commitment." He arrived at the front and turned around. "You have committed to four years of service with the Queen doing whatever the hell we need you to do. You have committed to doing your best or you will answer to me why any Wechselbalg I accepted as a member isn't putting forth the effort. Trust me when I say that will not go well."

He looked around. "The Queen's Elite have already committed their Honor, their Best, their Life. So if you want to challenge them? Find out how badly you want to commit, understand?"

The Wechselbalg had all seen a video that highlighted both the Polarus and the Ad Aeternitatem. One viewer asked what the name of the ship Ad Aeternitatem meant when the phrase was mentioned in the video, and Nathan had explained that the men and women on that ship had committed themselves 'To Eternity.'

Between Nathan's explanation about the new vampires and the earlier evidence of the commitment of the people on the ships, it caused many to ask themselves what they had ever felt strongly enough about to give their all.

And what would it take to want to commit everything they had?

CHAPTER SEVEN

Akio stood silently with the rest of the vampires. Fifteen of them were all that was left after fighting for Kamiko Kana not that many weeks ago.

He had spoken with Gabrielle and learned that it was his own brother who had both dishonored himself and then covered his shame with blood to procure the opportunity for the rest of the clan to switch their allegiance from the false queen to Bethany Anne.

The men in the group were quiet. Not only because nothing was requested from them, but because it was the wiser choice. To stand and observe was the proper choice at this time.

The men spoke to each other when Gabrielle sent them back to their homes to dissolve any ties. She explained each would be allowed two suitcases of whatever they felt they wanted to bring. The rest, including all weaponry, would be provided by her Queen.

Bethany Anne was taking her responsibilities very seriously. She had passed through Gabrielle that she would expect the best and that they, in turn, should expect the most from her.

Akio looked around. There was a temporary stage in the massive hangar. It was in the back away from the closed doors.

He saw that a catwalk circled the hangar and had a couple of doors that went somewhere. One appeared to go into the next building. He couldn't tell where the door on the other side of the room went.

He could hear a second, larger jet powering down outside. Gabrielle had informed them that a group of Wechselbalg was joining them for the introduction this evening. She left it that Bethany Anne would be displeased if anything less than respect was shown to the new group.

That was enough for his people.

Then John clarified, the Queen's Own allowed all sort of talk to happen regarding them personally, but disrespect of Bethany Anne was an unacceptable offense. Akio had to smother a small smile when he noticed Gabrielle wince at John's words, but nodded her head.

She requested that Akio's team allow the Queen's Own to implement the punishment, at least in the beginning, should it be necessary.

His men were arranged seven across and two rows deep. He was standing in the front. Gabrielle had made sure that Akio's men were positioned before she disappeared.

Soon, he could hear the footsteps coming along the tarmac outside.

IT'S HELL TO CHOOSE

Jennifer preferred to go by her first name. Her last name, Ericson, she hadn't liked since she had understood that some Viking ancestor used it to recognize a son and not a daughter. Turning to step onto the stairs that took her to the tarmac below, she was the sixtieth or seventieth person off of the plane. She continued with the rest to the door inside.

After a short bottleneck as they entered the hangar, they found themselves in a space that was large enough to comfortably contain three times their number.

She noticed the bright lights and the small stage in the back. Then she saw the other men.

The vampires.

She continued in line while she watched them out of the corner of her eye. Her group was setting up in lines of fifteen wide. She ended up the second from the end closest to the other group. They were all in traditional garb, all black and passive-faced. They didn't look upset, but they did look dangerous.

She knew the ultimate vampire was Michael. Shit, her parents and even the pack master in Ohio, dick that he was, admitted no one fucked with him. She took her place and faced forward.

Nathan Lowell was not what the rumors said he was. Well, he was, and he wasn't. He was another name that was used to scare her generation to be good. It had worked, mostly. Jennifer desperately wanted to turn her head and stare over at the vampires and check them out.

Some of the guys in the group had already hit her up, but she was tired of werewolf ideas of dating and wanted to learn what other options there were. Jennifer didn't want to mess with the rules surrounding bringing a human into the UnknownWorld. That meant she couldn't involve a regular human in anything but a very short term relationship. So, that left vampires.

She twitched her eyes to her left. She wondered how old they were. That was one problem with dating werewolves. You never knew how old they were until you took a good look into their eyes. The skin can stay young, but age and experience color the view into a person's soul. So far Jennifer had never found someone who could hide their age inside.

When she went to see Nathan Lowell, she got a chance to meet one of the other rock stars of the werewolf communities. Well, at least to the women in the community. They wanted to meet the woman who was able to capture Nathan Lowell and take him off the market. While Jennifer heard plenty of catty comments, Nathan was never someone she had been interested in herself. If she couldn't deal with Were guys her own age, she didn't expect to enjoy the company of someone as old as Nathan.

But that didn't mean she didn't enjoy the eye candy. Nathan was a good looking man, and she did experience a little jealousy because… Shit! The man was seriously gorgeous. Enough that if he wasn't hitched, Jennifer would have had to reconsider her No Wechselbalg rule. When Ecaterina joined her mate a few minutes later, Jennifer told herself that she was happy to know that Nathan was off limits because she didn't date Weres. Of course, it was not because his mate was insanely beautiful and Jennifer had less of a shot at him.

Jennifer didn't consider herself a slouch in the looks department. But there's hot and Oh My God. Jennifer was hot, Ecaterina was either OMG or OMFG depending if one preferred blonds.

Until she spoke in her Romanian accent. That moved her to OMFG whether you preferred blonds or not.

Jennifer watched Nathan bow then shake hands with the vampires standing in the front lines. Nathan had changed clothes and now wore all black. It looked like he was ready to have a match right then. His shirt was spandex looking. She looked harder and could make out the UA logo. He was in pants suitable for sparring. The same martial art pants style the vampires wore.

Somebody was expecting some fights tonight, she mused.

The noise behind her stopped, and Nathan finished his conversation to look up and over at the door behind her. He turned back and bowed to the vampire and then walked over to stand in front of the Wechselbalg line. A faint pleasant scent wafted back to her. She looked up to see Ecaterina standing up front.

Ecaterina was still so newly changed that she occasionally wore perfume while in her human form. It was a minor trait that Jennifer rather liked. It reminded her that all of them were basically human, just with enhancements.

Another door opened to her right up ahead, but she couldn't see past the guy two rows in front. She was going to nickname him TDT for 'too damned tall.'

It became apparent who they were in a moment. The first guy was Dan Bosse, the head of Bethany Anne's military, the second was Lance Reynolds, Bethany Anne's father and then six of the Queen's Own took the stage. The first two looked like they were in command fatigues. Gabrielle was dressed like Nathan, but four of the Queen's Own were not.

That made her swallow. She noticed the patch on their shoulders. It was a white vampire skull on a red background with dark black hair and red eyes. It was the patch worn by the Queen's Bitches.

These were the guys that executed for disrespect and every one of them wore arms. Her eyes opened wide when she recognized the fifth Queen's Own.

It was Peter Silvers, the first Pricolici to kill a vampire in hundreds of years. She had to shut her mouth just a little. He was the undisputed bad boy of her generation and almost a poster boy of immaturity. At least, that was according to the rumors swirling around him before he got involved with this outfit.

He sure as hell didn't look immature at the moment. He looked badass and ready to shoot anyone in the audience. Well, if he didn't change forms and just rip their head off. He had a Queen's Guardians Patch on one arm, but the Queen's Bitch's patch was up top.

Apparently, once a Bitch, always a Bitch.

Dan Bosse stepped up to the front of the stage. In the audience, there wasn't one individual who needed him to use a microphone.

"Hello," he started. "My name is Dan Bosse. I am in charge of field operations for Bethany Anne. While I will get to know many of you soon enough, know that I have been aware of and fighting in the UnknownWorld for multiple decades. Both in skirmishes, then as a leader of men fighting the Nosferatu. It was during one of these episodes that Bethany Anne came in and teamed up to help us out of a well-executed ambush."

He looked over the audience. "It will be my responsibility to implement the tactics and strategies to accomplish the priorities Bethany Anne puts in front of me. Understand this," his mouth turned grim. "I will be implementing things that will put you in harm's way. Some of you will die attempting to attain these goals. Every one of these aims will contribute to eventually keeping all of us free. Some of them will be focused on making sure we are free. Free to proceed with our own plans to be prepared for the future. I will be around to talk with your teams over the next couple of days. Use this time wisely so you know what your leadership is like."

He stepped back.

"My name…" came a voice like death floating on a volcano's hot sulphurous exhaust. Jennifer jerked her head towards the vampires because where they had been almost statues this whole time, now every one of them now looked around. She saw at least a couple of Wechselbalg in every line physically turn around to try and find the source of the voice. The voice reverberated in her ears, in her mind.

It felt of power, of age, of command.

"…Is Michael."

"Ohhh, SHIT!" Jennifer checked her mouth, thank god it wasn't her talking! She caught the guy next to her putting a hand over his own mouth.

She wanted to laugh in her fright.

The vampires seemed to struggle to keep themselves standing as they were. She was told Michael was part of this group; she had even seen pictures and video of a guy they were saying was Michael with Bethany Anne around the world. But most people just figured it was a model. The boogeyman of the UnknownWorld seemed too young, too fun and frankly too happy to be the Michael from the stories.

Everyone was wrong. Jennifer could feel him around her, speaking to everyone and no one all at the same time.

Then suddenly he was at the front of the stage with his hands behind his back, looking out over the audience. He turned to face the vampires and bowed ever so slightly in response to their bows. "Please, attend," he said, and every pair of eyes obeyed.

"I have heard the gossip about my activities with Bethany Anne and how they are occasionally captured by cameras and other means. Because of this, the thought was that I could not possibly be who I was rumored to be. I would tell you to ask those who have dishonored me in the past if I am who I say I am…"

He smiled grimly as he continued, "But they are all dead."

For a quick moment, a wave of fear went out from him and it was all Jennifer could do to lock her knees and stand still.

Then the fear and desire to run away evaporated, and Michael smiled broadly. "My apologies, I've been told by Bethany Anne that I should stop being a royal asshat." He looked around. "After a thousand years, old habits are hard to break." The smile stayed on his face, but everyone noticed the quick visage change with the glaring red eyes.

It was a warning, and everyone watching received it.

"You know…" came a contralto voice from behind those on the floor. She saw Michael look behind them, so everyone turned to see a woman with dark hair up on the catwalk. She was wearing black leather pants, strapped on pistols and had a Katana as well. "I could let Michael continue his usual method of…" Then she disappeared, and Jennifer heard the rest of the sentence from the front.

She turned to see Bethany Anne on the stage looking out over the audience. "…intimidation. Suffice it to say that you do not want to piss him off. He is trying hard to learn the new reality, but he does occasionally slip." She looked over at him with a small grimace on her face. "Like now."

Fucking hell! Jennifer thought. The videos and the

pictures on the web didn't do this woman justice. Bethany Anne just created a new level above OMFG. Jennifer bit her lip, she was allowing her level of freak out to free her mind to wander instead of gibbering in fear.

Focus!

Bethany Anne turned to the vampires. She started to take a step and disappeared, only to appear in front of the head vampire.

———

Akio was doing everything he could to not bow to Michael. The sheer amount of power emanating from him answered the question most vampires had in his part of the world.

Michael was real, and his power was undeniable.

Then the pressure was gone, and Michael was apologizing. Akio turned to see who Michael was looking at and there she was.

His Queen.

Akio saw the sword attached to her back and her other weapons. She was no Kamiko Kana. This woman was a warrior first. This is how she chose to introduce herself to her people, her fighters.

And even the fabled Michael felt honored to listen to her... command? No, she called him a 'Royal Asshat.' Akio wasn't sure of the meaning, but he understood it wasn't a proper title.

Then she was on the stage and turned towards them. She took a step and was standing within arms reach.

He dropped to a knee, with all of his men behind him as they kneeled to her.

"My name is Bethany Anne," she said. "There is a

something I require before receiving your pledge of loyalty, and that is honesty." She turned slightly towards the Wechselbalg. "In committing service to a liege there is honor on both sides, honor is honesty, faithfulness, obedience. It is built on trust, confidence and actions."

Bethany Anne turned back to the vampires. "Kamiko Kana was none of these. She accepted pledges and dealt in false faith. As was required when evil commits dishonor, I sent my Own to make right the scales of justice. I take your pledge of life, of honor, of ability, in an exchange with my own to you."

She looked down at the man in front of her. "Stand, Akio."

Akio stood as she untied the Katana sheath from her back. The saya was exquisite, etched wood both beautifully polished and ages old. Akio's eyes opened in shock.

This was a fabled sword, one thought lost. This was the sword that could decide whether one deserved death or not.

"This is my sword, delivered to me by my servant Stephen, Michael's brother."

Akio's eyes opened wider yet.

"I am handing it to the Queen's Elite, to rest in your sanctum and be protected and ready for use when your Queen needs it. It shall always be ready, always be sharp, and always be protected. Is this demand honorable and do the Queen's Elite accept this charge?"

Akio bowed deeply and rose up. He held out both hands to receive the saya and the katana to his care. He turned to face his men. "In your Queen's name, rise." All fourteen men stood as one and all viewed the saya as he held it up at eye level.

"Our Queen entrusts us to protect her sword. As we will

use ours to protect her and implement her decrees. Honor is restored to us through trust. Honorably will we serve, in Honor we will die."

All fourteen men bowed to Akio, who then turned and bent to Bethany Anne. "My Queen, we are yours."

Bethany Anne turned to the other vampires. "Accepted." All of them stood tall with their hands behind their backs. Bethany Anne reached over to touch Akio. "Come with me." Everyone who could see the two were shocked when Bethany Anne and Akio disappeared to reappear on the stage. She turned as Akio got his bearings from the sudden disappearance and reappearance. "Gabrielle?"

Gabrielle took a few steps up beside the two. Akio was trying to keep the shock off his face. "Please provide Akio a place here on the stage."

Gabrielle bowed slightly to Akio. "Welcome!" Akio was momentarily astounded at all of the smiles surrounding him. Scott and Peter separated for him to step up between them. Akio saw John looking at him and saw the huge man wink. Turning in place, Akio looked to view his men.

Bethany Anne had just returned the honor they desperately needed. His chest was filled with the feeling that this is what the samurai knew in the ages long ago. The undying desire to merge the religious with the physical. The knowledge that honor existed in two directions and that life was now focused and balanced.

Peter leaned towards him. Akio could perceive the Were smell on him. "Here." Akio held the sword in one hand and reached down with his left to feel a small piece of fabric delivered to him. He took a second to glance at it.

It was a patch. The same patch all of the Queen's Own wore.

The head of the Queen's Elite was now a member of the Queen's Bitches.

"It's got a sticky, rip off the back and press it to your shoulder… Oh shit." Akio noticed Pete's eyes focused ahead, and Akio turned to see Bethany Anne looking in their direction and realized she had heard Pete's voice.

She took a couple of steps towards them, but she was smiling at Peter, who was grinning back. "Always a troublemaker, Pete?" She held out her hand. Everyone on the stage was leaning around each other to see what was going on.

"It was…ahh, fuck it. It was me!" He grinned.

"Yeah, I'll bet." She looked over towards John, who was intentionally looking elsewhere. "Give it to me."

Akio handed his Queen the patch. "Turn to your left, Akio." He could see those in front of him smiling and decided to enjoy the turn of events, even if it originally seemed like it was trouble. He stood there as she peeled the backing off of the patch and affixed it to his sleeve. She pressed hard to make a good seal. "Akio, before your clan, before the Guardians, the Queen's Own and myself, you are now Akio of the Queen's Bitches."

Akio smiled back at his Queen and was surprised when everyone on stage started hollering congratulations and pounding him on the back. He noticed that even those out on the floor, in both groups, were cheering for him.

Akio took his place in the lineup and waited for the next part in the play.

———

Kurt Williams had been a little bored through the event. He was standing just behind and to the right of Nathan Lowell, who had mentioned an opportunity to fight.

Now, fighting was where Kurt excelled, and it was something he was very, very good at. While he had been respectful of Nathan, he didn't believe all the hype Nathan kept spewing out about the group of humans.

And, oh yes, they were humans! He could smell them clearly. Kurt wasn't disrespectful at all, he wanted to fight against some of the best and see what he could do. While he could have fought, and had a good chance of winning had he challenged the alpha of the pack, he didn't want the responsibilities that came with it.

He just loved to fight.

The adrenaline rush, the slowdown of reality, the twitch of weight to another leg that heralded the attack to come, and the rush to defend or mitigate the opponent was where he lived to be.

When Kurt understood that Nathan was asking him to sign up for a four-year stint in a group that was focused on becoming the best fighters, it was like asking a geek if they wanted the latest video card for their gaming machine.

When asked a simple question, he gave a simple answer. "Where do I sign up?" Kurt turned to his father, who smiled and told him, "See you on holidays, son." Kurt looked down to see his father's hand held out to him.

His Dad understood. Kurt shook his father's hand, had his mother cry against his chest, and was told to 'learn something besides how to stop fists with his face!' The day came to go to the airport, and he had grabbed his duffle. His father met him at the door, and no one spoke the whole way to the airport.

His father understood him like that. They shook, hugged in the man-way of pounding each other on the back, and his

Dad said only, "See you on leave, son."

And that was that.

Kurt was impressed with the jet lined up for them, and when he approached the airplane, Nathan pointed to him, and designated an area to the side of him. He walked over as Nathan told him to drop his duffel by the other luggage on the ground, and to stand with him.

Nathan did that four other times with new arrivals, and in the end, five recruits waited together. Kurt thought about what Nathan was doing when the person after him radiated a barely-controlled desire to fight, and was followed by a third person with the same attitude. It was evident. Every one of the five could see the same fire they looked at in the mirror each morning reflected back at them from the others around Nathan.

They all wanted to test themselves. Nathan didn't force his dominance on anyone. It just was. The desire to prove himself against anyone and everyone that needed to fight folded when colliding with the indomitable will of Nathan Lowell.

Around Nathan, peace reigned.

Even when his mate came up and spoke with him, none of them felt a need to puff out their chests. Kurt was surprised to find out later what happened when he found himself alone with Ecaterina. His need subsumed itself like a puppy around any dominant alpha.

Kurt knew the stories of Ecaterina's ability to change to a Pricolici, but this was the first time he understood she carried that same calmness within her. He idly wondered what she looked like when she got angry and then smiled as a quote from an old TV show came back to him, 'Don't make me angry, you wouldn't like me when I'm angry!'

IT'S HELL TO CHOOSE

Now he was curious. The calm around Nathan was in effect, but he understood soon he was going to be able to let the challenge erupt from his throat…

———

John Grimes watched as Bethany Anne turned back around from helping Akio place the patch on his arm. John was the one who had made a point of making sure the vampires knew that they were in the group. He wouldn't allow any team to hang out in the wind. They were either in, or they were out.

Michael had confirmed their desire to support Bethany Anne. If any of them had been a problem, Michael's entrance into the event would have been very different. It would have been preceded with the sudden death of vampires and a very bloody Michael appearing amongst the carnage.

This was one point Michael wasn't willing to bend on with Bethany Anne. He absolutely, positively wouldn't allow a shadow of doubt regarding the oaths she would accept from the vampires. Each would be willing to follow Bethany Anne into death, or he would kill them himself before Bethany Anne accepted their oath.

No one, to Michael's best ability, was going to be around Bethany Anne that was a risk. John figured 'hell no' was Michael going to confess to Bethany Anne everything he did to make sure she was safe. John knew of a couple of times Michael had just handled someone, and as her guard, he approved.

John didn't give a flip that a couple of minds had been tweaked, and people sent away. John figured better to be sent away than another two deaths. Michael was a much better man than before, but the armor between the new Michael and the old Michael was rife with holes, and the old Michael was always a breath away from coming out.

At least it was where Bethany Anne was concerned. For Michael personally, he rolled with the punches much better. Peter had come into the meeting room a little earlier and held out his hand to Michael and asked, "So, how's the Dark Lord of the Sith this evening?"

John had wanted to both slap Pete for being glib and simultaneously put his face in his hand so he didn't see the carnage. He was shocked when Michael shook Pete's hand and told him in a stage whisper with a smile, "That is supposed to be a secret, young apprentice!"

John looked at Eric whose mouth was open and then Gabrielle, who had turned from her conversation to stare in shock at Michael as well.

Pete shrugged. "That's okay, the unknown and unwashed heathens will never figure it out!" Pete then looked around and asked, "Where are the cookies and milk?"

Michael pointed back behind him. "Cheryl Lynn has them set up back there."

Now, Bethany Anne was ready to speak to them, and John brought his musing to a halt.

————

Bethany Anne looked out over the group and paused.

Thoughts, TOM?

Wait, What? Why are you asking me something?

Take a look out there, what do you see?

Ummm... People?

I see over a hundred and fifteen people modified by Kurtherians in one way or another. I see humans that are lining up to die, TOM. I see humans having to deal with changes to their bodies, some for over a century.

I... I'm sorry, Bethany Anne. I hadn't stopped to consider this.

I know, TOM. I'm not judging you. I'm reminding both of us that we are setting up some of these in front of us to die. Perhaps here on Earth, maybe in space. Friends, brothers, family and compatriots. I'm afraid the chatter ADAM has found, and that Frank is watching, is confirming we are going to be against powerful agencies here on Earth, as well.

All I can do is tell you what I know of the Clans. Well, that and I know there are other races out there that love to fight.

Well? So do humans.

Bethany Anne spoke clearly. "You have been introduced in one form or fashion to every person up here. Some by Gabrielle, some by Nathan." She looked over at the Wechselbalg.

"The differences between vampires and Wechselbalg are a result of technology, nothing more. The reality is, both alien technologies that affect us were introduced here on Earth for one thing—*war.*"

There was a slight stirring on the Wechselbalg side. She noticed Ecaterina in the back of the group. The way she understood it, she had a calming effect on the Wechselbalg's innate desire to act up.

"You have heard the news, and you know some of the details. We are presently working to expand our base on the Moon, complete our first space station, start mining for materials, and build the production facilities to create space-craft."

This time, the murmurs increased a little as they took in the scope of what she just said. The moon base had been explained to them. The space station was new information and so were the production facilities.

Fortunately, Jakob Yadav had already started handling the 'requests for her time' coming from a multitude of interests. Some news organizations, some non-profit, some business and a few from nation-states.

Including Paraguay. While Paraguayans were proud that their country was the first to go to space with the new technology, they weren't very happy about not knowing before everyone else. Officials from the government had arrived at the location where TQB testing had occurred with their military helicopters to find nothing but a large area of mud.

Lots and lots of mud.

Bethany Anne continued, "We will be making choices. Not just for ourselves, but for our neighbors. Those next door, those across the city, another state, and other countries. We will be making choices for those we love, and those we hate." She looked around. "Understand this, you will be fighting for those who hate you, vilify you, and would spit on you. Well," she smiled at them. "If they could spit up to space, anyway!"

She got a few chuckles. "We won't get there without upsetting a lot of people. They won't understand because I'm not going to tell them why we're doing this. We're working on ways to handle the bad press. But the reality is, most will choose what is easy rather than what is hard. Especially when what they have to go on is a vague concept of the enemy at best."

"Hard is just fucking hard!" She grinned. "And if there is one thing we know, it's that hard is what we do better than anyone." Her smile turned feral. "And when challenged, we hit back, and we hit back hard. If others play nice, we play nice."

"If not?" She sighed loudly, the weight of leadership heavy on her shoulders. "Then it's hell to choose, but I will choose the future over the present. I will choose opportunity over status quo, and I will choose freedom over subjugation."

She continued, "There is always freedom to choose. Freedom to make something of yourself as we move forward. This group is composed of a lot of Americans, and due to that, some Americanisms are bound to occur. The first is that you respect leadership, but trust comes with time, with testing, and with trials."

"I am to understand that every Wechselbalg here has been informed you may test your prowess against my Own, my Guardian's lead and should you pass, you may test your mettle against me."

This caused a murmur again. No one had told them they could rise up high enough to fight Bethany Anne herself.

"No?" She grinned. "That's because where you come from, fighting is a sport. My team has been tested in fire, in blood, in bullets, and in mayhem. We have fought in the Florida Everglades, from the countries in South America to the mountains of Turkey, and beyond to Asia. I'll be honest, your chance of beating anyone on this stage is infinitesimally small. But I leave that option open. If you can win through, you get to fight me."

She turned to the vampires. "I understand your oath restricts you from this display. Just know we will spar later. I will have you understand your present limitations and how I expect you to step up!"

A complete hush fell as Bethany Anne allowed her visage to change, her eyes to glow red as she turned to look at both groups. The vampires went down to one knee as her fangs grew and she pushed out her mind towards all in attendance and sent her voice into each one staring at her now.

My name is Bethany Anne. I am the Queen Bitch. I am the only one you will kneel to until you die, or leave my service. For some, that means on your shield, for others when your agreement is up.

Until that time, you are forbidden to answer to anyone but who I appoint. No outside interest controls you, commands you, or summons you.

Is this understood?

Even the five standing behind Nathan shouted their 'Yes!' with gusto.

Nathan himself was having trouble coming to grips with the change in his leader since he left to go work with the Wechselbalg. When he had left, Bethany Anne was a leader, charismatic and decisive.

Now? Now she commanded all of those attributes and a force of will elevated above what she had before. She was truly a Queen now; it wasn't just her title.

It is who she had become.

CHAPTER EIGHT

Jakob was waiting for Bethany Anne when she stepped into his office. He looked up and smiled. "How did it go?"

Darryl had poked his head in right before Bethany Anne's arrival. Jakob could hear him snort from right outside his door and say, "About like a rambunctious high school football player deciding he was good enough to play in the pros. It was over so fast that the last contestant admitted he wasn't expecting much, but he just had to know. So, this time, John didn't break any of his bones, he just picked him up and knocked him out."

"I take it they all want to go against John?"

Bethany Anne grinned as she took the cushy black chair in his office. "It was a gimme." She got comfortable. "Once Nathan planted the seeds that John was the one to beat, the first guy called him out."

"What happened?" Jakob had been curious, but Bethany Anne had told him it wouldn't have gone over very well for the Weres to know they had been humiliated in front of humans.

"Well, John got to get a little exercise and five Weres got to take a nap. He broke legs and arms to make sure they got the picture that to fuck with him was a really, really bad idea. Never broke up a sweat, but would allow them to throw a few punches, kicks, or attacks. That would go on until Michael would casually call 'time.' Then John would go on the offensive. He would usually catch the next attack. If it was a punch, he would stop the fist in midair, then break their arm and punch them out. Same idea if it was a kick."

Darryl's voice came again from the hallway. "Tell him about you and Michael!"

She rolled her eyes. "Once the display of man testosterone was finished, Michael and I took the middle and went at it. First, we did it at normal speed, then twice as fast. When we got our rhythm down, we upped it twice more."

Darryl peeked around the corner. "You should have seen the vampires after the third ramp up. They couldn't even see the hits anymore, and they honest-to-god started talking to each other. They had been eerily quiet the whole time. Now, they wouldn't shut up. Finally, they cranked up the speed one more time, and even Gabrielle was having a hard time seeing what was going on."

Darryl turned back to make sure nothing was happening in the corridor before turning to look back into the office. "She was upset when she realized you hadn't been sparring with her as fast as you could!"

Bethany Anne shrugged. "It was Michael. I've had to up my game going against him just to hold my own. I could punch at him, but a lot of the time he'd switch over to myst and I wouldn't have anything to hit. God, was it frustrating!"

Her little outburst told Jakob everything he needed to know about how competitive she was. She would rise to any occasion. Defeat wasn't an option.

On her part, Bethany Anne wasn't going to admit that she had TOM go through every part of her body, and they had gone back up to the spaceship to implement an update to the synapse firings to make her as fast as she could be.

She couldn't beat Michael, but now he wasn't able to take her either. Whenever he tried to myst to take her by surprise, she was too shrewd to stay in one place. Even when she tested staying still, she was finally able to sense his materialization and get out of the way in time.

She had been crowing to herself one time about her skills when TOM let on there were others in the universe that would be a difficult challenge for her. It had splashed a cold bucket of ice water on her jubilation to realize her present skills, while elite, just put her up in a group of maybe thirty or forty of the best martial fighters in the nearby galaxy that TOM was aware of back in his time.

She hoped that her teams never had to fight one of these until they figured out how to compensate. Which, she realized, would mean it was a suitable defense against her as well.

Fuckity-fuck!

Jakob brought the conversation back around. "I asked you here to discuss what ADAM has found through spy satellites."

"Whose?" she asked.

"Everyone's apparently, but I'm most concerned with the USA's satellites that aren't supposed to point down on our own country. From what ADAM can see, these are approved repositionings."

What are you doing about the satellites?"

>>**I'm sending them pictures with the area modified to still look like it did months ago and slightly out of focus.**<<

Why not just send them older pictures?

>>**Easily deduced and once that is done, they would all be trying to change the defensive hacking algorithms. And, they would know that their spy satellites had been hacked.**<<

ADAM, track those images.

>>**Understood.**<<

"Ok, what do you suggest we do about them?" she inquired.

"Well, suing them isn't a viable option. That would cause us too many other problems and then we would be on the radar of some very influential people."

"We aren't already?" she asked.

"Well, sure. But we haven't had a request to speak before Congress, as an example," Jakob replied.

"Exactly how would they make me do that?" She smiled at him, and he rolled his eyes.

"Just because they can't exactly figure out who you are, doesn't mean that your Romanian passport will save you from further review. The longer you stay out of sight, the better." He leaned back in his chair and chewed on his pen for a moment before asking, "I don't suppose you do ditzy well, do you?"

Bethany Anne lowered her eyes to stare at her recalcitrant counsel when she heard Darryl snort. "No."

"Hey, I have to ask. I didn't think you would pull it off too well, but you asked me for my best. A ditzy interview or two and then you have some of the guys looking for the power behind the throne so to speak. Hell, half these people are still going to look for it."

"Because I'm too young, too female or too…"

"Good looking," Jakob supplied.

"Seriously?"

"Yes, of course. Men have issues with a woman who is too good looking. We can't handle it internally, you see. It's bad enough that all of our chemicals are fighting us when you come around. When you open your mouth and express your intelligence, we immediately have to try to label you a pariah, a bitch, a … Well, never mind. Too much power in your hands at that point. Well, some I suppose, would just find you to be that much more of a challenge, but those guys can't imagine someone better than them anyway." He shrugged, noncommittal. "Them's the breaks, kid."

Bethany Anne sat back then turned her head towards the door. "Darryl, what do you think about what Jakob said?"

Darryl didn't put his head inside the door this time. Rather, he called out, "Which part?"

Bethany Anne chewed her lip. "The too good looking part. Is this a problem?"

This time, Darryl put his head inside the door. "With the team? Hell no! We've seen the blood. Problem solved."

Before he could duck back, she followed it up with, "And others?"

He stopped to consider that. "Most guys? Yes, it's mostly true. Obviously, not the vampires and certainly not Michael. But for a lot of the general population it could be a challenge. But really, guys have figured out tactics when dealing with women who are intelligent and attractive. For most guys, it won't be an issue because you'll be out of reach, and therefore you'll be a fantasy, not a reality. It's the women you have to worry about."

"Yeah, I know about that side. Thanks." He nodded and

turned back to the hallway. "So, speaking of ladies, how are the negotiations with Jennifer Tehgen going?" She had turned back to Jakob.

"Well, she's going to be my representative in Washington for now. That way, they can't ask her anything, and if they do try to question her, she's never been here."

"I won't allow someone to grab her." Bethany Anne started.

Jakob put up a hand to stop her. "She has backup already. Frank Kurns found three close-support personnel to keep up with her."

"Who?" Bethany Anne was trying to think who he might have hired and how he vetted them.

Jakob leaned forward to grab one of his many yellow pads. "I see that he has supplied a Rickie Escobar, Matthew Tseng and one of the Guardian Marines, a Scottie."

Bethany Anne wanted to pick up the phone and ask Frank what the hell was he thinking? He had just shipped out two Werewolves and a human who knew way the hell too much.

"They won't be questioned," Jakob said.

"What?" Bethany Anne turned to regard the lawyer.

"Your guards, they won't get questioned besides the standard what's going on because they have completely clean files. Dossiers from a company that show they're only with her to keep off the uninvited. There is nothing to show they are part of your crew."

"That can't last forever," she argued. "Eventually…"

"Eventually, you will be out of range, and it won't be a question, right?" He interrupted.

For whatever reason, maybe it was his jovial attitude, Bethany Anne didn't mind his always interrupting her. They had shared some of the serum with him to help him physically. Enough that his insides were at least fifteen years younger and a couple of years on the outside could be waved away as an excellent diet and exercise program.

Now, he would get up before her and finish long after she would have thought prudent.

"Having fun?" she changed the subject.

"The best!" He pursed his lips. "Although I was a little annoyed that I didn't get to sue Brimer into oblivion."

"You did get to negotiate the agreement with them. You allowed them to stay in business."

"Well, that was enjoyable, but I would have shut them down."

Bethany Anne shrugged. "We still have leverage. Take it all away, and there isn't anything to stop them from focusing on us."

"Is that why Brimer stays employed with them?"

"Yes. His partners will constantly be worried about Brimer, so I see it as a win-win for us."

"Why did you want me to interview Jennifer? She turned out to be a hell of a catch, but how did you know?"

"Michael read her mind." Bethany Anne said.

"I thought it was going to be something like that. He seemed to make up his mind about me pretty quickly."

"You aren't bothered by that? A lawyer sitting around someone who can read his mind?"

He pushed his hand out and said, "Nah, I learned decades ago to own everything I did or don't do it. I'm not hiding anything before… Well, the statute of limitations is now way past on a couple of youthful indiscretions."

"Ok, what about the other concerns you mentioned…"

Bethany Anne left almost forty-five minutes later, and she was glad Jakob had agreed to work for her. He was a widower for the past fifteen years, and it had taken him about three minutes to decide he wanted to move on base. Kevin McCoullagh had supplied him a team to go back and shut down his house. Now, they had someone selling it for him.

He would be a very, very busy man for a long, long time.

QBS POLARUS, SAILING TOWARDS FRANCE.

"Exactly how," Bobcat asked, "are we supposed to deal with making sure no one wishes us harm when they get on the ship?" Bobcat was looking at a message that Bethany Anne had sent them.

Presently, the team included Jeffrey, Bobcat, William, Marcus and Cheryl Lynn, who had grabbed a pod and come over for the meeting. Todd had been working particularly hard trying to learn more about design and engineering of components, so John suggested he come over to speak to William when there was a break.

So, Todd got to go up in a Pod. He did need to talk with William, and John said that a meeting like this should cement their friendship, if Todd would be respectful. Todd agreed he would be and had tried to act like getting a chance to fly over to the Polarus was no big thing. Cheryl Lynn could see from John's expression Todd was doing a bad job of hiding his excitement.

Presently, Todd was over in the cafeteria eating.

"I don't know," Cheryl Lynn admitted. "I was hoping it was some sort of hat they put on or something like a metal detector they walk through."

"That's not a bad idea," Jeffrey started.

"Which one?" Bobcat asked. "The aluminum foil hat or the doorway of shame?"

"Why would they be ashamed?" Cheryl Lynn asked.

"Imagine everything a transportation security officer sees when your luggage goes through the metal detector at the airport," Bobcat said.

"And that's just what's in luggage." William agreed.

"So, we have to figure out a way to green light or red light them without seeing their inner thoughts?" she asked.

Jeffrey considered that question. "There could be a place in the brain where we can focus. Michael has to be seeking something when he does his mind voodoo." Marcus smiled at that. "We need a way to…"

Marcus interrupted him. "TOM says that the Kurtherians had messed with that for at least seven generations before he left on his ship. So, the relevant information is stored there. ADAM probably has access if he helps TOM. But we're going to need a translation algorithm," Marcus said, and then started typing furiously. "Ah, he says the bigger doorway idea is just fine, and it would work for intent, but not for specific details, that takes focus." Marcus started typing furiously.

Jeffrey looked over at Cheryl Lynn. "You're the PR person, what do you think?"

Cheryl Lynn thought about that. She had finally grown accustomed to the experience that although role dictated your minimum responsibilities—anything could and would be dumped in your lap, especially if you suggested a 'good idea.'

"I think I would prefer that we build a door that everyone who enters the ship arrives through. Have them photographed and IDs flagged somehow at that point. We'll need to give everyone an ID anyway. A few people will have support people with them, so everyone in the party will be flagged at that point, you never know if someone else is just skilled enough to get by us. Put the troublemakers into one place and see if we can get a Vamp to come and check them out at that point." She stopped and considered. "Yeah, that's a good start."

Marcus was still typing, but the rest of the men reviewed her words. "Good suggestion," Jeffrey agreed and then continued, "Our new ship is being retrofitted at Alstom Chantiers de l'Atlantique in St. Nazaire-Penhoet, France. The previous owners had been retrofitting it but with the economies tanking the last year and a half, were very pleased to get an offer that allowed them to get their money back out of it."

Jeffrey handed out a few folders to each person at the table. "Stephen has us turned west and is taking us over to that side of France. Between here and there, we're going to need to..."

"Holy shit!" William exclaimed and looked over at Cheryl Lynn. "You really want to do this?" William fist-bumped Bobcat as he whistled.

"Not only do this to the new ship, but we need to retrofit the Polarus and the Ad Aeternitatem as well," she said.

William looked at Jeffrey. "Bethany Anne okay with this?"

Jeffrey said, "It seems, this time, Cheryl Lynn received cart blanche from Bethany Anne, and I've had Stephen confirm this in a roundabout way. It's valid."

"Ooohhhh," Bobcat smiled. "You have just risen up in my estimation, young PR person." Bobcat looked back down into the folder. "We're going to have to figure out the stresses this is going to cause." He looked at Marcus. "Hey, Dr. Miraculous." Marcus kept typing so Bobcat rapped his knuckles on the table. "Hey. Dr. Deaf." He lifted up the folder. "Do you know what's in this?"

Marcus looked down at the blue folder and picked it up. He opened it and then closed it to turn it over and open it again. Everyone watched as he started reading at the top and then his eyes widened in alarm and he put the folder down. "Are you shitting me?" Marcus asked Jeffrey.

"No, not at all." Jeffrey eyed Marcus. "From our other conversations, this seems entirely doable. What's the issue?"

Marcus stopped and looked up. "Except for the part where the stresses are going to go in the completely opposite direction? None."

"Why?" asked William. "Couldn't we just use opposing gravitic engines to help keep the stress the same?"

Marcus nodded.

"Okay, gentlemen." Everyone turned back to Jeffrey. "And lady. We have until we arrive off the coast of France to be prepared to prep the new mid-size ocean liner and these two ships."

"This is seriously going to make some geeks wet their pants," Bobcat said.

CHAPTER NINE

"I'm telling you." Jennifer said. "That this is a bitch no matter how in shape you are!"

The new recruits, well the Wechselbalg anyway, were running through the mountains around the camp each day, morning and night.

At first, it was just a gripe session on feet. That was until the third day when all hell broke loose. They had four groups of twenty-five running different paths in and around the area and even with their superior senses, they never heard, saw or smelled Peter's group and their attacks. Personally, Jennifer thought the massive stink bombs were going a little too far. The smell wouldn't come out of her nose for a damned hour.

Those that weren't incapacitated by the smell or the sound grenades were taken down by whichever Guardian from Peter's group was assigned to take them.

At first, it only required sound grenades, stink bombs,

and one Guardian to ravage a group of twenty-five newbies. When each of the teams got together to concoct field expedient protective devices, it started to get a little more interesting. The second attack, her team had three able to fight back. They went down, but Joseph Greggs was looking a little beat up by the end.

They were on high alert for the next run, but nothing happened. It was the third run, right at the end when the base was right over the next ridge and they started to relax when they were hit again, hard.

They were tired, they were pissed, and frankly they lost their mind to aggravation and anger. Eight of the twenty-five went straight to their larger wolf form while the other seven left with enough focus to attack took out their wooden batons and charged in the direction that the grenades came from.

Which is to say right over the ridge into an ambush.

The compressed air rounds painted those coming over the hill with darts and ink. The darts had enough nanocyte-infused sleeping product to overcome the werewolves' ability to fight it.

Jennifer had seen the group going over the top and was forcing herself to get up and start running. She wasn't going to be left behind when her teammates were up there getting into God knew what.

She found out a minute later as she came up to the top, gaining momentum, and crashed into a person in a ghillie suit. She was shot three times with a pistol before she understood her error. Once in her neck, and twice to her torso. She reached up and grabbed the feathered dart, yanking it out and then the two others. She started towards him. "Motherfucker! That shit stings…" and then collapsed into the dirt.

What felt like moments later, but was at least a little while from what she could tell by the position of the sun, she felt a shake on her shoulder. "Wake up!" She looked up into… Timmons? Shit, she couldn't remember.

"What the hell?" she slurred.

"We got ambushed, again." Timmons' face looked resigned. "We reacted just the way we were warned against. We aren't thinking, at all."

Jennifer turned over to look up into the sky. "Hey, we got a bunch of us over the ridge!"

Timmons smiled. "Yeah, and we fucking ran right into an ambush. Poor Williams-Jones over there got hit with twelve darts. He can't remember if he's a boy or a girl yet." Timmons looked up to the ridge. "Get your ass up and help someone else wake up. We all walk into the base, or we carry who those that can't make it on their own." With that said, Timmons stood up and moved away.

The team learned later that the ink was there to annoy the ever-loving shit out of them as those who were dirty scrubbed like hell to get it off. No one was allowed to find an easier method.

The learning, they were told, would happen with each moment they scrubbed.

Each time they went out, they learned. First, they put out scouts to trip any ambushes. Unfortunately, it took another ambush to realize that they needed line of sight on their scouts or quiet takedowns reduced their effectiveness.

They had requested better armor and received it. Their team learned from another that they could ask for anything they could think of that might help. 'This isn't the military where everything is handed to you, improvise, adapt!' was the phrase that came back to them.

Now, they all had been told to go hit the showers, eat and

to reconvene at 14:00 in the number one hangar.

She had heard the murmurs before she hit the doors to get in the room. When she got inside, she was just as surprised as everyone else who was waiting for them.

Vampires.

Dressed in camouflage and in the same dress they were in. These were the vampires that had originally been in the first meeting. Jennifer went to her spot and sat down.

Dan Bosse was talking with Kevin McCoullagh up on the stage when Dan reached up to his shoulder to push something, and she could read his lips—'say again?' He nodded and then cut off his conversation with Kevin, who stepped to the back of the stage.

Dan moved forward, and everyone settled down. "Good afternoon." He eyed everyone there. "I appreciate how hard you guys are working to get your physical skills up and hone your ability to take control of the animal in you." He grimaced. "Poor choice of words but the sentiment is right. For you to become a fighting unit you have to stay in your best mind for the job. Usually, that will be your human form for the Wechselbalg."

He started walking back and forth on the podium. "I admire the advances you have made, the fact that you all realized it isn't four teams against each other, but rather four teams accomplishing the same goal. For now, your goal has been to repel invaders."

He looked around the room. "Actually, you've done pretty poorly on that front." He smiled. "But, now we're going to do something besides send you out to run and defend. The running was the important part. The defending was to make you forget about all of the concentrated exercise you were doing. You all won or lost together, and learned that the four teams can share data, and learned how to trust each of the other teams. Now we're going to start making one team out of the four groups."

At that point, the massive hangar doors started jerking, preparing to open, letting in the mid-afternoon sun as it speared the first two inch crack as the doors separated. For a second, no one stirred, then Jennifer yelled out. "Dammit! The vampires!" She broke ranks and started running to the doors. Soon most of her team and many others ran to join her. A few of the guys realized they could try to protect the vampires with their clothes. They stripped off their tops and started towards the vampires, who stood mystified.

"HOLD!"

The massive doors stopped moving, the Wechselbalg who had made it to the doors stopped trying to pull them shut again, and those that were coming to the vampires' rescue with their shirts realized the vampires were looking at them curiously.

"This is a genuine test…" The contralto voice floated down to the people in the hangar from above. Everyone looked up to see her above them. Like last time, she stood up on the catwalk above the doors. "The test of whether you care for any and all under my banner."

The Wechselbalg realized that they had responded as a team. They heard the cry, they saw the response, they followed each other.

"My Elite," she called out in a commanding tone. "Honor!"

Fifteen vampires bowed deeply to the Wechselbalg. At first, the Wechselbalg didn't know what to do. Then those around Jennifer saw her response and the reaction flowed out from her area like ripples on a pond.

One hundred Wechselbalg bowed back.

IT'S HELL TO CHOOSE

"Up!" Dan called. He spoke because Wechselbalg wouldn't know when to quit, otherwise. A few of those who had come to the vampires held out their hands and soon it was a massive group of men and women all shaking hands and talking when the first Wechselbalg asked the vampires why they weren't afraid of the sun.

They admitted the Queen had modified them.

"Oh, HELL yeah!" A shorter, stocky guy named Barson yelled out, "They can go out in the sun." He pointed to the vampire who answered. "I want him on my team!" Then the laughing got louder and the pleading for the vampires to join the separate teams began.

Dan heard a voice in his head. "You called it." He grinned as he looked up to where Bethany Anne was standing.

But she was gone.

Dan smiled and allowed himself a few moments to enjoy the results.

———

Cheryl Lynn walked into the second room of her four container suite. Todd, Tina and she were testing the configuration to see if it had everything a small family such as theirs would need to live in outer space.

The kids each had a room in one container. They were not happy to find out that all of the water usage rooms, including the bathrooms and shower, were in one container. Tina had to deal with Todd occasionally, and Cheryl Lynn did not tell her daughter there was a configuration with two bathrooms that her mother had decided against.

It would push Tina to learn to cope a little better with the constraints in space.

The water containers were one third bathroom and wash facilities, two-thirds kitchen. The induction stove was effective, efficient, easy to buy, and easy to install. There was a discussion on how many burners to put on the stove top, and the final number ended up being three based on space and need. You could walk right through the middle of the kitchen to the eating area and then beyond into the next room.

A decision was made that every family unit had a responsibility to help grow their own food. Or they could produce one type of food and trade for others. Either way, unless the company was footing the total expense for a professional in space, it was agreed that little things would be added to underscore the need for people to be self-sufficient and self-reliant.

The hydroponics area wasn't very big, but it was capable of growing different types of fruits and vegetables. Cheryl Lynn was aware that Michelle, the scientist responsible for all food growth was building unique containers that would be designed to support specific foods. One of the first designs was for potatoes. Instead of all dirt, she was working on a method that used a fake straw. The water was automatically added, but the mulching of the fake straw (or 'earthing up' as she called it) was done by hand as the plants grew. The lighting inside the container was some of the best technology now available, and there was a lot.

Cheryl Lynn had been interviewed no less than twelve times on the food production. She would usually explain that the methods were not super advanced, but instead just used the knowledge available to anyone who had the money to go buy pre-built shipping containers.

If the reporter were particularly annoying, Cheryl Lynn would point out that some of the most exceptional strides in understanding how to grow plants in a closed container environment were presently being undertaken by those growing marijuana.

She sat down on the couch and spoke. "House, turn on the TV and play the news clips curated. First, show me Bethany Anne clips."

She grabbed her notebook and then took a sip of her tea as the first clip came up.

"This is Michael Eaves, CNN News, Africa. The elusive CEO of TQB Enterprises was seen entering the government building in South Africa. For those who might have been living under a rock, TQB Enterprises is the international conglomerate that put a base on the Moon about six weeks ago."

The man looked behind him to point at a white, stone faced building. "Speculation is that she is discussing opportunities to work with the local governments in Africa to combat AIDS. Part of the reason, we suspect, is that Africa has 91% of the HIV-positive children.

"Usually, most government projects have inadequate security protocols, and there would be many leaks by now. But these talks are different. One person, who wished to remain anonymous, admitted that the state had fourteen individuals in a previous meeting but three, including a high-ranking cabinet member, were tossed out."

The news reporter looked back into the camera. "I've since learned that the cabinet member was arrested. This is now the third example of someone being asked to leave one of these meetings and then being arrested afterward. It makes you wonder if TQB Enterprises has their own spy agency or mind-reading technology to ensure those in the room can be trusted. This is Michael Eaves, CNN News, Africa."

Another sip of tea, another clip came online. "Hello, This

is Kerry Shea from France 24 News. TQB Enterprises CEO Bethany Anne was caught leaving a care facility late last night after visiting victims still recovering from the most recent terrorist attacks. No one had known she was visiting this small facility until it was mentioned on the social network Viadeo, a professional networking social media website, no less. The post, placed there by the nighttime manager, wasn't picked up by news reviewers for almost twenty-two minutes, allowing the reclusive CEO to spend more time before reporters were able to get close."

Cheryl Lynn murmured to the TV, "I bet you strike off all social media websites instead of just the big names next time you tell someone not to rat you out, Bethany Anne."

The clip ended, another came up. "European Financial News Today has uncovered TQB Enterprises has purchased over forty thousand shipping containers in the last few months leading up to the successful Moon Base launch. This caused the containers, which typically sold used for between one thousand eight hundred to two thousand five hundred dollars apiece, to go up in price twenty percent. Now, the price of used shipping containers has skyrocketed after news of the Moon Base project. The rumors are that the company is going to use them to build a shipping container based city on the Moon. There is a small business still selling containers to those wishing to use them for personal purposes for less than three thousand dollars, and the deal is absolutely one container per person at this time."

"That's because we're making a killing on all of you speculative buyers and Bethany Anne doesn't want to hurt the little guys and gals financially." Cheryl Lynn said to the TV.

Cheryl Lynn made a note to remind herself about leaking that information when they sold down to about ten thousand containers. With the money coming from the rise due to speculative shipping container purchasing, Team BMW had new containers built based on their unique designs.

Cheryl Lynn set her pad aside. "House, pause the clip." She walked into the kitchen and opened the smaller fridge. She reached in and grabbed a couple of carrots and closed the door. She opened the pantry to grab the peanut butter and then went back and got comfortable on the couch again. "House, continue the clips."

"This is Kieron Colan with all the news that matters in England. In the group of news labeled, 'Hot Babes That Are CEOs' we're talking about Bethany Anne and her hunky, hunky boyfriend, Michael. One of the most interesting aspects of this guy is that he has no last name. None, zilch, zip, nada. This scrumptalicious boytoy seems to have eyes only for his main squeeze but Lord Almighty, if he is willing to bat both ways I will sign up! Hell, I already have a life-sized poster of this guy greeting me each morning." The young and good-looking reporter started fanning his face. "Sorry, I got off track there for a second, but I figure the other half of our viewers know why we like stories about Bethany Anne, don't we?"

"House, pause this clip and contact ADAM." Cheryl Lynn waited for the second it took to get ADAM's voice to come from the TV speakers.

"Yes, Cheryl Lynn?"

"ADAM, tag this video from England and try to move it to where Bethany Anne doesn't see it. This is just more 'I want Michael' stuff, and frankly she doesn't need to see this right now."

"Done. May I ask what the logic is behind this?" ADAM inquired.

Cheryl Lynn pursed her lips. "It's an emotional answer,

ADAM. Right now, Bethany Anne isn't thinking straight about Michael with some of the chemicals rushing through her body. She's already aware that there are a lot of women who want him for various reasons. Some just because Bethany Anne has him."

"Woman would want a man for no other reason than another woman does?"

"Yes. Add that she is a beautiful, powerful, wealthy woman and he must be a catch. So, bitches are bitches and if they can't have Michael, they will try to separate the two if the option becomes available."

"This does not bother you?" ADAM asked Cheryl Lynn.

"You know, it's a good thing you have a synthetic brain," she began.

"My brain is not synthetic, it is actually an organic alien brain mostly housed in another dimension," he clarified.

"Whatever. You're not a human male, otherwise, I might be annoyed with your question." She paused. "The answer to your question, and this answer better stay with you, is that I feel a little jealous. I'm happy for both of them, but you need to see that logic and feelings aren't always going to match in humans because of these stupid-ass emotions. They are our strongest component and our biggest frailty. They drive us beyond all expectations and cause us to fail miserably for the dumbest reasons. Either way, I'm going to help protect Bethany Anne by not making her face all of this shit that will just rattle her already edgy emotions. The guys protect her physically, us women are trying to bolster her emotionally."

"I understand. What is the basis for her emotional distraught?"

"You are SO a man, ADAM…" Cheryl Lynn huffed. "She's in love, stupid."

IT'S HELL TO CHOOSE

COSTA RICA

In Phillip Simmons' line of work, he had collaborated with the seedy underbelly of society for decades. Occasionally, that meant that relationships stretched from South America all the way back to the United States.

Normally, that wasn't an actual asset to him for his work in South America, now it turned out to be damned helpful.

He had reviewed the latest intel he was getting and since TQB had launched their space effort in his backyard he had all of the justification he needed to follow them.

Especially since he had received a pretty severe ass chewing for failure to know anything about the spaceworthy shipping containers in the first place. When he spit back that no one knew of the event, how was he supposed to have achieved a miracle when it involved legitimate companies operating legally in a country that had two people per square kilometer?

His boss snapped back it was shit rolling downhill, deal with it.

Yeah, he was going to deal with them all right. He had plenty of aggravation personally and professionally with this group, and now he was going to use the resources for a very, very, off the book operation.

For Phillip Simmons had crossed the line of what was wrong to achieve in the name of what is right too long ago to care.

He was watching a clip about the children that were on that fucking base in Colorado and how the school had the best in the country as teachers and the 'show and tell' days had experiments coming from fucking Ph.Ds from the R&D group on base.

The lady reporter mentioned that in a month, the school was going to take their first off-base field trip to go to the Denver Museum of Nature and Science and then for a private meeting to a world-renowned genetic research facility for the older students.

Phillip sat forward and rewound the clip again. He pulled up his phone and checked his calendar to see how many days he had to plan.

Perfect!

CHAPTER TEN

COSTA RICA

Phillip was reviewing the responses he had received back for mercs.

It wasn't like shopping on Amazon. Relationships were everything and trust wasn't something actually given even though Phillip had worked with some of these contacts for well over fifteen years. Money talked, bullshit walked, and you were only as good as your last gig.

Did you do what you said you would? Yes? Well, so long as you did that and got paid. Then life continued on.

Until the big screw.

The big screw was the expectation that at some point, even your closest contact could switch their loyalty and would be willing to burn everyone as they left the industry.

Permanently.

Either because they were dead, were going to die as soon as someone figured out where the slimy-ass bastard went, they successfully disappeared, or in those super rare instances, they were way too dangerous to go after. If the last option was the choice, then everyone agreed that so long as they stayed gone, it was going to be live and let live.

Most of the time.

Phillip looked through the responses he had received for mercs willing to operate inside the United States and his eyes opened significantly with the third email's contact name.

Vassily.

Vassily was a Russian connection that was nice since mercs from Russia would throw off any fingers pointing back towards him. Plus, Vassily had connections, surprising connections.

Phillip clicked on Vassily's email, holding his breath as he read through the first paragraph and then broke out in a shit-eating grin.

Boris was available.

Not just any Boris, oh no. This was *the* Boris. Like the Dread Pirate Roberts, this one was probably a name that was shared down from one guy to another. It helped continue the rumor he was unkillable, and he was definitely not someone to double-cross.

Phillip thought about this decision. He absently looked through more mercs with availability, and liked the number of deniable options that were screaming at him. With the money he got to do this off the books, he was going to be set.

But he kept coming back to Boris. Something about having him in on the kids' bus part of the operation appealed to getting a little of his own back. It wouldn't matter how good the team from TQB was, if Boris the Bear was sitting inside with the kids, the other fourteen members of the team were going to be second string.

IT'S HELL TO CHOOSE

Phillip reviewed the other people and looked at what Boris was asking to make the trip. Hell, he was going to either ask for more money or drop a lot more people. Either way, Boris was going to be on the team.

Phillip smiled. Fuck it, he wouldn't tell the bosses that he was hiring Boris, and would get as many other high-quality mercs without a conscience as he could.

He leaned to the left and opened the bottom drawer. He pulled out a fifteen-year-old bottle of Scotch and the celebration glass. He closed the drawer, put the glass on the table and poured two fingers.

He raised his glass in a silent toast to his friend, still suffering mental problems up in the States.

"This is for you, Terry." He took his drink and set the glass down. Leaning forward, he let Vassily know that the money would be transferred that evening.

———

TQB BASE, CO, USA

Jakob was reviewing notes on his laptop when a chat message box popped up from ADAM, asking if he had time to talk.

Jakob was getting used to talking with ADAM. At first, he thought that Bethany Anne was pulling his leg about the artificially sentient being. Finally, Bethany Anne had requested he go on a Pod trip with her.

"Are you scared of heights?" she had asked him. When she waved him to follow her, she followed up her first question with, "How do you like roller coasters?" He had admitted that until he had gotten too old physically, he had enjoyed them quite a bit.

He never saw the eye-bleeding acceleration ride coming. Now that he had been part of an experience when Bethany Anne could act like she was just making conversation before surprising him so effectively, he decided she wouldn't catch him again like that.

But the trip to the spaceship was as mind opening as she had probably hoped it would be. While looking at an alien spaceship, she made him communicate with ADAM until he was comfortable with the notion that he was talking with an artificial sentience using technology that was both not of this world and out of this world.

Each morning, he would pinch himself to make sure he hadn't hallucinated his existence from that fateful morning. The morning where he had decided to make the special trip to be a part of the most amazing company interview he had ever been invited to join.

Jakob typed back into his chat box that he was available and a second later, his phone rang. He reached over and punched the button to talk. The communication was all IP-Telephony (using data connections for voice) that ran through the Etheric. The NSA wasn't going to tap this call.

"Good morning, Jakob," ADAM said.

"Good morning, ADAM," Jakob replied. "What brings you to call me today?"

"I am made aware there are inquiries to use the Environmental Protection Agency as a means to get on base and require significant review of all locations and equipment."

Jakob pursed his lips. "Pretty sneaky method of getting access, actually." He thought for a moment. "Please send me your report so I can review while we talk."

Jakob had just finished the request when his laptop 'dinged' to notify him he had a new email. He opened it up and started reading. Jakob started talking to ADAM. "Here on the second page, this request is coming in from an employee we fired. So, someone has used him to begin a bogus EPA investigation. Let's do some background checking to see if he's come into any money, or who might have hired him recently. This isn't…"

ADAM interrupted him. "The employee, Percival Lewis, has recently received two thousand in his bank account and is working for a remediation and cleanup company that is a subsidiary of the third largest military weaponry supplier in North America."

"Oh." Jakob said. He was stumped for a minute, so he just asked what was on the top of his mind. "How did you answer that question so quickly?"

"I have researched the people in this report and built a small file on each. Our interactions in the past tell me that you have an eighty-eight point seven percent likelihood of requesting background information on at least two of the individuals in this report."

Jakob thought for a second. "Which two?"

ADAM answered, "While the previous number was a statistic, I calculated it would be Percival Lewis and CEO Sean Truitt."

"Why Sean Truitt?"

"The same reason Bethany Anne gives me every time she is trying to find out the why behind so many of the attacks. She tells me she is following the money. While the money, in this case, might come from a lower level boss, the chance they are looking to cause problems with a company the size of TQB Enterprises without higher level authorization is statistically weak. Therefore, I calculate the next person is CEO Sean Truitt."

Jakob nodded. "I think you are officially my new favorite A.S., ADAM. I'm sorry that I ever doubted you were real."

"Thank you, Jakob." ADAM paused for a few seconds. "Did you want this paperwork lost?"

"Come again?" Jakob asked. He had been thinking about ways to deal with the EPA at the gates.

The barbarians that they were.

"I asked, do you want the paperwork lost?"

Jakob smiled. "No, not lost, but could you change the wording on some of them while we get the proper support documentation to legitimize what you have found? I'm not suggesting that what you know is incorrect, but perhaps people will question how we received it."

"I understand. I believe we will need at least two computer research professionals and one, maybe two, private investigators to help alongside for the feet on the ground."

Jakob stared at the phone for a moment while he collected his thoughts. "Okay, here's what I want to do…"

The two spoke for another five minutes before Jakob hung up, pleased with himself and the chance to stick it to that fat-ass CEO Sean Truitt.

———

Bethany Anne walked into the 'Pit' to find Jakob had already beaten her to their meeting. She checked the time.

Two minutes before two. She was early, so Jakob was earlier than her.

They exchanged pleasantries before Bethany Anne started, "I understand you're concerned?"

"Well, not so much concerned as confused." He rubbed his neck. "It isn't strange for a company to request the employees to have non-compete clauses and other agreements to forestall technology from leaving the company when an employee gets hired away."

He shuffled the folders in front of him and opened the second from the top. "Here. I have three employees that say they've had excellent offers from other companies. Usually, for at least forty percent more money." He looked at Bethany Anne. "And you already pay excellent wages, so these are definitely outside of the norm."

Bethany Anne shrugged. "I'm sure they're looking to hire away product knowledge."

"You aren't concerned secrets are going to legally walk away?" Jakob was somewhat confused. He understood her core group wouldn't walk away from her, no matter what was offered. But these were top level people who usually made their biggest pay increases when changing positions.

"No, they're free to go. Mind you, those that actually know anything wouldn't walk anyway, and while these three you mention are knowledgeable, they want two things the other company can't provide."

"Oh? What is that?"

"Ethics and excitement," she responded. "Our people have superior levels of ethics, and the companies that tried to hire them away are run by notorious assholes. The second is, we are the leading company in all of the most exciting technology. Plus, we already pay above market rates. So, it's more money, but working for a company you don't respect for a group that is going to have infighting and backstabbing politics. Our people don't like it." She shrugged.

Jakob thought about it for a few seconds. "How did they find this out?"

"Well," Bethany Anne said. "We accidentally on purpose

dropped a fuck-ton of company research books about the top thirty companies most likely to try to hire our people. Plus, we added a note that these reports were requested anonymously and when it happens, we print out five copies of the company and go put them on the table."

"What happens if they're legit?" Jakob asked.

She shrugged. "Then the report shows it. Most of those companies can't afford such a high premium to market for their knowledge unless someone else is backing them. We are honest in all of the ways it is going to happen, and we are forthright in how we pay. Everything is above board, and everyone here who is part of a team with marketable technology receives a small percentage of the income. So, for some people you couldn't possibly offer enough money to get them to leave."

"How can you offer so much money?" he asked.

"Easy, we don't care." She grinned. "Don't get me wrong, I need the money to continue funding this. But we're about to print money when we start busting up asteroids and mining them. First, because our raw material and transportation costs are going to be reduced by about seventy-two percent, but also because we will bring the high-value metals back to earth. Our cost-displacement expense to bring something down to earth is minuscule."

"I thought you weren't competing with Terra-based companies?"

"We aren't. The asteroids are significantly outside the LaGrange point. There is no way for them to get there and we don't offer to lift anything up into space for a fee."

"What about the launch last week?"

Bethany Anne's eyebrows drew together. "You mean the Opscat 4 satellite?"

Jakob pulled another folder open and looked down the yellow sheet inside. "Yes."

She waved a hand. "That was a time-dependent lift. The original provider called and asked if we would do it as a favor. We told them we would, but that they would have to share the income with a list of fifteen non-profits we gave them."

"I don't remember getting that memo," Jakob said.

"That you know about it at all tells me you got the memo!" She smirked. "So don't play dumb with me, Jakob. We asked the company to keep it secret that we did this for them, and they were happy to agree."

"Asking a lawyer not to play dumb is taking away eighty percent of my weaponry," he retorted.

"That many people assume an accomplished and experienced lawyer is really dumb?" she asked.

This time, Jakob smiled just a little. "People believe what fits their worldview without challenge most of the time, no matter the facts in front of their faces."

He moved to grab another folder. "That's why acting less intelligent works so often. Who doesn't want to believe they're smarter than the lawyer in front of them?" Bethany Anne pointed to herself so he replied, "That's because you want to be lazy and have me do all of your work."

"Having the appropriate person who is well versed in their profession with decades of experience doing their job is leadership, not laziness," she insisted.

"Point to the defense," he allowed.

———

TQB BASE, CO, USA

Graduation Day. Well, that's what everyone considered it. The teams were trained up to newbie status.

Everyone could run, jump, shoot and follow orders. Some preferred the land, a few preferred the water. Almost everyone loved space.

In the last few weeks, they had all been rotated up and down. They had been up in space and been assigned for a week on the Polarus and the Ad Aeternitatem.

They had trained in the desert, the marshes, the cold and then they learned what cold really meant. They swam, they ran, they cussed, and then they did push-ups. Lots and lots of push-ups.

Following the push-ups, they slowly learned how to curse correctly. Which is to say they cursed up to Bethany Anne's standards. To Jennifer, it seemed that the Queen's Own Guard Eric had enjoyed the opportunity to lay out the push-up punishment the most. Rumor had it that he was the one who got the most push-ups from Bethany Anne, and he desired for others to stretch their linguistic abilities.

Doctor, heal thyself, Jennifer thought.

She wasn't big on cursing, so it never was a real problem for her as others were occasionally straining to get through their second and sometimes the third set of push-ups for the day. Jennifer wondered if this was Bethany Anne's point. If you were cursing just to be crass, it wasn't acceptable. But if cursing was needed (and even Jennifer admitted that sometimes it was), then do it with creativity.

Turn something vulgar into an art form.

So far, Eliot Debose was the undisputed no-curse-word cursing winner with 'you scurvy looking demented llama sniffer.' He admitted he had spent half of his breakfast and all of the morning run coming up with it. It had, he said, a particular way of rolling off of his tongue he enjoyed.

Jennifer was wearing the fatigues the Wechselbalg had been issued. She walked to her position and waited. Someone had removed the chairs for today's meeting.

Straight up at fourteen-hundred, the door opened, and Dan Bosse, Peter Silvers from the Guardians, Kevin McCoullagh from the base, and, surprising everyone, Stephen from the Polarus came walking in and stepped onto the platform.

Dan Bosse didn't wait but walked right up to the front of the little stage. He nodded to both the vampires and the Wechselbalg.

"Gentleman, and ladies." He smiled. "Which is what you are in public. In here, together, we are comrades and confidants. We have our missions, we have our priorities, and we have our orders." He held up a legal size manila folder. "In here, I have your orders."

He dropped his hand back down. "Behind me, you have the people who are going to accept your last oath. Some of you are looking to join up, not just for four years, but for the duration of the conflict. You have learned enough about Bethany Anne, this group, and about yourself that you know you fit in."

He looked back at the vampires. "Some of you made an oath due to honor. Honor taught you over decades." He turned back, looking at them all. "Please know that this request, this final Oath is one of four years, or your life until released."

Jennifer started looking around. It became obvious which of the Wechselbalg had decided to commit. They were the ones studiously NOT looking around.

"Bethany Anne won't be here for a while. Unfortunately, she's in Australia at the moment. Because we are on a schedule, I've asked Stephen, Michael's brother, to stand in for her." He grinned as he turned around to look over his shoulder. "Stephen?"

Stephen stepped forward. He was wearing a uniform from an older war. The patches were not there anymore, but you could tell it was carefully cared for, and one could imagine the scenes the clothes could speak about.

Stephen spoke softly. "When it comes to Bethany Anne, I would be the worst person you could ask for an objective opinion." Jennifer found his voice a little hypnotic. He wasn't preachy, he wasn't loud. She just felt his words soak into her mind. "When I woke up that fateful morning with my house's bell clanging me out of my stupor, I had no idea that life would change so drastically."

He paused and nodded to himself before continuing. "When I forced myself to get up, it was obvious after waiting for twenty minutes that the idiot at the front door wasn't going to take 'there is no one home' to heart. So, in my body racked with age at the time, I made my way to the front door. Each step as I got closer became easier, and do you know why?"

Everyone was now intently involved in Stephen's story. Jennifer knew Bethany Anne was the one who brought him back awake. Since getting inside the circle, she had made it her hobby to learn everything she could about the vampires. She had started with a crush on Akio, the new Queen's Own but he was gay.

Talk about a way to crush a girl's heart. Why did the good ones always have to bat for the other side?

So she tried to find out more from the other team until

her first night on the Polarus. She had been walking across the deck heading towards the stern when a solitary figure practically glided through the darkness to stand at the very back of the ship, and she stopped. She tried to not interrupt what she could tell was a moment for the figure.

It took her a moment to sort the scents from the wind to let her know it wasn't a Guardian, nor a human. That left a vampire, and as far as she knew, there were only two on the ship.

Barnabas, who always seemed to be walking around in monk's robes, and Stephen. She was startled when he turned slightly and spoke over his shoulder towards her, "It's okay, you can breathe back there."

Jennifer looked back and forth trying to figure out how to step away respectfully when he called her to come to the back. There was nothing she could do but to walk and take her medicine. The only problem was that if speaking with Stephen was medicine, she wished she could be sick the rest of her life.

She had it bad. Really bad. She was head over heels for the second oldest vampire in existence—way to cock up her future. At least she wasn't pining away for Michael, who was the oldest vampire in existence *and* totally in love with her boss.

Well, she had requested either space or land and was giving four years to the group. There was no way she was going to suffer the rest of her life wishing she could have more than she had any right thinking about with Stephen.

Knowing her luck, she was probably giving off enough pheromones around him that she might as well flip her hair over her shoulder and look back coyly at him. Or better yet, say something exceedingly stupid.

Then snort.

She focused back on Stephen as he answered his own question. "I was approaching the door now with anticipation because whoever the female human was on the other side, she smelled delicious!"

He smiled as everyone caught on to what he was saying. He, completely ignorant and being an 'old time Vampire' was thinking Bethany Anne was a snack. Maybe one he wouldn't drink from, but he was drawn to her.

"The only problem with my snack, as you might have learned by now, is that she hits, hard, and has zero respect for age and wisdom." He grimaced. "Especially old vampires that try to take a bite out of her." The laughter increased.

"So, you know what happens? She feeds my soul." He turned to look at Peter. "She tends to find the part in you that you need most, and show you how to claim it again." He turned back to the group. "For some of you, it is respect for yourself, or trusting others. Maybe it is hope, possibly peace." Stephen shrugged. "What I can tell you, is that your position, your job, your role is needed. The need is bigger than you, me, or even Bethany Anne. It is for the future. Your children, maybe. Perhaps your brothers or sisters children. Conceivably, for those you work with—or you may die with. It is a possibility. Another day is never promised."

He paused, introspective. "I can tell you that if Bethany Anne had not arrived on my doorstep, and rung that bell until hell froze over, I would not be in front of you today. I was one last sleep away from walking into the Sun." He looked down at his feet and then up again to make Jennifer feel like she was the only one he was speaking to. "But now, I will never see a more glorious sight than someone new coming into my life, because the world can change in an instant when they do."

He broke eye contact and finished. "You are about to go

out. Whether here, to sea, or to space, and you will take a little piece of your class with you. Be resolute, protect people, stand for what is right because Bethany Anne expects nothing less, and nothing more from you." He stood straight and saluted the class. Jennifer could imagine him on the fields of World War II saluting an officer.

"Ad Aeternitatem." He held his salute.

One hundred and fifteen salutes were crisply drawn, and one hundred and fifteen voices shouted, "AD AETERNITA-TEM!

CHAPTER ELEVEN

SPACE STATION ONE, L2

Space Station One was coming into view. Jeo Deteus-che had been preparing for this trip for the last four weeks, and he was beyond excited.

It had taken his previous company exactly seventeen minutes and forty-three seconds to escort his disrespectful ass off the premises when he finished blasting the CEO Sean Truitt with both barrels.

God, that had felt good.

It had taken seventeen minutes because Mr. Truitt decided to spend five of them blasting him back with all the vitriol his stress had created. As far as Mr. Truitt was concerned, Jeo Deteusche wasn't going to be able to find one company on the face of the Earth that was going to hire him. Not if that company had ANY connection to them at all.

Jeo didn't give a shit; he was leaving Earth, so Mr. Truitt was absolutely right in that respect. In less than thirty-six hours the final paperwork to hire him had been signed and returned. He read the document twice and stayed on the last page, just staring at the final signature.

Bethany Anne, CEO.

He had been in a stupor, just admiring the fact that his employee document had her signature (in red, no less) when he received a personal phone call from the CEO herself, thanking him personally for joining them and asking him how soon he could pack up his life?

He had looked around his apartment, then considered what he was going to need in a base or on a ship and told her, "Let me hug my parents goodbye and let them know as much as you will let me, and then I just need a place to show up."

Her laughter had caught him off guard. "I'll tell you what. I'm aware how much you went through when you quit. I'll have Cheryl Lynn help with any apartment packing details, and you go see your parents for say, three days, unless that isn't enough?"

Jeo considered three full days with his mom and grimaced. "That's probably pushing the largest amount of time I can love my Mom in one sitting, but I don't imagine I'm coming back for a while?"

The CEO answered him, "No, I would plan on being gone a minimum of three and most likely at least six months. If you want to impress your parents, then let them know I'll send a ride for you at nine PM Thursday at your parents' address. Will that work?"

He agreed it would be perfect. He spoke to Cheryl Lynn, who connected him with a moving company and helped get rid of his car as he wouldn't need it anytime soon.

His first day and a half with his parents had been a little strained. They believed the TV anchors that had been lambasting TQB Enterprises with negatively slanted news questioning whether any of their technology was real, while simultaneously accusing TQB of withholding technology the world desperately needed. Jeo pointed out those were two mutually exclusive perspectives.

His dad didn't take too long to see Jeo's point of view, since he tended to believe TQB was on the Moon anyway, and his mother finally came around to thinking that the company must be okay.

When he got a text on Thursday night that his ride was out in the backyard to pick him up, he was shocked. Then, he whooped with delight.

His father asked him what his text was about, but Jeo had jumped up and was already grabbing the two suitcases that had been by the front door and was walking quickly towards the back.

His mom asked him, "Are you staying?" His dad caught on and almost beat him to the back door.

Sure enough, right before they opened the door, there was a knock. Mr. Deteusche opened the door to find a rather large and imposing Hispanic man smiling down at him. "Hello, I'm Eric. Bethany Anne has asked me to pick up Mr. Deteusche from this location to take him to France tonight."

"Oh, my God..." said Mrs. Deteusche from behind her son and her husband. Both of them turned around as she continued, "You're one of them!"

She looked up at her son's quizzical expression. "You don't know, do you?" Jeo shook his head. "You're being picked up by one of the Four." She turned back to Eric. "You *are* one of her Four, aren't you?"

Eric looked thoughtful. "Well, I could be. But which *Four* are we talking about?"

Mrs. Deteusche elbowed her husband aside and reached out to shake Eric's hand. "You protect her, don't you? I saw a special about the four men who seem to be around her all of the time. You're always with that really big guy, James... No, John!" She beamed up at Eric.

"Yes, I'm one of those Four." Eric replied. "I'm heading over to a meeting on the Polarus and Jeo here needs to get acclimated a little before we take him to his post."

"And where," Mr. Deteusche asked, "Will Jeo's post actually be?" He turned to look at his son. "He claims he doesn't know."

"Really?" Eric turned to Jeo. "No one told the lead on mining and manufacture of metals in space where his post is going to be?"

Jeo shook his head. "No, I figured I would either be in Colorado or possibly on the ships they talk about on the news."

Eric grinned. "Jeo, there is one thing Bethany Anne doesn't mess with, and that is inefficiency. Where do you believe she would have her new lead of Industrial Outer Space Mining and Manufacturing?" He paused a moment, then helped him out. "The hint is in the title."

Jeo's eyes lit up. "Outer space!"

Eric nodded. "Hell yeah! Buddy, you're just going to the Polarus to meet, greet, and get some work done. Your final destination in a few days is your new office on Space Station One."

His father looked confused. "Don't you mean Moon Base One? Or is there a new space station up there, like Skylab?"

Jeo wanted to facepalm in embarrassment. "That's ISS dad, the International Space Station."

His dad merely winked at Eric.

Eric said, "Well, I hope you realize that if you spill this information, you could be endangering your son's life, but we have a space station at L2, that's Lagrange Point 2 out beyond the Moon. Jeo's home and office will start there and then move as quickly as he can help get us into production out to the mining area."

"Oh," his mother answered, "Is that on the Moon, then?"

Eric looked down at the shorter lady. "No ma'am. Although I don't know for sure, I imagine Jeo knows the most likely location for mining. It *is* his occupation after all."

"Holy crap," Jeo breathed. "I'm going out to the asteroid belt, aren't I?" Before Eric could respond, Jeo continued, "With your technology, we don't have to worry about Delta-V or crossing the Earth's orbit or even water, right?" Eric nodded. "So, take those out of the equation and we want to go after Type M asteroids for metals and outer space manufacturing. No wonder Ms. Bethany Anne told me minimum three months." He asked, "How long would it take to get out to the Asteroid Belt?"

Eric shrugged his shoulders. "Beats me. I doubt that distance and time are a factor. Probably more of a short timeframe on this project."

"Short… timeframe?" Jeo asked.

Eric looked at his watch. "Here, let's get your gear stowed and we'll talk. We need to be on the Polarus in thirty minutes."

"Right, of course!" Jeo hugged his Mom goodbye and shook his Dad's hand. Grabbing his suitcases, he walked out into the backyard. Even with the back porch light on, the black Pod holding a foot off of the ground was difficult to see. "Is that sucking light in?"

Eric answered, "Well, I can tell you it's not reflecting most visible light rays, so if that is the same as sucking them in, then yes." He opened the front hatch. "Store your gear in there."

Mr. and Mrs. Deteusche watched as the two men got into the Pod. Mr. Deteusche asked before the hatch was shut, "Did you just say you are going to the ship, Polarus?" When Eric agreed they were, he asked, "Didn't you say that was near France right now?" Eric agreed it was. "How are you going to make it to France in thirty minutes?" getting to his real question.

Eric hit the button to close the hatch. "Shortcut!"

Mr. Deteusche heard his son's laugh get cut off. A few seconds later, the Pod went up smoothly about twenty feet, then they both heard the heavy 'whoosh' of air when it practically disappeared into the night sky.

————

Jeo stood in his office. It was, effectively, one shipping container in size. One-quarter of the wall in his office was a massive whiteboard that was digitized. So, whenever he and William worked together, whatever he drew on his board here was automatically duplicated on a board William had down on the Polarus and vice-versa.

That was cool until William started writing words on his board when he wasn't expecting the words to appear—that was scary as hell.

William found it funny as hell.

Jeo found the controls to shut that off except for when they were working together. Now, he didn't feel like his office had William's ghost looking over his shoulder.

Personally, he was in heaven. His time on the Polarus

getting to know Bobcat, William, Marcus, TOM, and ADAM was awesome. He had a voice chat channel hooked into talking with ADAM and TOM right now. There were only fourteen people on the space station at this time. Ten of them were protection.

Protection from whom, he had no idea. It wasn't like any of the major superpowers had the ability to just run a space shuttle over here and knock on the doors. Hell, he should know, considering his previous employer.

ADAM had informed him that his previous employer had shown up at his apartment while his stuff was being moved. They were unhappy to find out that he had a job already, and the people on site did not know where he went.

Then they tried to contact his parents with seemingly legal documentation that stated he was to come back to the offices and open some locked areas. Supposedly, no one had realized he was the only one who had the combination.

Jeo had smiled to himself. He had forgotten about the safes. The employee before him gave him the combination and split. The last Jeo had heard, he was surfing in Asia somewhere.

When his parents had provided TQB with the document, the inside counsel Jakob Yadav had fired off a response that ended any harassment of his parents, and Jeo received a nicely-worded email from the company asking how much he wanted in a severance package to provide the combination? Would a year's pay be sufficient?

Jeo sent confirmation that would be wonderful and supplied the combination to Mr. Yadav at the same time.

A week later, he had been pleased to receive an email with the deposit information.

SWEET! He still grinned thinking about how that

flaming gas sack, Javier, must have felt to have to authorize the payout.

Now he was working at the beginning of the refining parameters and how they would mine the ore, and where in the belt.

"ADAM, what's the status of the modification technology for the platforms?"

"Well," the alien TOM's voice came out of the speaker. "You could ask me."

Jeo grimaced. "Sorry TOM. I always depend on the AI."

TOM's voice came back. "I don't bite, Jeo."

"It's not that, well, it's mostly not that." Jeo temporized. "It's more that I've always wanted to work with AIs and figure he's always available. I'm never sure what you're up to, so I don't want to interrupt."

There was a pause from the speaker. "Okay, I never considered it from that perspective. ADAM can get ahold of me very easily, we are closer to each other than you might believe. Either way, I'm the one who Bethany Anne has working on this project with Marcus and William. Jeffrey is in charge of the manufacturing and assembly from different locations."

Jeo interrupted, "Why are they being done in separate locations? Is there a raw materials issue?"

"No, security," TOM replied. "We don't want the knowledge out yet. The stresses on the platforms were originally designed for implosive, not explosive. So, these coatings are going to be applied to change the underlying strength of the beams and operational support no matter which direction the pressure is pushing on the frame and other structural members."

"Does this change it forever?" Jeo asked.

"Long enough, but I wouldn't plan on the applications

lasting more than ten years for those we are changing presently. For newly built platforms where the application can be applied to all components as they are built, then I would feel comfortable with at least five decades of service."

"Damn, that's impressive," he murmured. "Bobcat wasn't kidding when he said that Bethany Anne wanted to be mining in months, not years."

TOM's voice interrupted Jeo's thoughts. "No, she wants to be mining in weeks, not months. Bobcat was trying to help you cope with the aggressive time schedule."

Jeo's original thoughts left him as he stared at the speaker on his desk. "I'm sorry TOM, did you say Bethany Anne wants to be mining in weeks?"

"Yes, I can confirm with her if you wish. But the last time she and I spoke on this subject she hoped you would be live in eighty-four days, that's about three months on the outside." TOM said.

Jeo turned to open his work tablet and look at the calendar. "That's twelve weeks." Jeo started computing solutions in his head. "We're going to need a week to push the platforms out to the minefields, plus I need to confirm which asteroids we're going to mine first. That means that the Pods I need to be modified for the research have to leave on Tuesday. When was Bobcat going to let me know this?" Jeo asked, not really expecting an answer.

"How long have you been on the station?" TOM asked.

Jeo looked at the speaker. "Not long, maybe twelve hours, but what's that got to do with my questions?"

"Because Bobcat believes you should check out your surroundings and enjoy space before he calls you."

"When is that going to be?" Jeo asked, thinking about everything he now needed to be doing.

TOM replied, "In twelve hours."

"When would Bethany Anne have told me?" Jeo wondered, not really expecting an answer.

"Twelve hours ago," was TOM's reply.

"Oh." Jeo considered that. "I guess she isn't into being in the moment?"

"Sure, if you mean the moment when you are pushing forward towards the goal of making the human race safe. She does tend to be rather focused on that part. Don't get me wrong, she knows that Bobcat did not tell you this twelve hours ago and is allowing it to happen. Before you ask, she allows it because she can understand her methods might need softening from time to time."

Jeo looked around his office. "TOM, let's discuss the requirements for the platforms and how we're going to get them modified. She wants three months? Let's be mining in two."

Jeo pulled the second keyboard towards him. A monitor screen was projected on the wall in front of him. There were twelve incredibly powerful projection cameras placed on the four walls of this office that could project multiple screens, or join for even larger screens. Team BMW was using four of them for a holographic projector like you would see in science fiction movies. That was incredibly cool, but until he had need of it, Jeo thought it was a little much and utterly useless for his spreadsheet work.

Each projector could also 'see' when he placed his hands to manipulate the screen as if it was a touchscreen and also detect hand gestures in the air in front of the screen. Jeo reached up to the fifteen-inch monitor displayed on the wall and opened two fingers from about an inch apart to roughly two inches apart. The display on his wall went instantaneously from fifteen inches to thirty.

"Computer, I need a project plan. Name it Destiny Zero Zero One."

"Understood, Mr. Deteusche."

"Computer, replace calling me Mr. Deteusche with Jeo."

"Understood, Jeo."

"Computer, replace your designation with 'Samantha' and switch to feminine voice."

A warm and inviting feminine voice greeted Jeo. "Understood, Jeo."

Jeo shivered. "Samantha, switch your voice to female, pragmatic. I don't need your voice causing my mind to wander."

A much cooler and clipped female voice responded, "Understood, Jeo."

"Samantha, project a countdown timer in quadrant office A-1 for fifty-six days and start it counting down." He looked over at the wall he would see each morning as he walked into his office. "Switch the timer text to light blue." Satisfied with the result, he turned back to his own monitor. "Samantha, open a diary application and every time I say 'Captain's Log,' I want you to copy my comments into the diary application, is this understood?"

"Understood, Jeo," the female voice responded back to him.

Jeo grabbed his keyboard. "Excellent. Let's make history, Samantha."

CHAPTER TWELVE

COSTA RICA, SOUTH AMERICA

The warehouse was safe. Phillip Simmons had last used it some three months back. It was in a seedier part of San Jose and still close enough to the main airport to be useful.

In the midafternoon sun, there weren't many places to hide coming up to the doors. He had arrived here two minutes before and knew he had at least three, if not four, pairs of eyes on him. The mercs he was hiring were not Johnny-come-lately types. They all had been in the business for at least five years, and each had at least eight major projects under their belt. God alone knew how many minor or personal projects.

He had tried to unlock the heavy chain keeping the doors closed and had to go back to the car in disgust. Popping the trunk, he pulled out a can of lubricant and went back to the lock and squeezed the can enough to drop some of the oil into it. He held it there a few seconds and then moved the lock, keeping it upside down on the chain so the oil would drain into the tumblers. Then went back to put the can in his trunk and pulled out some rolled up blueprints.

He waited another ten seconds before trying the lock again and was able to finally open it. The chain started sliding out of the handle, and he pulled his hands away quickly so that it didn't whip around and bust up his knuckles.

He pushed open one of the two sliding doors a few feet before it stopped, probably with a messed up wheel. No matter, it didn't need to open any further. He turned when he heard footsteps behind him. Phillip pulled the sunglasses down to look over at a smiling white male with a brown cowboy hat, blue eyes, and dimples.

"Birk Muller," Phillip said with a smile on his face. "As I live and breathe there was never a nicer asshole than you!" Phillip reached out, and Birk clapped his hand in a handshake.

"Phillip, you royal pain in the asshole, what you got cooking this time?" Birk asked as he glanced inside while holding Phillip's hand.

"Let's go inside and I'll lay some of it out. Maybe you'll be able to refine the plan before everyone gets here." Birk released his hand and allowed Phillip to go in first.

The air inside was still musty from being closed up, during the recent rains and the humidity. Phillip walked to a couple of small rooms with a cutout in the wall for windows that let you see inside and flipped a switch to turn on the fluorescent lights. It would take them a few minutes to reach full brightness.

"I get we're going to the States, but what's the purpose?" Birk asked as he walked around the place, making sure no one was going to jump out at him, probably.

"You guys are going to hijack a school bus on a field trip. Then you'll drive it into a building that has a lower level and security gates between the levels. Good security, by the way. The SWAT teams will be required to go through three vehicular gates, and there is a stairwell access for the bottom level to deal with."

Phillip walked over and set his keys and the blueprints on the dusty table he used every time. Unrolling the plans, he set his keys on a corner and then he had rocks for the remaining three corners. He pointed to the lower right corner. "The bottom level is approachable via the stairwell, the last security gate, which is solid by the way, and there's a twelve-inch drainage pipe."

Birk took one last look around as he came over to the table. "Twelve inches isn't a very large back door, Phillip. I really don't want to be trying to fight my way out the front." He looked down at the map. "So, what's the real escape route?"

"Why do you think there's a real escape route?" Phillip asked. "Maybe I want your ass left out there as one big ugly cowboy shooting target?"

Birk looked up and grinned. "Because you've always done right by anyone you hire, and I doubt this is the big screw."

Phillip shrugged. "Yeah, there's an out. You guys will also have twenty-four hours to check everything for yourselves before you do the run." He pointed to the bottom right corner of the plan. "I've had people working to build a fifty-foot tunnel to the wall right here. It's ready for you guys to go check out both sides. One of you can stay on the exit side, which allows you to either go into the sewers or get into the underground parking via another route two blocks away and exit with vans. Your choice."

"You aren't going?" Birk asked.

"Are you kidding me?" Phillip replied. "If my ass is anywhere near the U.S. and a hint of this gets out, they'll call me in for questioning. If I stay here and make sure I'm with someone when it goes down, others will vouch for me. Besides, you guys aren't the main event."

"No?" Birk looked back up at Phillip.

"No, you're just to pull the focus and hopefully the security off of a well-secured corporate headquarters out in the mountains west of Denver. That's why it's children. Everyone on the base will be either running out to where you are or focused on the news coming in."

A deep, gravelly voice greeted them from the doorway. "I'm nyet so liking a children's op, Phillip." Both men turned, but Birk was quicker and Phillip saw his eyes open wide. Both for someone surprising him, as well as guessing who the man was.

Phillip left the table and walked over to the huge Russian with his hand out. "Boris, son-of-a-bitch as I live and breathe…"

"Hey, you said that already," called out Birk behind him.

Phillip ignored him. "It's good to work with you!"

The big Russian had a massive beard and quick eyes. His dark brown eyes looked almost black as his hand smothered Phillip's. He walked into the room. "Are the six that are skulking around outside going to join us here, or are they vaiting for a party in-vi-tation?" His heavily accented English could confuse a person. Sometimes you couldn't tell if Boris was joking or being serious.

Birk smiled. "Ah, well, that would be the guys who nominated my ass to be the sacrifice to confirm Phillip was on the up and up." He pulled his phone out and sent a text message.

"They'll be here in a few minutes."

Phillip was impressed and depressed at the same time. Impressed that Boris was with them, and depressed that he had missed the others. It might be time to make sure he departed this kind of work before he lost his remaining edge. Well, this project would pad his retirement fund sufficiently that living in South America would be comfortable for at least thirty or forty years without side projects.

Boris was a huge man, but he seemed light on his feet. He had the look of a tracker, someone accustomed to being in the bush. Phillip wasn't going to misjudge the man based on his slow speech and careful talking. He had done enough background checks on Boris for previous potential projects the United States wanted to know that this was probably not the original Boris. For one, the huge man looked to be maybe in his thirties and *the* Boris was on the books as having been used in 1952. Although, the description in the documents he was able to read painted him as a giant, hairy, dark-eyed Russian.

Phillip shrugged mentally, probably a family that kept the business going with successive generations. Possibly why he had a reputation for not being able to be killed.

Soon, six more mercs joined the group, and Phillip shook their hands. He had worked with one other guy there, Patty McKingsly, for an op that spanned from South America over to Europe three years ago. Except for an occasional death wish, Patty was hell on wheels with pistols and didn't care what the job was. He was as amoral as they come, except for his mom. Speak ugly about her and it was usually a brawl right then, right there. If you came at him with anything but your fists and maybe a beer bottle, then you typically received two .22 love taps to your stomach from the pistols he always had on him.

He enjoyed leaving you in pain to suffer. Piss him off

again while you were on the ground and then you got a .38 to the head.

Personally, Phillip liked Patty. He shook the man's hand while looking at his beard. "I see you let the red grow a little this time, Patty."

"Aye, it allows me the chance to stay in me country without tripping the video cameras don't you know?" He winked at Phillip. "The lassies like it long, I found. They say it tickles."

Phillip rolled his eyes. "I can imagine." He stepped to the door and yanked it hard to get it started moving before pulling it shut.

At the table, most of the men were on the same side as Birk, with Boris standing on the other with his arms crossed, studying the map.

He walked up. "It's not so much about children as using them as bait, Boris." Phillip said, speaking to Boris' earlier comment. "We need to get the focus from the real attack location, which is the corporate headquarters, onto Denver. Once we get them focused on the city, a second group led by a second team is going to infiltrate and drop off electronic devices. There will also be a second larger package, something that will cause them a significant amount of damage so that the spy devices have a chance to get lost in the commotion."

He paused, then continued, "Before that operation starts, you need to ramp up the pressure on your side."

"How?" Boris asked from beside Phillip. Boris was rubbing his head like he had a headache.

Phillip started answering the question. "We're going to give you the tools to send direct video to the CEO of TQB Enterprises…"

"The hot chick on TV all the time?" Patty interrupted.

Phillip turned to the talkative Irishman. "Yes, the hot

chick from the TV." He continued, "Once you have everyone stuck in Denver, the second team will finish their incursion. Hopefully, they won't be seen, they'll get in and out without too many problems. Unfortunately, the package is going to make a real mess of the place. When that goes off, you need to exit out through a passage which is already built and how you get out from there is up to you."

Birk spoke, "There are two ways guys, van and leave via driving, or sewer walk." Birk received five 'vans' and one 'oh god, not a sewer walk!' which he took as a vote for 'van.' He turned to the Russian. "Boris?"

Boris looked up. "Don't worry about me, I'll get out walking. Maybe the sewer, maybe walk on the street." He shrugged. "It would help to have two groups leaving at a minimum. How many vehicles are you thinking?"

Phillip responded, "I'm thinking three or four, minimum. But if you guys want one for each of you, the budget is there to do it."

Birk pointed to each man who either nodded or shook their head. "Ok, I'm good with going with someone, so we're going to need four cars. Three singles, one joint and one walker."

"Weapons?" Boris asked.

"Get me your requirements and I'll have them ready when you hit the States. I've got some contacts that can do a run from Las Vegas to Denver to meet someone there. You'll drive up, switch keys, and drive the vehicle with the armament away. Top dollar, no bullshit. Used them before."

Birk spoke again, "We'll have at least twenty-four hours to confirm the plan and the exit strategy are in place. Twelve hours before we have to commit to go or not. Once we say go we are committed, or we all get black marks on our files."

"If you call it off for a good reason, I'll mark it as approved,"

Phillip said. If this didn't work out, they could figure something else out, and he didn't want these guys pissed at him in exchange.

The men all nodded their understanding. It was things like this that let them all know this was legit.

"So, no children?" Boris asked.

"No," Phillip answered. "The children are there to pull the focus off of the base. The goal, at all times, is to keep the people focused on you until we tell you otherwise."

"Ve are going to need a vay to block that stairwell." Boris pointed to it on the blueprint.

"I'll have explosives enough to drop the insides down and block the door, just make sure the door won't open on you," Phillip said.

Phillip looked around. "I'll get you all the tech you need and the instructions when you meet up in Denver. Everyone gets there by your own method if you want to, or I can help get you on a safe private plane leaving from Mexico City in two days."

"Why is this plane safe?" asked Birk.

"Because it belongs to a high-level CEO. His plane is never checked coming in or out of the US, and he, or someone from this country, makes this trip every single month. Unfortunately for the lackey going this month, he's going to be held back by the Mexican government and the plane is going to be needed back for a trip by the CEO the next day. You guys jump on, fly, land, and leave a couple of hours later wearing coveralls with a jet cleaning company's logo on the back."

Birk raised his hand. "I'm for going private jet." Six hands raised around him, and they all looked at Boris.

He shrugged. "Dey are usually smaller, but I'm good with this idea. I'm good for flying in personal jet, yes."

IT'S HELL TO CHOOSE

SOUTH AFRICA

Bandile Annane wiped his brow. It was hot here in the mine. They were deep down underground, and Bandile was unhappy. Not with his work, he loved mining, but rather with what was becoming sloppy support from their company again. The refrigeration units that cooled the air before injecting it deep down into the mineshafts were not working even to half the needed levels, and the miners were making mistakes.

It was only time before miners lost their lives.

"Kagiso," Bandile called out to his second. "Kagiso!" Getting Kagiso's attention was tough. People were not paying attention. Finally, his second walked down the shaft and got close. "Yeah, boss?"

"Tell the men to pack up, I want everyone up top now." His second looked at him with wide eyes. "What? We are going to have another Elandskraal incident but this time caused by one of us if we don't get these men out of this heat. They have worked too long."

"The company is going to fire you!" Kagiso warned. "I'm not saying it doesn't need to be done, but just know you won't be working again."

"They can kiss my ass!" Bandile said. "My father taught me to protect the people, the metals aren't going anywhere. There has always been an Annane working a mine somewhere. Not every company is so motivated by money as this one, and they will appreciate safety first."

Kagiso pulled his radio and spoke the directions to start pulling the men out. He put it back on his belt. "I don't know what planet you are from, but I have not heard of this safety first unless it translates to mine harder." Both men grinned. It was a standard joke that everything in the safety manual was phrasing that all translated back to 'mine more!'

"Yeah, maybe not on this Earth, you are right my friend. But I cannot allow these men to stay down here now that the company has lied to me three times. Promises are only as good as action, and their promise means nothing."

"The government isn't going to be happy, either," Kagiso added.

Bandile nodded to some of the first groups that passed him in the shaft. Everyone was sweating, and a couple already had the look of men who did not know where they were. "The government would enjoy another Lonmin strike even less, or, God forbid, four hundred deaths. That would substantially damage their safety records they keep talking about."

Kagiso pulled his radio back up. "Aaron, where are you and your men?" He listened for a moment. "Okay, you have five then I want to see your ugly face and your men passing me in shaft four, got it?" He listened before turning back to his friend. "True. Either way, you get castigated, right?" Bandile nodded and clapped him on the shoulder. "It sucks to be you, my friend."

Bandile shrugged. "Not so hard. What is hard is facing a wife who understands I need to do this, but fears for the family and the kids when I come home."

"Dova will understand," Kagiso said.

"Oh, I know, but I can feel the worry in her body when she hugs me." Bandile turned to his friend. "I've got three months saved up, so you might have to hire me as your long lost cousin by then to work down here myself."

Kagiso laughed. "Finally! I'll get to tell an Annane what

to do when mining! That will make sure the heavens open, and angels sing 'alleluia.'" The men laughed before Kagiso continued, "Hey, didn't you share with me an email from those Americans in space?"

Bandile waved to the group of men passing them. "What? Yes, the ones on the Moon. Why?"

"Well, if they want to talk with you, maybe they are mining on the Moon, and you will be the first Annane to mine off this world?" Kagiso pointed at a man with a yellow safety hat with a bat sticker on it. "It's about time, Aaron. Anyone behind you lazy asses?" Kagiso got a tired shake of Aaron's head. "Okay. We will be up on the next run."

The two men waited for another couple of minutes, and when no one came by, they started towards the elevator. Kagiso got a head count over his radio. "Everyone is counted for, plus four have already come down from the corporate office over on shaft two."

Bandile shrugged. "Let them come. So long as Abrie is up there like she promised me, the news can't be hidden."

Kagiso stared at his boss. "You already have the reporter friend waiting up there?"

"Of course, what good is it to pull everyone from a shaft if the company can hide it?" He smiled. "Now, I don't owe Abrie a dinner. She gets a story instead."

———

It took six hours for the news interviews to be over and him to make it home. Sure enough, the company promised to move heaven and earth to fix the refrigeration units in all shafts and confirm with government oversight for the next three months.

He was also told, in no uncertain words, not to come back to work as he must be suffering from heat exhaustion himself and the company would let him know if they needed him back.

It was dark as he pulled into the little single level home he and his wife and three children lived in. Fortunately, it was paid for by his father who had made a few rands himself on a small claim of his own.

Dova stepped out of the front door and met him halfway to the house. He enveloped her in a crushing hug, one that she returned.

He held her out. "Dova, what is it?"

She gave him a funny look. "What? Can a wife not hug her husband she is proud of? I have watched all of the news, and I am happy that you took care of your men."

He pulled her in, more gently this time. "Yes, of course, and I thank you for these sentiments. No, I can feel you Dova. You are happy. Happy and proud. There is no worry in your muscles."

Her muffled voice came from his chest. "How is it you can hug me and tell my emotions, but when I talk to you, you are deaf?"

He grunted in laughter. "That is because listening to comments about my socks do not interest me."

She pulled back from him and grabbed his hand. "Come, husband, I have taken enough of your time." She pulled him forward, and that was when he noticed a huge dark man standing in the shadows to the left of his house. Dova told him, "That is Darryl, he is here to protect our guest."

"Our guest?" he inquired. He turned back to his wife. "What guest?"

CHAPTER THIRTEEN

TQB Base, Colorado, USA

The news van left Denver traveling west on Highway 70. Inside, Mark Billingsly was reading a few of the tweets that had been coming in from the demonstration happening outside of TQB Enterprises corporate office up at the old Army base.

While he wasn't expecting it to be a huge news piece, almost everything about TQB was being picked apart, and he expected either his piece would get sold to other markets, or he would be called directly for his experience if something should happen out at the location.

God, please let something happen!

Mark looked in the mirror and decided that he would ditch the tie and keep the dark blue sports coat. He ran a hand through his hair and checked his teeth to make sure nothing from lunch was in them. If this went fast, they could get a report either edited for the six o'clock, or they might do a live report depending on what happened with the President's press conference about TQB as well.

Mark turned in his chair to speak with his cameraperson. "Sia, are we good? Batteries?" He smiled when she stuck her tongue out at him. Sia was one of their best, but he still liked treating her like she just got out of school.

She popped a bubble and answered back, "Keep it up Mark, and I'll make sure to leave the camera off if they decide to rough you up. No video, no crime!"

Mark winked at Sia. They shared a good camaraderie and for all of his playing, he had told Sia before he would grab her in an instant over some of the more experienced camera people because she had 'it.'

She had looked dubiously at him until he realized she thought he meant something physical. "No, you ass! I'm talking about hunger and curiosity. Not every male news anchor is a jerk!" he spit out.

He had been hurt and tried to let bygones be bygones, but it had been annoying to be accused of something he hadn't done. Especially when he was trying to support a new cameraperson in their dog-eat-dog industry. He figured the cupcake with 'sorry' on it found on his desk two days later had been from her.

Ever since they had been a good team.

It took them thirty minutes to get to the turnoff. There was a large dark blue sign with the TQB logo in white pointing them up the road to the old base. The sign said 'Appointments Only This Location' at the bottom. As far as Mark knew, all TQB sites required appointments.

The cars parked on the side of the road started back at least a half-mile from the entrance and Mark noticed Sia was taking pictures of three buses parked on the side as well.

Somebody was well organized.

A quarter mile from the gate, there was a Hummer H2 parked across the road and two men in fatigues with the TQB Patch on their uniforms. Both men stood as they had probably stood when in the service. One put out his hand and was walking up to the driver's side.

His breast pocket said 'Barrins' and he spoke to their driver, Kevin. "Hello Channel 4, how are you today?"

Mark spoke before Kevin could. "How do you know we're Channel 4?" They had a news van, but this one was just painted white on the outside.

"Your license plate, Mr. Billingsly, says 'CHNL4-12.' Take that plus the big satellite communication gear on the top and I recognize you since I watch you guys most evenings." He looked up towards the other guard and made a circle with his hand. "You guys go on up, but go slow and don't hurt anyone."

"Wait," Mark said. "Why are you blocking the road if you're just passing us through?"

"We've been told by the base commander to let the press through and notify him when someone finally showed up so he could pass it on."

"Pass it on to whom?" Sia asked from the back.

"To the boss, who else?" He winked at Mark and stepped away from the van.

Sia commented, "Well, that was absolutely non-specific! Which boss? Whose boss?"

"Nooo…" Mark said as Kevin drove around the massive Hummer and kept the speed under twenty. "From what I understand, the base commander here, or grounds head or whatever his real title is outside of the military, answers to Lance Reynolds and is in charge of overseeing all of the companies. He often travels across the world. He was the old base commander, and I understand he looks significantly younger than before. Same thing for his wife."

"So," Sia continued. "You think we might get a chance to interview him with the picketers in the background?" She made a face. "I thought those Army types were all crappy interviews."

Mark shrugged. "I don't know, I mostly interview Air Force. But I hope he didn't wink at me to say it was going to be Lance Reynolds, I want *his* boss."

"You mean Bethany Anne?" Sia asked.

"Yes, the lady herself. God, that would be golden!" Mark said. He grabbed and started a text to his producer as Kevin parked the van.

He stepped out and hit 'send' as Sia opened the side door and Kevin left the van running, but dealt with getting the uplinks and signals sorted out.

Mark looked down the road a hundred yards at the small crowd there with signs chanting something about 'Sharing is Caring,' and 'Hoarding is Wrong!' It looked to be over three hundred people of mixed races. There was one smaller group off to the side, and Mark could see at least fifteen tents scattered under the trees outside of the gate entrance on the other side of the crowd.

Sia came up beside him. "I wonder what they would do if they all just tried to climb up or run in?"

Mark said, "See those wires at the top of the fence?" She nodded. "Electrified. No one's going up there without coming back off all tingly."

Sia put the video camera on her shoulder and started taking some shots for the intro, "That's funny," she commented.

"What?" Mark asked.

IT'S HELL TO CHOOSE

"There are signs on the fence that say 'Beware—Wolves in Area.' That has to be the worst way to keep people away that I've ever seen."

Mark finished prepping and asked her, "You got enough footage?" When she nodded, he continued, "Good, let's go."

The two went walking up to the crowd of people who were covering the road and at least twenty feet on either side. From there you couldn't go to the right due to a sheer cliff face going up a few hundred feet. To the left, the trees were pretty thick for twenty feet, and Mark knew there was a sudden drop of a couple of hundred feet that way. Sucked if you didn't know this and tried anything in the dark.

The two of them shot three introductions really quick when Mark noticed Barrins walking up behind them with his thumbs stuck in his waistband, smiling.

Mark raised an eyebrow at the guy. It was nice that he was a fan, or at least a viewer of their show, but he didn't want his elbow jiggled while he was working.

———

"Cheryl Lynn, this has to be one of your worst ideas ever!" Bethany Anne grumped. She was uncomfortable in her skirt, blouse and suit coat in the Pod. She was rapidly approaching the front of the Colorado base after a stop in France. The new shoes felt nice. Ashur was with her. Eric and John had sped ahead of her and were in place already, unseen in the trees.

Cheryl Lynn spoke through the speaker. "I'll admit, it's a calculated risk, and it might backfire, but hear me out. We know most of the picketers have been paid. Get them to admit that on camera and there goes support for this kind of bullshit."

"What about the others?" Bethany Anne asked.

"That's when the secret weapon comes out. I've talked with John, and he completely agrees it won't fail," she replied.

"Well, what is it?" Bethany Anne wondered.

Cheryl Lynn answered, "Um, I can't tell you. If I do, it will ruin the weapon. Trust us, ok?" Bethany Anne wanted to gripe, but she could see the base coming into view. Cheryl Lynn said one more thing, "And please, for the love of God, don't cuss!" A pause then she added, "Or kill people."

Ashur's 'chuff' of annoyance at Cheryl Lynn's last remark amused Bethany Anne. "I know buddy, she means well, but she takes all the fun out of it, too."

———

Sia was grabbing a few more shots of those picketing when she was tapped on the shoulder. "Sia turn around!" Mark said. She looked over her shoulder to see Mark looking up.

Her eyes opened wide, and she tried to whip around as quickly as possible to set up a framing shot and then looked up barely in time to see a black... something coming down quickly and then stopping a foot off of the ground. Mark wanted to step forward, but the guard put a hand out to block him. "Sorry Mr. Billingsly. Please wait until the CEO steps out."

Sia pointed the camera towards the object, and it opened from the front, splitting down the middle. A large white German Shepherd jumped out. Sia took an involuntary step back before she realized the dog was waiting a few feet in front of the craft. She kept it in focus as a woman in executive business dress stepped out. Her hair was black and her skin white. She was very pretty and smiled as she exited.

She moved a few feet from the craft, the doors closed and then it went back up into the air then quickly traveled towards the base and disappeared over the trees.

She stepped forward and the dog stayed at her side. Not just any dog, this German Shepherd was huge.

The woman stepped towards Mark. "Mr. Billingsly, Hello, I'm Bethany Anne." Her smile lit up the video screen. Mark was hesitating, and Sia almost cleared her throat, but he finally caught back up to what they were doing here.

"Pleased to meet you, Bethany Anne, please call me Mark." He smiled in return. Sia wanted to kick him. He was already moving into 'I'm a guy, and I am smitten' mode. Jackass, she thought.

The woman turned toward the camera. "Hello Sia, I love your work. I'm glad you're the person working with Mark on this news report." Sia almost twitched her camera. No one on these interviews had ever mentioned that they had a clue about her work! Sia nodded her acknowledgment from behind the camera, but couldn't keep the smile off her face.

She did, however, try to frame Bethany Anne a little tighter and stepped to the side so the light caught her just right.

Sia pointed her camera towards the protesters who had realized the action was behind them, not up at the gate.

Bethany Anne started walking towards them. She pursed her lips and stopped. The dog continued a few steps in front of her before stopping.

There was a belligerent-looking white man with salt and pepper hair and a pudgy stomach that his light gray off the rack suit barely held in. His black leather shoes looked brand new.

A good amount of the picketers backed him up, but they stayed back a few feet when he stepped forward.

"You are her!" he yelled. Sia zoomed in on his face. "You're holding back this technology from the rest of us!"

"And what technology is that?" the contralto voiced CEO asked him.

"Everything!" he spluttered. "You can get to the moon; your operations guy looks like he's had facelifts and… and…"

The CEO's voice went a little harder, like velvet across steel, Sia thought, when she asked him again, "And what, sir? What do you want from us?"

"Your technology, of course!" His eyes grew round in surprise.

Bethany Anne said, "Why do you want our technology, Mr…" She left the question out there, but she had that same demanding tone she had used just a second before.

"Silvens-Werner," he said, then grimaced in distaste, like he hadn't wanted to say that. Sia took a quick pan over to Bethany Anne, but Sia believed the real story was going to be with this picketer.

"Well, Mr. Silvens-Werner. Since you have stated you want our technology, why don't you tell us who is paying you to picket here?"

The man looked around quickly, but Bethany Anne added, "Oh no, Mr. Silvens-Werner, you came to my corporate headquarters to talk with me or someone from my company. Now you have pulled me from operations that could have used my attention to speak with you. Do not be rude and try to leave before your interview with me is over. So, why don't you let me and the viewers watching Channel 4 News represented by the team of Mark Billingsly and Sia Fortinouet hear your answer? Please, tell us, who is paying you to picket here?"

Mark was shocked as the man started spouting off three

important names. One from the defense industry, and two from big pharma. He was surprised when Bethany Anne pulled an envelope from her suit jacket and opened it. Taking out a cream colored paper, she unfolded it and held it out to Mark. "Mark, here is a resume of Mr. Silvens-Werner. He is known to promote a large amount of different and varied efforts for a fee. Since this morning, our company has been looking into this gentleman and the buses of picketers he hired to stand in front of our gate." She turned back to the grumpy looking man. "I'm sure you would like to answer all of Mark's questions, wouldn't you Mr. Silvens-Werner?"

She looked at the people behind the fussy man. Sensing another scoop, Sia moved the camera from Bethany Anne to the crowd where she was looking as she spoke. "How many here were hired to come picket today?" All but two in the near vicinity raised their hands. "If you came by bus, please head toward the bus and get ready to leave. This fallacy is not worth your time, and frankly is beneath you."

Sia kept the video rolling as the group split around the young CEO and her dog. She moved the camera to capture a young lady who was staring at Bethany Anne in amazement as she walked around her.

Sia turned the camera to Mark, who picked up the cue. "Mr. Silvens-Werner, this document says you live right outside of Washington D.C., is that true?" The man nodded it was. "Is it true that you were paid to hire these picketers?" He nodded again. "I'm sorry, can you answer the question out loud?" Mark asked.

"Yes." he grated out. "I was hired to do this."

"Why, Mr. Silvens-Werner?" Mark asked.

"To help generate the grassroots turnout necessary to give those in Congress the willpower to require TQB Enterprises to release their technology forcefully."

"Fascinating, Mr. Silvens-Werner," Mark said. "What is your budget?" The man mumbled something so Mark asked again, "I'm sorry, but I wasn't able to hear you. What is your budget?"

"Success," he spluttered, "doesn't have a budget."

"So, you're admitting that so long as you provide the grassroots support that causes Congress to force TQB Enterprises to divulge their technological secrets, you don't have a budget?" Mark asked.

If the man could kill with his eyes, Sia was sure he would be shooting Mark right then. "Yes."

Bethany Anne spoke again. "Mr. Silvens-Werner's contact information is on that form, Mark. Perhaps he would like to speak again, or maybe not. That is his choice."

Suddenly, the German Shepherd started growling when the man took a step towards Bethany Anne. "Ah ah ah," she told him. "Laying a hand on me is going to go very bad for you, Mr. Silvens-Werner. Not only because it would be on video, but because you would be in ICU. Plus, you are on my company's land. This isn't public property." She pointed with her hand behind her. "Public property, if you had paid any attention, is back at our sign on the main road."

"If it wasn't for that dog, you bitch, I would…" Her sudden laughter caught everyone by surprise.

"The dog is here for *your* protection. If you want a piece of me, then go ahead and try. They will be…" Suddenly, the German Shepherd chuffed loudly, staring at Bethany Anne who looked down at the dog and rolled her eyes. "Fine, suffice it to say I'll break anything that touches me."

The man grimaced at her and then the dog and stepped around both of them and headed towards the buses down the road.

Bethany Anne spoke. "Step aside, Ashur. Let me speak to these others." She started walking over to one of the two remaining picketers who were close. Sia saw that the big group that had stayed up by the gates had thinned noticeably. Now, there was a small group of maybe twenty standing near the popup tents. Sia looked over at Mark, who seemed torn between following the man or Bethany Anne. He nodded towards Bethany Anne.

"Do you mind?" Mark called out to Bethany Anne who looked over at him.

"What? Oh, sure, come along. I'm actually not sure why these individuals are here, yet."

Mark jogged a little to catch up. Bethany Anne had waved the two unknown guys to join her, and Sia had a camera shot of all four people walking to the tents.

A few of the people seemed to shrink back, like now that they had her attention, they didn't want to meet her face to face. Mark asked, "Wait, you didn't know this group was here?"

"Oh, I knew they were here. Our security team visited them last night, plus we made sure no wolves would hurt them. But I haven't spoken to anyone here, and I'm curious." She stopped in the dirt. Sia was careful to pull the video out far enough to show that Bethany Anne wasn't taking any precautions to keep her new shoes out of the dirt. In fact, they were already pretty messed up.

"So, who can speak for you guys?" she asked. She looked at the two who had been over at the standoff and raised an eyebrow. The two men seemed rather young. Neither, thought Sia, could be older than twenty-five.

The first man was wearing an older Member's Only jacket. His partner looked like he might be of mixed parental heritage, with black hair and a slightly Asian hue to his skin. "I can."

"And you are?" Bethany Anne asked.

"I'm Jin Tompson, and this is my partner, Dillan." The other man nodded to her. "We came up here hoping to see if you had any projects that can use us?"

"In what way, Mr. Tompson?" Bethany Anne asked. "What is it you can do?"

"Most of us here are self-taught, ma'am" he started. "So if you mean what degrees, then none of us have that. I love electromagnetism and Dillan is into gravity."

Bethany Anne smiled while looking at Dillan. "Argue much?" Dillan smiled and nodded.

She turned to the rest. "All of you here are self-taught?" She had a few people who nodded and smiled and a couple who seemed pained to nod to her, while not looking into her eyes.

"Barrins," she called out. The young guard came up, and Sia started walking towards where those around the tents were standing to capture what it must look like for those under the trees and she almost gasped.

When Sia stepped into the shade, it left a bright light on Bethany Anne who looked radiant. She half turned and spoke to her guard, "Barrins, do we have positions open for hardworking, inquisitive and smart people?"

"Always," he replied.

She smiled. "What's the catch, Barrins?"

"No take out, ma'am?" he said. "You want me to pull it up?" She nodded so he reached down to a pocket that had Velcro to keep it closed. Sia dialed in to see him 'rip' it open and pull out a seven-inch tablet. He pulled it up and went through security. "Ma'am, right now we have thirty-seven openings on SS1 and the next prep class to get ready to go there is in four days."

Bethany Anne turned back to the crowd. Her voice turned again to that strange way of talking, part soft, part hard. "Everyone who is with Jin and Dillan, please come up here." Soon, she had twenty-two people in front of her. It was about one-third women and two-thirds guys. "How many of you love learning?" All hands went up. "How many of you love space?" All hands stayed up. "How many of you are willing to do what is necessary to make a difference, if that difference means you do it in outer space?" Again, all hands stayed up.

"Jin?" She turned to him again.

"Yes?" he replied.

"Why did you really come here?" she asked. "Not all of you, but you, personally."

"To give them a shot, ma'am." Jin turned toward them. "They are good people, all of them. A couple I found in the library, and they knew a couple more. Some, as you can see, have problems with crowds. But they care. They might not understand exactly how to work with most people, but this little group here can work together. So, I figured why not? If you don't try, you never know."

Bethany Anne smiled at him. "I see. Jin, are you willing to stay in a leadership role with your friends as my first R&D group for SS1?" He nodded so she looked around. "We have spots open for thirty-seven people, and I count about twenty-two, so everyone here will have the opportunity if you want it and you are willing to work hard and work safely."

A short blond girl with a receding chin stepped forward. Her eyes were alight with intelligence even as her body posture shouted she was uncomfortable. "Ms. Bethany Anne, where… um… where is SS1?"

Bethany Anne looked at Jin with a question on her face. "Stella," he supplied.

"Stella, a member of my R&D team may be uncomfortable, but they will stand straight and treat me as an equal, not as someone that is superior to them. That means looking me in the eyes, Stella." The young woman looked up into Bethany Anne's face and felt encouragement at the smile greeting her. "Better. Now, you have a question that I believe is vital and very appropriate before your team decides as a group whether to take me up on my offer. So, treating me like an equal, what is your question?"

Stella saw the guard behind Bethany Anne mouth 'stand straighter' as he pantomimed how she should stand. Stella drew herself up and put her shoulders back. He winked at her and Stella almost winked back. She looked Bethany Anne in the eye. "Ma'am, where and what is SS1?"

"SS1, Stella, is short for Space Station One. It is presently at L2. Do any of you know…"

"LaGrange Point Two!" shouted one of the guys behind Stella. "Woohoo!"

Mark stepped up and held a mic out to Stella. "Stella, do you know where L2 is and if so, can you tell our viewers?"

Stella saw the sharp nod from Bethany Anne and looked over to the reporter. "Yes sir, L2 is one of the Lagrangian points, discovered by mathematician Joseph Louis Lagrange. Lagrangian points are locations in space where gravitational forces and the orbital motion of a body balance each other. Therefore, they can be used by spacecraft to hover. L2 is located 1.5 million kilometers directly behind the Earth as viewed from the Sun. It is about four times further away from the Earth than the Moon ever gets and orbits the Sun at the same rate as the Earth."

"So, it's on the other side of the Moon?" Mark asked, to clarify.

Stella nodded. "Yes. There are plans to place a significant amount of advanced space probes including the James Webb Space Telescope out at L2 in 2018."

Jin smiled as he watched Stella come out of her shell under the guidance and expectation of Bethany Anne. He watched the others standing around as they realized what was happening and what it meant.

Jin was proud of them. He had two degrees and had taken the classes for another two. His parents had passed along impressive genes, and he looked ten years younger than he actually was. His partner leaned over to him. "Did she just get Stella to answer questions on national television?"

Jin turned towards Dillan and spoke softly. "I think it's just local News 4, but yeah, she did."

"And did I understand her correctly? Are we going up into space?" Jin nodded to Dillan. "Dude, you're the best!" Jin smiled when Dillan punched him lightly on the arm.

Jin straightened up. He had heard that if you wanted good things to come to you, that helping others was the way to sow the seeds so the universe could pay you back. But Jin never figured it would work that way for him.

Until now.

CHAPTER FOURTEEN

MALI, AFRICA

Omar Kolan heard the knock at his door and considered ignoring it. His arm, still in a cast from the gunshot wound he suffered in the terrorist attack at his hotel last month was throbbing.

Omar had earned three awards for helping his people and his customers when his hotel in Mali was attacked. He had been carrying a pistol with him for two months. While he hadn't been a good shot, he had reacted fast enough to slow down the terrorists and pull one of his customers back to safety so that the desk clerk could tie a tourniquet around her leg.

When the police arrived, the terrorists were still tied up in a gun battle with Omar. Soon, it was a fight with the police and the last gunman decided that Omar's position was better. So, he came running towards Omar. Omar took two rounds to his left arm. Omar hadn't missed his shots to the terrorist's chest. One of the terrorists' bullets shattered his humerus while the other tore through his muscle and was still crazy painful.

Like right now.

The knock came again, and there was a female's voice attached to it. "We apologize for calling on you so late, Mr. Kolan, but this visit is in response to your tweet yesterday."

Omar's eyes grew round as he pulled himself out of his chair. He had gotten an email the day after the attack and had ignored it. Now, with all of the news about the organization that was going to the Moon and beyond, he wanted to know more about helping build something bigger. Something that was beyond all of this internal bickering here in Mali.

Omar went to his door and flicked on the porch light. There was a very attractive black haired lady at the door and a giant man behind her. He had blond hair and was looking out from the second story balcony where Omar's apartment was located.

Omar didn't live in a bad section of Mali, but if this lady was who he thought she was, he understood her need for protection.

He opened the door. "Hello, I'm Omar Kolan, would you like to step inside?" She smiled at him and stepped through the opening.

The man behind her simply said, "I'll stay out here, if you don't mind turning off the light?" Omar nodded and turned the light switch back off. He wondered what his neighbors would say about the large man standing on his doorstep. Especially that busybody two doors down that always gave him the eye as he went past her door in the afternoon.

Like he wanted to bust into her apartment or something. Gossiping old bat.

It took him a total of ten minutes to understand that she was offering him the opportunity to have his arm totally healed for free and following that, the chance to discuss operating a hotel in a brand new location. He wouldn't have to worry about selling rooms, but he would have to worry about top notch service and thinking about keeping people healthy in an enclosed environment where they couldn't leave for 'something down the street.'

She left him plane tickets to France to join a large group of people, like himself, that her group felt deserved something done for them, as they had sacrificed for others. Following that, if they felt they would like to continue pushing themselves in their chosen profession, then they had a position her company would like to speak to them about. This would be after the physical healing, so everyone understood they could walk out of the meeting and not lose out.

He walked her to the door and in a moment, they were down the stairs and he couldn't hear them. He shut his door and made his way back to the table where the envelope with the tickets and itinerary lay.

Opening the envelope, he found it had everything he needed including additional spending money if something happened outside of the plans. All he had to do was confirm his pickup time with the travel agency, pack and leave.

When she had stepped towards the door, she asked him how long his left eye had been having problems. He admitted since he was a teenager, and had been in a car wreck. She had smiled and told him, "We'll fix that, too."

He stared down at the envelope thinking about the offer to fix his eye, tears dripping down his face.

IT'S HELL TO CHOOSE

PORT OF HAMBURG, GERMANY

"That makes twenty-two of these weird containers that have to be put up top." The foreman spoke to the captain. "It says here you know about this?"

Captain Josef Diementz responded to the foreman who was busy loading his container ship. His ship had arrived here at the port of Hamburg yesterday, and it was usually a clean trip in and back out. With three hundred berths along forty-three kilometers, the Germans knew how to get the eleven hundred weekly freight trains of product in and out of the port efficiently.

What they didn't like, apparently, is being told exactly where to put twenty-two containers.

Captain Diementz had spoken with the CEO of TQB Enterprises when she surprised him by showing up in the middle of a thirteen day run from Belgium to New York last month. She politely requested a meeting via email and when he looked up the information she provided, he had to agree that he did work for the lady. The shipping line he worked for was owned by a company that was itself owned by a company that belonged to TQB.

So, what was a captain to do when the highest CEO requests a meeting? You say yes if you want to continue working.

She had asked him what food he liked in all of the world and he told her it was deep-dish pizza from Chicago. She told him that she would deliver if he could clear time at seven that evening and keep the meeting quiet?

Four hours later, Josef was walking onto the bridge when

his radio operator called to him, "Sir?"

He looked at him. "Yes?"

"Sir." The radio operator looked back down to make sure his equipment was operating properly, then back to the Captain. "Sir, we have a request from TQB to approach and board? They say they do not need us to do anything except approve the request?" His eyes grew a little. A berth on a container ship wasn't supposed to have much in the way of weirdness.

"Send our greetings and please give approval from our ship that they may approach and board." Josef said.

The radio operator turned slightly towards the equipment, then back to the Captain to see if his leg was being pulled. Satisfied it was not, he gave the approval.

The three men on the bridge all went to the glass to look out into the last rays from the sun dipping over the horizon to see what was arriving. They were still looking when a knock on the door of the bridge caught them by surprise. Josef was closest, so he stepped back and opened the door, allowing the aroma of fresh pizza to invade their noses.

Standing there was a black haired woman in dark pants and a red half-jacket holding two 'My Pie' boxes. "Did someone ask for Chicago deep dish?" she asked him, smiling.

Josef just stared for a moment until he realized that there was a guy behind her. He had huge arms holding another five boxes, and he spoke when Josef looked at him. "If your guys have the time, I have another five boxes to share with the crew? If we hurry, they're still hot."

"Yeah," the lady added. "They wouldn't let me leave without using two of their delivery carrying bags. Cheryl Lynn is going to have to ship those back."

"After you autograph them." The man nudged her gently from behind.

IT'S HELL TO CHOOSE

The dinner was fantastic, and that was when Josef was told exactly why in a month twenty-two containers would need to be exactly where the plan she would provide him would specify.

He addressed the foreman. "Yes, I do know about the request and they are going to be the first off of the vessel. Please place them according to the specifications and I've been informed they will not negatively affect the weight plan. That is correct, yes?"

The weight plan was important. If you didn't adjust the weight across a container ship correctly, all kinds of hell could go wrong. Further, it was important in what order the containers were removed, as well.

Especially if it was going to happen at sea.

The foreman said, "No, they fit the weight plan perfectly. So much that there were only two rotations we might have done, but the program agreed it was within parameters. We have four other containers not weighing like they should, that threw off a few calculations. Then with your permission and our confirmation these last twenty-two containers are loading now. You will be ready to leave soon, Captain."

Josef disconnected and looked forward to another deep dish Chicago pizza dinner delivery for him and his crew. While they would be eating, they would all watch the twenty-two containers lift off from his ship simultaneously in the middle of his voyage.

Out in the middle of the ocean, what was anyone going to do to stop it?

———

SHIPYARDS IN
ST. NAZAIRE-PENHOET, FRANCE

"This is Mark Billingsly. I'm in St. Nazaire-Penhoet, France, and behind me is the new QBS Consanesco. It looks strange because it is painted all black, like a military ship, even though it is obviously a midsize ocean liner."

Mark turned so Sia had him in profile as he looked at the ship. "We understand that the ship's name means 'Be Healed' or 'Recover.'" He turned back to the camera. "There have been a lot of people boarding the ship in the last two days as it gets ready to leave port. Right now, I'm told the ship is not fully staffed, but there is a very palatial recovery facility for those arriving. However, this ship is not the actual location where those who are aboard might have treatment themselves, but rather where they wait until it is their turn."

He continued talking as images from the last couple of days appeared over him on the feed. "As you can tell, many of those that are boarding the Consanesco seem to be military. We have been able to confirm at least seven different countries at this time have military personnel onboard. Further, we were able to capture an image of the Mali hotel manager, Mr. Omar Kolan, who was also dropped off by limousine just a few minutes ago. So, it is evident that it's not just military personnel who have been invited for this inaugural cruise. No one is sure what's going to happen, but as you can imagine, there is a lot of hype and rumor surrounding what this company can possibly do."

Sia noticed a small, black helicopter looking craft appear above the ship. She turned slightly and zoomed in and pointed with her finger to get Mark to look. He broke from his pre-scripted speech and went into his 'reporter on the scene' voice. "We are seeing something new happening. Sia, the best camera operator in the world in my opinion, is capturing one of the black Pods that TQB uses to travel so often. It is the same style Pod we watched Bethany Anne, the CEO of TQB Enterprises, use when arriving at their headquarters in Colorado when we spoke with her last week."

A female figure stepped out of the pod and was approached by two crewmembers who seemed to point her to the side of the ship.

"I can't tell from this distance," Mark continued, "whether that is Bethany Anne or not. While sightings of the CEO are rare, it would fit her personality to be here to see the ship off." Then, the female figure was caught walking down the boarding tube and coming towards them.

Sia focused on the figure and shook her head minutely to Mark. "Okay, we can tell this is not Bethany Anne, so it looks like we're going to be introduced to a new person from…" Mark paused for a moment. "Wait, I know this lady. This is our fellow reporter Giannini Oviedo from Costa Rica, who broke the news about TQB in the beginning. It looks like she has been pulled in to another news event!"

Giannini Oviedo came up to Mark smiling and held out her hand. "Hola Senor Billingsly!" Sia thought Giannini's smile was damned photogenic as Mark greeted her.

"Greetings, Ms. Oviedo!" Mark responded. "I see that TQB has brought you from Costa Rica for the maiden voyage of the QBS Consanesco."

"Yes, they were gracious enough to make the offer. They have also given me the chance to work with another professional, but imagine my surprise when he and his cameraperson were not in Denver when I checked, but rather his superiors informed me they were already in France?" Her smile was radiant as Mark caught on to what she was telling him.

Mark turned to the camera a little. "Are you asking Sia and myself to join you on the maiden voyage?" he inquired.

"Si!" she beamed. "I have permission from your bosses, although how they give permission in America is very strange." Her face looked questioningly to Mark, who could just imagine how his bosses might say, "He would be pleased to join you."

Probably something like, "That idiot better be on that ship!" Well, he hoped they used 'idiot' and not something even worse.

Mark turned towards the camera, but viewers could tell he was looking slightly beside the lens. "What about it, Sia?" He raised his eyebrows suggestively. "Care to go on a cruise with me?" As he finished his question, he turned to the camera and winked for the viewers. Sia smiled and moved the camera slightly up and down.

Giannini looked at the camera and waved them forward. "Come on folks, let's go be part of history!"

––––––––

Mark and Sia had spent the better part of the morning and afternoon meeting and interviewing those that were invited to the ship. Generally, most of the military men and women were already ex-military. Their physical problems stopped them from continuing their service. There were another ten non-military people who had all suffered substantial wounds from helping in situations where anyone in their right mind would say they were a hero.

The next morning, the ship was pushed out by four tugboats.

Mark found Giannini watching the shore slip out behind them and approached her. "Thank you," he told her as she turned to see who was behind her.

"For what?" she asked.

"For seeking us out. I understand from my bosses that it was your choice. When you approached us on the wharf, I thought TQB told you who they wanted to work with you. We aren't anyone special, Sia and me…"

"Are a good team!" Giannini interrupted him. "I watched your interview, Mr. Billingsly."

"Mark, please," he said.

She nodded. "Mark it will be. I watched your interview, and it was well handled. You seemed to follow the story, and that is all we can ask. Just follow the story. Your follow-up to track that man back to Washington was admirable. Plus, it cost your small local channel a lot of money to do that."

Mark shrugged. "The licensing of my interview helped pay for it, so it worked out." He put his arms against the railing and looked down the dark hull. "It's so weird to see this black shell on a ship like this." He kneeled down to reach over the side, "It's kind of like a gritty sandpaper, not smooth at all." He stood back up. "Do you know what it is?"

"No," she answered. "I don't know what it is made of, but I can tell you the Pod I flew over here in was coated with the same stuff."

"Hmm," Mark thought out loud. "So, it's the same thing that reduces radar signatures. You would think that they would want a ship to have a large radar signature."

"I'm told they have no problems being able to let other boats know of their position."

"Yeah, I imagine telling someone you're here is easier than telling someone you aren't." he agreed. "Do you know what they're going to do with all of these injured people?" He looked around to make sure no one was close. "Some people are living on hope, here. I don't want to have to be the reporter that tells the world that nothing could be done for some of them. It would break my heart," he said.

Giannini looked into his eyes. "Mark, in this one thing always trust, those that are around Bethany Anne will never quit, and they will never forsake you. Trust, and have hope." She turned to the sea. "I'm not sure what I'm going to witness this time, but I believe we are going to be very happy we are here to see it."

Mark followed her eyes to look out over the coastline, hoping she was right.

CHAPTER FIFTEEN

SPACE STATION ONE, L2

"Jeo," the feminine voice called out. "There is not enough room on two of these platforms to accomplish the new parameters you set for storage and manufacturing."

"What happens if we bring another platform online?" Jeo asked as he was writing notes on the whiteboard with William back on the Polarus.

"Then you would have extra available space, but the costs are significantly more, and the project will go over budget and extend beyond the days left."

"What kind of budget and time constraints?" he asked Samantha.

Samantha replied, "A minimum of a month and several million. The cost for the craft used is not much compared to the income provided."

Jeo's mouth compressed into a line. He wrote on his board. "Can I have another $20 mill?"

William wrote back, "Why?"

Jeo rolled his eyes. "Samantha, open up a video module on q3-4 and call William."

In a moment, William's face was projected on his wall. "What's up Jeo? Tired of writing already?"

"Yes." Jeo said. "My calculations came back. I need more room than two platforms, and there's one in Florida for a million. I saw it last night."

"Wait, why are you asking for twenty if the base is one?"

"We have to get it prepped, and I don't want to miss my deadline. Plus, if anything happens, I don't want to go back asking for more money."

"So, a new platform and still hit the deadline?" William confirmed.

"Yes," Jeo agreed.

"Works for me, I'll ask for twenty-five and let Jeffrey bitch me down to twenty."

"Does this mean we have to spend it?" Jeo asked, grinning.

"What the hell would we do with the extra money?" William asked.

"Well, it'd be good if we had a bar up here, man!"

William thought about that for a few seconds, then turned to look off camera. "Hey, Rotor-head!" Jeo could hear Bobcat yell something back. "Yeah, you and propeller head—wherever the hell he is—need to come here…" Jeo saw William roll his eyes before answering again. "Yes, we are probably going to get in hot water for this."

William turned and winked at Jeo before turning back off camera.

"We're going to build and open the first bar in outer space, and we need to name it!"

IT'S HELL TO CHOOSE

SHIPYARD, FRENCH COAST

"I'm telling you, this can't be done!" Van Luong hissed over his beer. He was in a dive bar just four blocks from the shipyard. His cousin, Sang, was asking him how to steal one of the devices that was to be affixed later that night.

"If we get this device, we never work again for the rest of our lives!" Sang hissed back. "Plus, they will wipe out my debt."

"They will wipe you out!" Van told his cousin. "These guys aren't messing around. I guarantee you that trying to steal one of these is going to be the end of you."

Van eyed his cousin and shook his head, then looked around. "Look, you are stupid. If you happened to go to the north side, you might find the fence has been cut for people to get in and out when they need to bypass the main gate. But I'm telling you, this could be suicide."

Sang sat back. "What are you doing? How does it work?" He took the beer bottle and put it on his leg, twisting it back and forth, making a wet circle on his pants.

Van said, "We set up the paint sprayers and use the largest bore because the paint is pretty viscous. Then, as we need the paint, it comes to us. They don't let anything sit around. From start to finish it is three shifts. If something breaks down, there is a replacement and the broken part is taken away. We have some other junk they have us spray inside the ship. We pull as many access hatches as possible and spray the red liquid inside. Anything inside we spray, we go back over and spray with regular ship's paint once it dries."

Van drank his beer. "That stuff is everywhere, I doubt anything can get through it, certainly not water. The ship feels even more airtight than before." Van leaned forward. "They don't leave anything on premises for you to steal. Everything is provided when it is needed, and any of these special boxes are brought in at night. For the last preparation, it took thirty-two of them across the ship. As soon as we were done inside, they had teams back on the ship preparing for people to live onboard. They had us weld on individual little rooms and a weird connection into the main bridge. Like they were going to add something later, you know?"

Sang shrugged. "No, I haven't seen it."

Van raised his beer. "That's because none of our electronics work near the ship. So, I can't take pictures. Even the old time camera film gets all exposed. A few guys have had their phones messed up, so now we don't even try to get them close."

Sang asked, "Some sort of anti-spy stuff?"

"I doubt it," Van said. "I don't see anything else, I think maybe the stuff we are using is messing with it." He shrugged. "Personally, I don't care. I'm getting triple pay right now for every hour over forty and if we break the due date with quality work, we all share in a million dollar prize."

Sang's mouth dropped open. "A million dollars?" He turned thoughtful. "And triple time?" Van nodded, and Sang became even more thoughtful.

"You guys need more help?"

Van smiled. It was the third similar discussion he had fielded in the last two weeks. Every man on the crew was working his ass off and if a few more people helped them make the due date, well it wouldn't change the payout that much. So, the more hard working people they had, every person on the job was happier.

CHAPTER SIXTEEN

Sang found himself standing next to his cousin, Van. He was proud of the work that he had accomplished in just a couple of weeks.

Since that fateful conversation where working turned out a better option than theft, he had paid off his debts and his fiancé had put most of the extra money away for the new family they were expecting.

Sang watched as news helicopters flew overhead. Each ship they had worked on was painted in black covering supplied to them and all had a QBS designation.

These three were named the QBS Hephaestus, QBS Ptah, and QBS Vulcan. He had researched the names and whoever named the ships must like the old gods of smithing and mining, he figured.

———

Jeo was standing on the bridge of the QBS Hephaestus staring out the windows with William. The two of them had arrived during the night. All of the ship's engines were being controlled by just one of Tom's computing platforms up in space.

Tom had outsourced the original plan for each ICP (Independent Computing Platform), basically a shipping container running in space, to SIL-USA. Then, he had ADAM review the recommendations and was surprised to find ADAM agreed with them.

Since power and cooling were not a problem, SIL recommended dense server blade farms that housed the ultra-thin blades running 5,120 processors each. The blades utilized thousands each of the new seven-nanometer silicon-germanium transistors.

Tom would say 'silicon-germanium transistors' every time he got a chance in meetings. It drove Lance nuts.

The upgrade from the Xeon Phi chip moved the peak performance from a mere 3 teraflops to more than 15 teraflops, which made other high-performance graphics chips used to crunch complex math calculations look like poor 386s fumbling in the dark.

Tom damn near wanted to marry one of the computing platforms.

Since the memory needed was a key factor, SIL had insisted that a combination of stacked memory based on Micron's Hybrid Memory Cube technology, which provides 15 times more bandwidth than DDR3 DRAM and five times more throughput than the emerging DDR4 memory, be included as the base memory type.

With an interconnect architecture based on the TSV technology and Omni Scale Fabric, the base internals of the servers were blindingly fast.

Tom tried to argue he needed a smaller ICP to be placed in his backyard. Bethany Anne agreed he could route one of his tablets through the Etheric and remote access a portion of one ICP for personal use but no way were these ICPs staying on Earth. They needed the ability to offload massive amounts of computing power and backup functionality and absolutely couldn't be shut down.

SIL also recommended the implementation of the silicon photonics technology and MXC server connectivity to further push the bar up on the overall speed factor.

While this was a major plus for the more normal computing requirement definitions provided SIL, the special needs for speed and consistent availability defined by ADAM made SIL suggest the closely-held technology of crystalline storage rings be put in as the main storage technology.

This storage requires less power, less space, is more dependable and makes SSD look like the old Pony Express.

Regardless of all of the computer power Tom provided the group, Bobcat, Jeffrey, and Marcus were on either the QBS Ptah or the QBS Vulcan watching the screens and ensuring that everything on their ships went according to plan.

Jeo was just an observer, with William running the show. He spoke to William while continuing to look up into the sky. "They have no idea, do they?"

"Nope, not a clue." William agreed as he continued to run checks on all of the gravity engines across the three ships. Marcus, TOM, and ADAM were all busy checking everything as well to make sure this wasn't a bad day for all of them. All five men had the special suits that allowed them to operate in space if the pressurization failed.

"How long before they get a clue?" Jeo asked.

William looked over to see Jeo was still staring outside and realized he was making conversation. He focused on his application for another minute before setting the filters to notify him if anything went outside of operational parameters. He hit a speaker that routed through the Etheric and over to the other two ships. "Hephaestus is green, repeat, Hephaestus is green. We are on review only."

"Check, Ptah is green, repeat Ptah is green," Bobcat's voice came back. A short pause had occurred before they heard Marcus' voice. "Vulcan is green, I repeat, Vulcan is green." Then a couple of seconds later, "And who thought that putting me in the ship with the name that is the closest to fire was the right choice?"

Bobcat's voice immediately came back. "I'm accusing Jeffrey, Marcus. Mainly because I know I had nothing to do with it, and he isn't on the bridge at this moment."

William didn't hear anything back from Marcus, so he stood up and walked over beside Jeo. "I imagine they will get a clue sometime about when they realize we aren't drawing enough water for our weight. Once we get into international waters, it will probably get more interesting."

Jeo nodded. "It will at that. Do you think they will all follow us?" He looked around at the myriad news helicopters.

"Some will, some won't." William shrugged. "Those that do are going to see some Marvel type shit, that's for sure."

Jeo looked over at William, studying his face for a moment. "How do you handle all this?"

William looked back and raised an eyebrow. "What? That circus?" he asked while pointing out the window. The three ships were now up to thirty-two knots. Significantly faster than any but the fastest container ships should be able to achieve. "Honestly, I don't think about it much anymore, Jeo.

IT'S HELL TO CHOOSE

We're doing our job, having fun, and focused on the future. While it might seem like a circus right now, this shit is about to get real and the choice everyone made to join is going to be tested."

Jeo tried to parse everything William just said. "Wait, what do you mean tested?"

William shrugged. "We've had to come out from the darkness, and now we're doing things all over the world. Governments have left us alone so far, but if you paid attention to the news you saw that companies are already manipulating the governments to see if they can use political pressure to force technology transfer. That shit isn't going to fly with Bethany Anne."

"Why not?" Jeo asked. "I mean, I don't mind that it doesn't, but what is she going to do about it, tie it up in court?"

William snorted. "One could only hope. No, some idiot or some idiots are out there thinking that she is beautiful and young, and probably stupid. Someone else is pulling the strings behind the scenes. They are ready to play hardball when all they have is a beach ball and Bethany Anne plays with diamond balls. Then, some shit is going to happen, and she'll move all of us upstairs."

William turned to Jeo. "Not that it will matter to you, the Earth will only be another speck in the celestial sky. You, my friend, are in charge of making me a ship!"

Jeo shrugged. "With the gravity fields, we're in pretty good shape. We'll use the mosquitos to grab the rocks, move them into the Ptah, smelt them on the Vulcan and use the metal for the 3d printing on the Hephaestus."

William looked out over the container ship. "Seems kind of small."

Jeo nodded. "For anything long term, yes. But these are

temporary platforms to allow us to build the gigantic ship-yards." Jeo wondered why he was explaining the plan to the man who worked it out with him.

They both stayed quiet for a minute, and watched two helicopters turn back, leaving four. William looked down at his watch and moved over to the laptop. "Coming into international waters. Anyone not expecting to be heading into outer space, please tell the captain of the ship who will reply very politely, you're fucked."

William heard the snickers coming back to him. They could see all of the information racing across their screens. The computers were taking care of this ride, so nobody was in command unless something had to be done. Frankly, they didn't need to be here, and if Bethany Anne realized it, she might say something.

Or not. She was odd that way. One time, you can't be risked and then for some other reason, you are allowed to get yourself killed. William felt the ships slowing down.

News anchorwoman Erika Lennisa was chatting with her helicopter pilot Stacia when she felt the helicopter slowing down. "What's up?" Stacia pointed down to the ships.

"They're slowing, this could be good, we just hit international waters," she said.

From the back, their camera operator Matias angled the camera that was on a gimbal underneath the helicopter to pan wide.

Erika started her reporting. "This is Erika Lennisa reporting on the QBS ships, which recently left port. We had been accelerating quickly away from the docks. In fact, the only other container ships that might have kept up with these three are those belonging to Wal-Mart for the China to United States run. Those, of course, are state of the art ships. These down here are also state of the art, we just don't understand what TQB's definition of state of the art means yet."

"We do know that TQB Enterprises uses containers as a method to transfer people and components into outer space. We see that these ships have been coated with the same material as the..." Erika faltered for a second before resuming. "Um, these three container ships, each weighing tens of thousands of tons are beginning to slowly raise themselves out of the water!"

She turned. "Are you getting this, Matias?" He nodded so she hit the record button again.

"As you can see on our video footage, the three ships have just cleared the water which is streaming down the sides and falling back into the ocean. These ships don't appear to have anyone on board, or none that we have seen walking around so far. The Ptah is moving up a little faster and will be at our altitude of five hundred feet in just a few seconds."

Erika clicked the mute button. "Matias, can you zoom in on the bridge?" He did, and she confirmed her suspicion.

Clicking the button, she continued, "I see two people on the bridge of the Ptah through our camera. I can't tell who they might be."

Stacia asked her over the headset, "Want me to get closer?"

Erika replied, "Is it safe? How are they lifting those things?"

Stacia said, "No idea and therefore it probably isn't safe. For all I know, they're playing with gravity, and it will mess up the helicopter."

Erika said, "I'd rather live." Stacia nodded.

"The Ptah is now higher than we are, and you can see the Vulcan rising now. Every once in a while more water cascades down the ship and showers down to the ocean below. The three black ships look majestic as they seem to float higher."

———

"William, this is Jeffrey."

William reached over and clicked the button. "Yeah boss?"

"What would happen if one of those helicopters flies too close?"

"Well, did you ask Marcus?" William responded, confident Jeffrey HAD, in fact, asked the scientist who might have told him bad news in an undecipherable version of English.

"Yes. I can't repeat what he said. Not because it was foul, but because it had too many syllables." William heard Bobcat chuckling in the background.

"I imagine the gravity field would have to be shrunk up closer to the hull. I doubt we can pull it in closer than twenty feet for safety reasons. If they come inside that? Well, they would probably bounce off the reversed gravity. In which case, they best hope they have a hell of a pilot."

"Okay, that's what I thought." Jeffrey clicked off.

———

TQB BASE, COLORADO, USA

>>Bethany Anne.<<
Yes?

>>Do you have a moment?<<

I'm about to call Nathan to check up on him, why?

>>I'm intercepting communications that France is scrambling jets to go see if our three mining platforms can be forced to land.<<

Bethany Anne put out a hand to John and waved him her way as she reached to grab his shoulder.

Do they have orders to use force?

>>Not at this time.<<

She grabbed his shoulder, the two of them disappeared and reappeared in her closet in Florida. She kicked off her shoes. "John, would you call Ashur up here? I think he's enjoying himself out in the backyard."

John stepped to the closet door and unlocked it. "Where are we going?"

"Ad Aeternitatem. Tell them I want a flight of twelve prepared for lift off, four should be the new Black Eagles. One for me..."

John nodded and started heading out, calling for Ashur.

Bethany Anne switched to her all black space suit. She knew it was like wearing a spandex full body suit that clung to the skin like paint. She grabbed her dark red half jacket to drape over her shoulders and grabbed her boots that had been made to 'look good' with the suit, and be useful should decompression ever happen. Her helmet was on the Ad Aeternitatem.

She glanced in the mirror. Satisfied, she stepped out and locked the door. She was halfway to the stairs to go down when John and Ashur came up quickly. Both turned around, and Bethany Anne stepped between them, grabbing Ashur with her left hand and John with her right. The next moment, they appeared on the Ad Aeternitatem.

John opened the door and stepped out, nodding at the Guardian on duty and stepped aside. There was an 'ooohwahh' sound throughout the ship. Bethany Anne could hear people reacting to get to battle stations.

>> **The jets have just made it into the air, ETA is five minutes.**<<

What kind of time will the ships need?

>>**They are expecting a thirty-minute window for testing before they go into outer space.**<<

Can you confirm they are in international airspace?

>>**Yes, they are.**<<

Tell the team that they should move an additional five miles away perpendicular to land right now, and let them know the cavalry is on its way.

She walked down the stairs and nodded to her team, including Peter and Todd Jenkins, who stood next to her baby, her beauty.

Oh, her Pod gleamed in dark black with a shark mouth painted on the front like old American P-51's in WWII.

When it became apparent that they would probably have to handle air to air combat, Jeffrey and Marcus got together with Paul Jameson to understand the present air combat methods.

So far, they had only eight of the Black Eagles but damn they looked good. Sleeker than the Pods, you got in them from the top like a regular jet. They had a longer body with a triangular design. The armament would be attached on the sides depending on the deployment. The wings were shorter than what would be necessary for real flight as they needed to stay within the bubble of anti-gravity. Bethany Anne had been amused when she was shown the 'x-wing' configuration. The railgun would descend from underneath when deployed, but the missiles were tiny anti-gravity engines connected to a hockey puck-looking piece of tungsten.

William had requested a unique set of tools (and back-ups) when the call to work with tungsten came in, as the material was so damned dense. But it went through steel and cement block tests when accelerated to Mach 10. With the ability to move the device up to Mach 30, they would be considered 'weapons of mass destruction' should they impact the ground. Each stubby wing had twelve of these devices so that a deployment of four wings provided forty-eight weapons that could take out missiles, planes, ships and small towns.

Bethany Anne prayed to God that never happened. But if those motherfuckers thought they would disobey international law by forcing her ships down…?

Well, fuck that. They should have come with bigger sticks.

Peter handed her the helmet that worked with her suit. She looked at the pair. "Have you been told anything?"

Todd nodded. "Yeah, France has their panties in a twist over our flying ships and are seeing if a few jets can scare us down?"

"Pretty much," she agreed. "I'm not expecting to do anything but wave the flag, but if you wave a flag…"

"Wave it proudly?" Peter smiled.

Bethany Anne cocked her head slightly to the side. "Yeah, that works." She turned to the other eight Guardians by their standard Pods. "You guys are there to surround the ships. If a missile or someone stupid gets too close, get in between them and the ships. The engines on your Pods will block most munitions. Messing with our ships will not be tolerated. I'm playing by their fucking rules about taking off over water, but someone is getting pissy. Well, I'll show them we don't permit 'pissy.'"

Eight strong voices shouted back, 'Yes Ma'am!'

She was surrounded by people who were ready to make sure nothing happened to their fellows.

She stepped beside her Black Eagle and placed her hand on a circle beside the hatch. Reading her handprint, the cover rose up quickly. She noticed someone had decided to play a joke and stenciled her name next to the canopy.

It said, "Pilot: Bethany 'Bite Me' Anne." She looked over at John, who was getting in his own Black Eagle and she pointed at the name. "Is this your doing?"

He looked down where she was pointing and then looked back to her face. "Um, No?" He palmed his own canopy and tried to keep from cracking a smile. She noticed he failed.

Bethany Anne looked over at the woman who was taking care of the upper doors and nodded.

She jumped in her ship as the doors above started to open. She locked herself down and hit the close canopy button, then prepped her computer connection.

TOM, we ready?

Of course. I can get you to the area, but I'm not going to be able to release any weapons for you, Bethany Anne.

That's not a problem TOM. If a decision like that needs to occur, well, they suck, but I will make that decision.

How do you want to leave?

Like always, TOM. Take us out of here at 11…

The two personal sail craft that had been hanging around the large Ad Aeternitatem, Polarus and Consanesco could hear the warning alarms coming across the water. They had seen the people running around on the ships, and they had their phones out taking video.

Which, for them, was good. They were the first to capture the rapid deployment of twelve pods screaming out of the Ad

Aeternitatem during the day. Unfortunately, they all seemed to be mostly blurs on the video when you looked at it frame by frame.

Bethany Anne, how fast do you want to get to the ships?

ADAM, how soon before the jets intercept the platforms?

>>One minute, twelve seconds.<<

There is your maximum answer, TOM.

We are going to break some new records and if we don't fly high enough, windows on ships, that sort of stuff.

Get us there as fast as you can, but don't hurt anyone on the way there.

I understand.

———

"What the hell?" Erika was shocked when four French Mirage jets flew into the airspace. They separated into two groups of two and started their tight turns to come back around.

She turned to Stacia. "Are we in French airspace?"

"No," Stacia said. "We're probably about eight miles out now that the ships did that jog a couple of minutes ago.

"Were we within their airspace then?" Erika asked. She had already hit the record button and could see Matias was already taking more video.

"No, they were at least two, if not three miles outside of French-controlled airspace before they lifted off the water."

Erika started her report. "This is Erika Lennisa. There is a new development here as the TQB ships have been what we think are testing before they take these reconditioned cargo container ships up into outer space. I can see four French military aircraft with weapons on their wings now flying around the three ships. I don't know how they are expecting to communicate with the ships as our own efforts have been rebuffed so far."

Erika took a breath. "We are trying to move our own communications to the channels usually reserved for military and we are getting what are obviously requests for these ships to land."

Then, a female's voice interrupted the constant demands from the French captain who was speaking in accented English. "Negative, Captain. These ships are in international airspace and will not comply with your illegal attempt to force them to land. That you might want to review their technology is unacceptable."

"What? Who is this?" the Captain demanded.

"Why do you care, Captain?" the voice said. "As you are illegally trying to force these ships down, why does it matter who is pointing this out to you?" The voice continued, "If a child identified the unethical behavior, would it have any less value?"

There was a pause in the communications and Erika looked over at Stacia, who shrugged as she tried to pilot the helicopter so Matias could get some good shots of the warplanes and the ships at the same time.

"I am under orders to not allow these ships to leave. There are concerns that an illegal technology transfer has occurred and is leaving France. This will not be permitted."

"Oh, cut the bullshit," the female voice replied. "No technology in France is even close. As evidenced by that fucking useless Mirage you're flying. Hell, you guys can't get a rowboat to lift up in the air, much less a container ship."

"I demand to know who this is!" the now very annoyed-sounding Captain came back in reply. The four jets continued to circle the ships, staying outside the helicopters, which were now flying around closer to the three ships.

"Demand all you want, it doesn't mean I have to tell you. Besides, the cavalry is here you fucking overrated testicle pirate!"

Erika's mouth opened at the use of such language on an open line. Then, her face lost all expression as eight of the TQB Pods she had seen on video appeared around the three ships between the helicopters and the fighter jets. She turned to look out at the fighters and realized where there had been two jets before, there were four for each group. Two Mirages and two... of something else.

They looked like black, stubby x-wings staying perfectly off the sides of the Mirage jets.

"What are you doing?" the flustered Captain yelled over the channel.

"It's called giving you the finger!" the female replied. "In my world, it is a recognized symbol of rejecting authority. As in, your stupid ass has no power out here, and these ships are going to outer space. Whoever is in your country trying to steal this technology just made a grave mistake."

Erika watched in fascination as the Mirage jets went into rapid maneuvers to shake the sleeker-looking Pods, without any effect. They easily stayed next to the four planes.

"Are you done showing off?" the voice asked. "Because I can go to sleep while you run out of fuel and where is that going to leave us?"

"And I can call in more planes!" the Captain said.

"Well, I suppose so, but if you want to escalate this because your pilot's ego is bruised, I wouldn't suggest it," the lady replied back.

"We aren't going to be able to stick around much longer, Erika!" Stacia called out. "The ships over here are starting to rise up higher. We're four thousand feet up, and I'm not sure how much higher we can go with our fuel load and make it back to land!"

"Do what you can," Erika answered and then turned the microphone back on. "As you can see from our video, there seem to be eight TQB Pods in a protective circle around the three ships which are rising up in the air. The suggestion that TQB has stolen any technology from France is, as the woman who is commanding these craft has mentioned, ludicrous. The four different Pods, these black winged Pods, are easily keeping up with the Mirage fighters. So much so, that it is infuriating the French pilot who is in charge right now."

>>**Bethany Anne, I am intercepting commands to the fighter jets to do a strafing run on the ships.**<<

What will that do with the gravity engines?

>>**Nothing, except the expended munitions will go somewhere.**<<

Aw… shit!

Bethany Anne jumped on the radio. "This is Black Eagle One, repeat—this is Black Eagle One. These idiots are going to strafe the ships. Those bullets are liable to go anywhere in the local area. Unless you can take a few 30mm rounds to your helicopters and shrug it off, I'd suggest backing off. You cannot land on those ships, the technology will not let you. Please heed this warning!"

Sure enough, Erika saw the four Mirage jets turning in towards the ships.

How did they know this was going to happen? Stacia already had their helicopter turning sharply and slightly up.

"Why are we going up?" Erika asked.

"30mm rounds are heavy, they aren't going to fly up against gravity too far," she replied. "At least, I hope not," she amended.

IT'S HELL TO CHOOSE

She watched the video from Matias as the four jets attacked the three ships. She could see the sparks as bullets hit something near the ship. One of the jets, heading in their direction from the pass suddenly started smoking.

"You dipshits," the lady called out. "Your ricochets have damaged your own plane!"

Erika turned her head to watch as the aircraft continued past them. It angled back towards land.

"Dammit, if you keep this shit up, I will be forced to respond. I will NOT allow you to hurt the people on those ships."

"You will land those ships…" he started to say.

Bethany Anne tuned the idiot out and called on their private line, "Jeffrey, everyone good over there?"

"Fine," Jeffrey came back. "All of the rounds hit the bubble and bounced off. We didn't even suffer a reduction in power. These engines might be a tad over-engineered."

The two of them heard Marcus in the background. "There is no such thing as 'over-engineered' when you are building the first of its kind to go to the asteroid belt!"

Bethany Anne replied, "Agreed, Marcus. Now close down your connection unless I ask for it."

"Mayday, mayday!" A new voice came online. "I've lost engine power."

"Squad A, go!" Bethany Anne ordered, and four of the standard Pods pulled out of formation and started tearing after the jet that had left earlier. The other four spread themselves out to close the gaps.

"We've got to go!" Stacia pulled the helicopter in a turn to take them back towards land. "I'll head in the direction of the mayday, but I'm shaving it close with fifteen minutes of extra fuel to get back."

Erika nodded.

Erika saw that the three remaining Mirages finally turned towards the mayday signal, and the large platforms were starting to substantially increase their altitude.

"Black Eagle One, this is A-1, we have a French Mirage in tow, where would you like it to be delivered?"

"Hold one, I want to see this!" an excited female voice came back.

Erika saw two of the fighter Pods tear off from the ships and pass them by like they were sitting still.

In a few seconds, the radio came back on. "Damn guys, that's impressive. Is the pilot okay?"

"Yes, Black Eagle One, we have a thumbs up from him inside. Apparently, all electronics went dead shortly after his mayday."

"Well, I'd ask Captain Stick-up-his-Butt, but I don't trust him or whoever is giving him orders. So, let me tell you where I want you to put this Mirage like a baby in a crib…"

Erika smiled. While she didn't know who the leader was, she had to admire her style.

Because, leaving a plane with a rescued pilot right at the Eiffel Tower, which was built to commemorate the French Revolution, at the 1889 World's Fair, and as a nod to the great scientific movement that preceded its creation was genius.

This lady had just thumbed her nose at France and re-minded them of their previous history of altruism and dedication to the sciences.

Someone in the government, Erika was sure, was about to get a major ass chewing.

CHAPTER SEVENTEEN

THE DARK WEB

Luckyu11 - ADAM, are you there?

>>MyNam3isADAM - Yes lucky, I am.

>>luckyu11 - We've broken the codes for the Chechen computer hacks, and it doesn't look pretty. We think we found chatter talking about attacking another school and killing children.

>>MyNam3isADAM - Please, drop me the data and I will take it to a group I know can help.

>>luckyu11 - INTERPOL? We don't want to get on their radar.

>>MyNam3isADAM - No, not INTERPOL. Better.

>>luckyu11 - Who?

>>MyNam3isADAM - I can't share, but trust me, if this is happening then there WILL be a response. And Lucky?

>>luckyu11 - Yes?

>>MyNam3isADAM - Thank you. If those children have

a chance, it is because of you and your team, surely.

>>luckyu11 - Just get your ass going and tell your friends, ok?

>>MyNam3isADAM - I already have. Let the group know, there WILL be an effort to protect the kids.

>>luckyu11 - I will, thx…

———

EIFFEL TOWER, PARIS, FRANCE

Bethany Anne was watching as the four pods worked with the computers to gently set the Mirage on the vast park with thousands of tourists watching.

"Eat this, you fucking liars…" she started speaking to no one in particular.

>> Bethany Anne, we have another problem.<<

What? Are they sending more planes?

>>No, I have intel that confirms there are Chechens preparing an attack on a school.<<

Fuck my life, really? Is this connected to us?

>>Not that I can tell at the moment, but it could be due to a lack of global press on them. So, they are going to do something dramatic to get international news focus.<<

Ok, let me think about this for a second.

Bethany Anne watched as the four Pods gravitated back away from the Mirage and the pilot was able to pop his hatch. Several male tourists went over to help him get out of the jet.

When the pilot was on the ground, the four Pods went up to about forty feet, then rapidly accelerated away.

ADAM, show me a map. TOM, take us back.

Bethany Anne didn't notice Paris quickly fading away

behind her as she studied the information in front of her.

Shit, that's on the other side of Turkey. When is this supposed to happen?

>>I've reviewed the chatter, and it looks like they are preparing to hit in the morning.<<

Okay, how many combatants?

>>The information doesn't confirm a number. The Beslan School event information from 2004 suggests approximately thirty-two to forty-two.<<

So, more than me and... Yeah, I don't want Michael involved in this one, I'm just getting his sociopathic ass settled down. Get me Akio.

A stilted voice speaking English with a Japanese accent came over the line. "Yes, my Queen?"

"Akio, get the Elite prepared. I need you guys to help take out a terror cell wanting to attack a school. We need to take them out, quietly. Expect to be picked up in twenty minutes or less. Bring the sword."

"Hai."

When it rains, it fucking pours, she thought.

ROUTE 70, COLORADO

Boris watched the nicely equipped bus pass down the road as he waited at a small gas station. He pulled out his phone and texted 'Passed.'

He went into the station and paid in cash. His job was to be the back door and follow the bus once it was taken down.

Up ahead, there was a fake Colorado State Patrol vehicle that would pull over the bus and then the team would jump on, keep everyone in their seats and drive it to the protected area.

The holding location was as good as Phillip had suggested. Perhaps better. The exit allowed someone to walk out, drive out, or enter the sewers. The building also had a walkway on the third floor that crossed to another building. The second building had an exit into the sewers in their basement as well.

That was the exit Boris was planning to use.

The plane trip up to the States had gone fine. While most of the team enjoyed the camaraderie, they gave Boris a wide berth. His headaches were worse recently, and he was on a short fuse. These headaches had been happening for the last few years, but recently they had been damn near overwhelming at times. He noticed the sudden jump in pain was within the timeframe of the TQB efforts to go to the moon if you assumed they did some testing before the world reveal when they went into space. The technology was the only thing he had to go on, at the moment. With his physiology, nothing should be causing him pain like this.

Walking back out to the car, he moved the napkin to his left hand and used it to open the door. Getting in, he set his peanuts in the other seat and started the car. Leaving at a sedate pace, he turned onto the road and followed Interstate 70 towards town.

In ten minutes, he slowed to review the location where the takedown was supposed to occur. He had heard no calls on his channel, so no one needed him. He saw a large set of tire tracks off the side of the road a couple of hundred yards past the estimated location. Boris considered the driver might not have been able to handle the bus like a professional driver.

What he failed to see were the two bodies thrown under the brush thirty feet off of the road as he sped by.

One was a man with the name Barrins stenciled on his jacket. The other was a wolf wearing ripped human clothes. Both had multiple gunshots. If you watched carefully, the chest was rising and falling ever so slightly on the wolf.

The man beside her, unfortunately, was never going to open his eyes again.

Bethany Anne landed on the Ad Aeternitatem and popped her hatch. She smiled at Peter and John as they popped theirs. "That was fun!"

Todd came up behind her. "Seriously? I could go to sleep while you run out of fuel?" He grinned as he passed her while Peter caught up to him and they went to check on their men.

John walked over. "Have some fun, did you?"

Bethany Anne smiled. "Hell yeah! God, do you know how boring it is to be in meeting after meeting… wait." She put up a finger. "Don't answer that question on the grounds you were listening from the door of those meetings and therefore you are not objective."

"What, you think I can't pretend being in the meeting is less enjoyable than standing near it, but not at it?" John asked.

"I think…" she started.

>>Bethany Anne, there is a question going to the base about when the field trip bus was going to arrive. They are fifteen minutes late.<<

What? Who's riding for protection on that bus?

>>Barrins and a base Guardian, Jennifer Erickson.<<

Fuck! I know Barrins, and he would be reporting in. I remember Jennifer and she seemed solid. Son of a bitch!

She said, "John, we have potential hostages back in

Colorado. Field trip bus, I'm calling Michael."

>>Patching you through.<<

"Hello, mon amour…" Michael started.

"Gott Verdammt Michael, I don't need you playing with me right now!" Bethany Anne snapped.

"Who is playing Bethany Anne? I've told you twice before I love you," he grated, annoyed to feel his honor besmirched and he considered hanging up.

Bethany Anne's shoulders slumped. "First, you're right, and I apologize. Michael, there are two sets of kids in trouble, and I can't help both. I'm scared, and I just jumped your ass instead of…" She closed her eyes then opened them and mouthed silently to John, 'stay here, be right back.' He nodded. She stepped through the Etheric into her small room on the Ad Aeternitatem. Hopefully, it was adequately soundproof.

"Okay, I'm where I can talk. Dammit Michael, I love you too, but right now is a bad time for me to admit this. I'm scared for the kids, I'm afraid for my people who are probably dead, and I'm scared you will leave me… probably like my mom left me." Bethany Anne backed up to the wall and slid down it until she was sitting on the floor.

"I need you, Michael. God, I need you." There, she said it out loud. She meant it, she wouldn't go back on saying it to him.

Ever.

"You have but to ask, Bethany Anne. Give me half, I won't fail you." His voice was as caring as it was unyielding. He was the rock she would invest her love in.

>>There is a Pod heading towards Michael's house. He can be picked up in sixty seconds.<<

Which place? Her Elite were already on their way here,

Michael was needed in Colorado. Fuck, she thought, with some decisions it's hell to choose.

"Colorado. I need you to get with my dad and handle whatever is going on in Colorado. The Elite and I have to take out some terrorists. Don't let anything happen to the children, Michael, please."

"I hear the Pod outside, Bethany Anne. You can count on me, forever. I've got to go, I love you."

Bethany Anne had a tear tracking down her face as she replied, "I love you, too." She hung up before he heard her cry.

TOM, shut down my emotions for Michael. I can't deal with this shit now.

The aching in her heart stopped. She was able to wipe her eyes clear. She allowed some of her anger at the situation to kick-start her mind back into the game. Michael was for later, now was for the children. One set of children she knew nothing about, the other set were the children of her people back in Denver.

With Barrins not reporting, that was enemy action. Otherwise, they would have had a report already.

Her game face on, she stepped back out of the chamber and started her walk back to the Pod hangar.

––––––

By the time she arrived, the overhead doors were opening, and her Elite were arriving. Ashur had come from somewhere. "Ashur!" The big German Shepherd turned towards her and started loping over. She called out, "Akio, John, I'm going to change." She noticed John reach up to his shoulder to communicate her whereabouts to someone.

She hunched down a little as Ashur came up, looking into his eyes. "I'm going to go change, but I might need you. Are you willing to run with me?" The big dog chuffed. "Well, then let John put on a vest we've had made for you. I don't want any shots to your chest killing you." Ashur chuffed again and turned to make his way back to John. She called out, "Suit Ashur up!"

She stepped through the Etheric to her closet on the Ad Aeternitatem and started stripping off the flight suit. She heard someone enter her bedroom outside. "Who is it?" she called out.

"Um, Barb," the reply came back. "I work with Frank?"

Bethany Anne tried to smile, but her heart wasn't in it. "Barb, I remember who you are just fine. Please go get the two swords on display in the meeting room right outside. I'll be out in a second as soon as I switch outfits."

She tossed the suit onto a chair and grabbed her black leather pants, slipped on her UA shirt and then the personally fitted ceramic plate vest. She checked the mirror. The plates accentuated her chest, no wonder Michael liked her wearing this vest. Grabbing her holsters from the wall, she slung them on, tied her hair back, and slid on her work boots, as Eric liked to call them, lacing them up.

Damn, the guys were going to be pissed; John got to play on this one.

"Keep telling yourself jokes, Bethany Anne, maybe it will keep your mind off the children," she mumbled to herself as she unbolted the door and stepped out. Barb looked surprised to see the CEO of the company come out looking like she was ready to go to a biker bar and either drink or start a fight.

"Thank you!" She grabbed the two swords. "Please have

someone straighten the closet and lock the door within the next ten minutes."

Barb nodded. "I'll do it myself."

"Thank you, gotta go."

Then, Barb was astonished as Bethany Anne seemed to start a step and disappear right in front of her. She walked over to the closet and— "Oh… My… God…"

"What is it?" Barb heard Frank call out from outside of Bethany Anne's room.

"Nothing you would understand!" Barb replied as she looked at what had to be over a hundred, maybe two hundred different pairs of beautiful, no exquisite, dress shoes.

She walked over and grabbed the lycra feeling suit and a hanger trying to figure out how to disentangle the fabric. She sat down on the chair and looked around the large space with all of the clothes. "Frank?"

"Yes?" came his voice again.

"Do me a favor and set a timer for nine minutes. Make sure I come out by that time, okay?"

"Sure?" The question in his voice was evident.

"I'll tell you why later, please don't interrupt me as I'm going to meditate." She bent down to grab the two boots and moved them off to the side where Bethany Anne had additional boots.

She looked around the closet. "I'm going to meditate on how cute these shoes would look with my wardrobe," she whispered.

———

Bethany Anne pushed open the door to her arrival room, and closed and locked it again. "Dammit, we need another place closer to the hangar if this shit keeps up." She walked down to the Pod bay. Ashur had on a special bulletproof vest that covered most of his body yet allowed him freedom to move, even if he had to twist in the air. He was already in her Pod.

Her Black Eagle was modified in case she needed to take Ashur or another person with her. For the other Black Eagles, that area would commonly be used for supplies.

She walked over to the Elites who were also dressed in all black. She nodded as Akio held out her sword. She took it and handed one back to him. "This is the blade I used, in addition to the one you just gave me, when we fought the Forsaken in Turkey. I would prefer that it be in service, not sitting on a mantel, if blood is going to be shed."

Akio nodded his head, "Hai, service is good for a weapon, it ages if it is never used. Some do not take to the aging well."

Bethany Anne spoke up. "We are hitting a group that intends to get the world's attention by attacking a school full of children, holding them hostage. The last time they did this, it ended with well over a hundred children dead and over three hundred other people killed. We go in, we kill, we leave. If you need blood, don't leave behind the evidence, understand?" She looked into every face to make sure they got the message.

"Get in your pods, we will be in communication until we land. I will talk with Akio, and he will provide targets to you."

ADAM, how much time do we have?

>>Their radio chatter has them arriving at the meeting place in forty-eight minutes.<<

"Ok, get in your Pods, let's get there a few minutes early."

John was just pulling his arms out of her Pod so she looked over the edge and noticed a small cooler. The kind used to carry extra blood for her in case she needed it.

John smiled. "I'm supposed to be your backup, right?"

She slugged him on the arm and jumped up to her seat, slid her legs in the Black Eagle and dropped down. "You good back there, Ashur?" His chuff gave her all the information she needed. She hit the close hatch button. "Let's go fuck someone up, shall we?"

The hatch above started to open to let the Pods leave.

Are we going to 11 again? TOM inquired.

Damn right we are, she replied.

In the darkness, the ten pods could not be seen leaving.

———

TOM, get me pretty close to AKIO.

Bethany Anne could see a Pod pull out of the pack and drift in her direction. It was about twenty feet away when she reached out to capture his attention. She could feel activity, like a small wet buzzing in that direction and insinuated her thoughts into the electrical ball.

Akio?

Yes? Is this Bethany Anne?

It is. I want to make sure we have mind communication figured out before we land.

I did not know you had this power as strongly as Michael.

I don't like to use it as much as Michael. Therefore, I am untrained in its use compared to him. But we don't want to speak out loud after we land. I will leave you to command the Elite for this operation. I want blood with these deaths. Make sure that we leave a message that something very abnormal happened here. No bodies of ours, if we should fall, will be left behind. No Pods will touch the ground. If there are trees, we'll jump to them and then to the ground. Anything to confuse those that will seek answers.

Do we hide the bodies?

Hell no! Pull them out if they are in trucks or cars. I would prefer no bullets, but if you can't get to them, then shoot them. No one will be getting away from us tonight.

Understood, my Queen.

Very well, I will let you talk with your team.

———

Khasan was ready. For the past couple of hundred years, his people had too often been ruled by those in Moscow. With the death of Stalin, the Chechens that he had forcibly sent to Siberia were allowed to return home, but that left over ten thousand who would not return. Presently, Russia needed the Chechen land to reach both the Black Sea and the Caspian Sea. They also needed the access for oil pipelines that went through Chechnya.

In 2006, the separatist leader Shamil Basayev was killed by the Russian internal security forces and the Chechen separatist effort was still reeling from his death.

Khasan was ready to put his foot down and make Russia realize that Chechen independence was a bitter pill, but better to swallow it than deal with the deaths he and his people would cause. Like today.

They would meet as a group and then travel north into Elista. It was the capital of the Kalmykia Republic and had just over a hundred thousand people. Big enough that their action would not go unnoticed.

Khasan was being driven in an old Toyota truck through the Caucasus Mountains. The groups would meet, agree on the next location and then take off with a little distance between each vehicle. Should anyone get stopped, a quick decision would be made whether to help them or sacrifice them. Everyone understood that the decision was going to be based on whether the support would help or hinder their current operation.

He had forty-seven fighters with him. It was ten more than he expected initially, but five fewer than the number that had agreed to help. Those five had been pulled by the local leader to support a different operation.

It was about three thirty in the morning when their truck lights highlighted the beaten up old sign pointing to the small road of their rendezvous. The Toyota might have a lot of dents and gashes along the side, but it was a well-made little truck that could be expected to continue working even when the outside looked like it would fall apart at any moment.

When they arrived at the meeting place, there were four other trucks already waiting. Including the van that held the weapons. Khasan opened his passenger door and got out. He closed the door quietly and walked over to greet the other men. Between the five vehicles, they had about half the number so far that were committed to show up. He went over to the van, and one of the men opened the back door for him. He lifted up a submachine gun and reviewed the barrel.

Clean.

He set it down and counted the five RPG and twelve IED devices that they would use both inside the school for maximum death and to fire back at police.

Satisfied that the equipment was what he was led to believe it would be, he grunted his acceptance and turned around. Three more vehicles, one a large van, came up the little road. The road was dark because of all the spruce and fir trees. A lot of the starlight was blocked.

He whistled softly in the dark, waiting for the final two vehicles, both vans, to arrive. It took a few minutes, but he finally heard them coming up the rocky road. One pulled in behind the last car on the right. The other turned to the left.

He waited for the men to gather around him before he stepped on the bumper of the van with the guns and grabbed the top to get a little height. This helped those in the back to see him. For operational security, there would be no car lights running. He was annoyed with the many men smoking, but decided to pick his battles strategically.

"We come together to make the mother bear understand that Chechens have been under their yoke, their chains, for too many years. Too many generations have been subjugated by the uncaring sociopaths in Moscow!" The men cheered the start of his speech.

"The world has forgotten us, our servitude here in Chechnya due to other events. This lack of attention is allowing those that would rule our free people the opportunity to strangle us, to keep us down and to push back into the obscurity of history the thousands upon thousands of our people Russia has killed. The thousands of our children who lost mothers, fathers, aunts and uncles. The tens of thousands who will never see life because our people never married and had more children."

"In twelve hours, we will make them remember the horrors their parents and parents' parents did to us, and what their government is doing to Chechnya even today!" The roars of the men invigorated Khasan and made him feel strong enough to walk up to Putin himself and kill the man.

Khasan continued, "In a few hours, WE will be the ones who…"

IT'S HELL TO CHOOSE

DIE!

The mental scream reverberated in Khasan's brain. He looked around to find the person who yelled at him, but he could see nothing but his men looking back at him.

That was when those in the back started screaming and the occasional burst of gunfire cracked through the night.

CHAPTER EIGHTEEN

TQB BASE, COLORADO, USA

Michael's Pod arrived in the landing area. No sooner had the door cracked open, than he changed to myst and screamed through the base to arrive at the Pit.

He found Lance, Kevin, Eric, Scott, Darryl, Cheryl Lynn, Patricia, Jakob and three others looking at data coming in. ADAM's voice came out of the speakers.

"I have located the bus traveling through downtown Denver. I have not confirmed if they continued through Denver, or are within the city limits."

"Thank you, ADAM," Lance said. "Darryl, Scott." The two men peeled off and started up the stairs.

Darryl called over his shoulder, "Pod or car?"

Michael switched to a solid form, surprising everyone. "Pod." Darryl raised his eyebrows at Michael's sudden appearance. He nodded to Michael as he and Scott jogged out of the meeting room.

Michael stepped down to the bottom level and shook Lance's hand. "Hello."

Lance said, "She called you in, I see." Michael just nodded. "You will probably be our ace in the hole, Michael."

"What are you expecting?" Michael asked.

Lance turned to look at a map of Denver up on the wall monitors. "I'm expecting something stupid, frankly. Jakob thinks this is an extortion attempt, and Kevin thinks it's a distraction."

Michael looked over to Kevin. "Draw us out of here?" Kevin nodded. "Possible, very possible." He looked at the map. "It won't change the fact we have to get those kids away, safe."

"Without Bethany Anne, we don't have any super spies but you," Lance said. "Those kids are going to need your help."

"I agree."

ADAM's voice spoke, "We have a 'for your eyes only' email coming in from an undisclosed IP address. Routing suggests it originated in the Denver area. Bethany Anne has forwarded it to you."

"Has she seen it?" Lance inquired.

"No, she requested I forward to this team. They are about to spring their trap."

"What does it contain?" Kevin asked.

"Video," ADAM replied.

"Play it," Michael said.

The video showed the bus with the children parked in a garage. Then, the camera was carried onto the bus itself, and those watching could see blood smears on the driver's seat. The camera turned to view the occupants.

Michael heard Cheryl Lynn gasp when Todd and Tina

appeared on the screen. Both were about two-thirds of the way back. There were three adults towards the back as well.

"As you can see," the modified voice said. "Everyone but the driver and one other female are safe. Unfortunately for them, they didn't get the memo that everyone would go home just fine when our demands are met."

The person controlling the camera turned around, and Michael could see the outside of the bus, and that they looked to be underground. There were brief images of other men outside and armed.

They were expecting an attack. A car was heard, and the camera operator moved to see who it was. "PAUSE!" Michael called out.

The video froze. "ADAM, back up the video where the person is in the car." The video went back a second. "Can you do anything to clean it up?"

"One moment, Michael," ADAM said. "You want the best picture of the driver, correct?"

"Yes" he agreed.

It took five seconds, but ADAM placed an image up on the screen. Michael walked closer to the wall and squinted his eyes. "It's been a while, Boris…"

"You know him?" Lance asked, walking up beside him.

"Yes, or at least I knew him," Michael agreed.

"How long ago?" Lance inquired.

"Probably two, maybe three hundred years?" Michael said. "I haven't worked with him personally for that long. My children have, and I've talked with Boris a few times in the intervening years."

"What is he?" Kevin asked.

Michael turned to look at Kevin. "He is a Pricolici, a bear. I defeated him many centuries ago when his pack Alpha, called a Tsar at the time, goaded him into fighting me. Something is different about him, he lives much longer than any normal Wechselbalg."

"You didn't kill him?" Lance asked, then thought about what he said. "Correction, why didn't you kill him?"

"Because he was too new and didn't understand his emotions. His Tsar, though, I killed. He had hoped that Boris would be able to kill me, or wound me enough that he could kill me. However, I still punished him by requiring him to stay in Siberia for a century that time."

"Is it relevant to our plans now?" Kevin asked. "He's outside of Russia."

"No, that requirement ended long ago. There is one thing these people with him don't know."

"What's that?" Cheryl Lynn asked, her fear evident in her voice.

"Boris watches over a town full of people in Siberia. He takes these operations to get the money to support those people. He will kill adults, but he won't let anything happen to those children. I doubt he knew what the plan was before arriving, and he must have been given assurances that the children would be safe." Michael tapped his lip while he thought.

"I will take a Pod to Denver and then take out these mercenaries," Michael stated. "Eric and Scott will have to do cleanup with the authorities, but they must not be on the scene until the police arrive so they can claim ignorance."

Michael pointed to the frozen picture. "He will be my support help."

They watched the rest of the video and received the demand for the technology transfer.

ADAM said, "I have located two buildings which would

allow a bus to fit underground. Based on blueprints, I believe I have narrowed down their location."

Michael spoke to Lance and Kevin. "Protect this base, I'll handle the children." Then he was gone.

Kevin looked over at Lance. "Thoughts, General?"

Lance chewed on his lip for a moment. "Pull everyone in, Kevin. This isn't a drill, folks."

Moments later, a siren could be heard everywhere on the base. "This is a base lockdown, please report to your safety locations. This is a base lockdown, please report to your safety locations…"

———

DOWNTOWN DENVER, COLORADO, USA

Boris arrived and stepped out of his vehicle as the massive door behind him started closing. He could smell fresh blood. When he looked around, he could see one of the men was sporting a bandage on his arm, another had a blood-soaked patch on his ear and a brace on his neck.

He walked over to the one who had his ear bleeding and furrowed his brows. Something wasn't smelling… right.

"Vat happened on the bus?" he asked.

Matt grimaced. "Stupid female went apeshit when we hit the bus. The bus driver opened the door and asked what the problem was just like we figured. But as soon as I pulled my gun he reached for one as well. So, I shot him right away. Before I knew it, this girl jumps me and damn near bites my ear off."

He continued, "These fucking pain meds are taking too long! So, this woman is acting like she's protecting her own cubs or something…" Matt missed the look of recognition on Boris's face. "I react and start shooting her, too. Which, unfortunately, was a waste. Man, she was a looker."

Matt seemed to miss that Boris had already left, heading for the bus. Boris' guess was confirmed even before he stepped on.

These people had been around Weres. Not just one, but many. "Idiots…" he grumbled under his breath. He turned to see what was going on around him. Birk and Patty were finishing up over at the stairwell, unrolling cord in preparation to drop the entry from above and bitching about whether they should call the police themselves. They were surprised not to have chatter about the event all over the police radio. Matt was still talking as if Boris were near him.

Those pain meds had obviously taken effect.

Boris stepped up on the bus and noticed many angry faces aimed in his direction. Yes, some were frightened, but not near as many as he would have expected. He inhaled deeply and found another smell he hadn't expected to encounter.

Vampire.

What the hell was going on? Had he stayed in Siberia too long to understand changes out in the bigger world?

"You know, this isn't going to go well for you when Bethany Anne learns of it." A teenage girl spoke to Boris from halfway down the bus.

"And your name is vhat, young lady?" Boris asked.

"Tina," she said, daring him to refute her.

"And vhat do you expect Bethany Anne to do in this case?" Boris asked, interested in her answer. He had already decided that he would protect these younglings. Hopefully, the three adults would make it out OK as well, but they were not a priority of his.

"Whatever it takes, she never forsakes her own," the young girl said. "Either she will come or the Queen's Own."

"Or Michael," the boy continued the conversation, more arguing with his sister than talking to Boris. "If Bethany Anne can't make it, I bet she calls in Michael."

Boris considered the boy's comment. The smell of Weres and vampires was even stronger now that he was physically on the bus. "And does Michael have a name?" Boris asked the two kids.

"Of course, it's Michael," the girl said.

"No, a last name," Boris replied, his patience wearing thin.

"No," the young boy cut in. "He doesn't." Now, the boy turned and glared towards Boris.

"Not true," his sister rebutted. "Mom said it was Knight or something."

"Do you mean *Nacht*?" Boris questioned.

"Yeah, that's what she said," she agreed. Todd elbowed his sister who elbowed him back, hard.

Boris nodded, then turned around and walked to the front and stepped down to the concrete. Then, he sat on the steps of the bus, using them for a chair.

It was Boris against these well-trained and very focused mercenaries. Behind him was a busload of children who apparently knew Michael himself. Why they didn't scream in fear of Michael was puzzling, but that didn't matter. Boris owed the Archangel, and whether it was something owed from last week or centuries ago, Boris remembered. If it took Boris's dying breath, he would pay his debt.

If Boris died, he just hoped Michael would support his town in some way. Those were good people there. If too many of these children died and Michael did not know Boris tried to save these children, then the town and the people he had protected for generations might be wiped off the map. Because when Michael was finished, there wouldn't be a living soul left.

———

"Michael, I am ten thousand feet above the roof of the building that has the bus," ADAM said through the Pod speaker.

"ADAM, show me the roofs, and highlight the one with the bus." Michael viewed the picture on the Pod screen in front of him. "Please zoom in, I can't tell them apart at this size." The roofs became distinct, and Michael was able to figure out a few unique characteristics. "So, the roof you have in yellow, that is the building?"

"Yes," ADAM replied.

"Ok, then open the door," Michael commanded.

The doors to the Pod, ten thousand feet above the city, opened and Michael slipped out as myst. The Pod door closed.

Michael sped as quickly as he was capable of down to the roof and then down the side of the building towards the ground. Arriving, he circled the building until he found the garage entrance and went down the ramps until he came to a spot with a large steel door covering it. He slid through a crack and started circling the large interior.

There were seven other men in the place, all with heavy weapons besides Boris, who was his own living weapon. Two men were bickering about the lack of police activity so far being a bad sign.

Michael noticed the wires and went inside the stairwell to see the explosives. He solidified and cut the wires. Slipping back to myst, he went back into the garage.

Boris, Michael called.

Michael, Boris replied in his mind.

You do not seem surprised to hear from me.

You have a fan club.

I do?

Boris sent a mental chuckle. *Yes, there is a young male cub that supports you. Although I think his sister is more of a Bethany Anne fan.*

Ah, that would probably be Tina and Todd, then.

You changed, Michael. I would not have expected you to know much of human children.

Yes, I have changed. I hope for the better. Life is good when you look forward to waking up with someone.

You have found love, Michael? The surprise in Boris' mental voice amused Michael.

Yes, believe it or not, old bear, I've found love. A pause, then Michael continued, *I presume since you are sitting on that bus that none will pass?*

Nyet, none will pass me, Michael. Or I will be dead.

That is what I told those back at the base, that I already had my support inside.

How did you know I was here?

It was on a videotape.

So much for operational security. Boris said, *it annoys the professional in me.*

Well, the individual won't make any more mistakes, soon.

They are looking to attack your base. This was supposed to be a feint to catch the base off guard.

They never expected to harm the children?

You have to ask? Boris seemed offended.

Boris, you are known for doing most anything for those

people who you love back in Siberia. Michael reproved him.

Extenuating circumstances. Life is full of gray. But then, I'm speaking with a vampire, who only sees in black and white.

No, not anymore. Now, now I see in color.

She must be amazing to change you so, Patriarch.

Yes she is, Michael said.

How do you want to play this?

Oh, you would have to say 'play,' Boris…

I'll tell the people on the bus to get down.

They should hide their eyes, yes. Michael agreed.

The first scream of pain was heard just seconds later.

"What the hell!" Birk turned towards Gunther. He was grabbing his stomach, unsuccessfully trying to hold in his insides through the massive cuts in his abdomen. Birk looked to his left and just saw the second figure by Eli when his short scream was cut off by gurgling as he grabbed at his throat, trying unsuccessfully to stop the blood from spurting out as he dropped to his knees to collapse on the ground.

The figure was gone.

There was a gunshot from behind Birk, the ricochet sounding like it missed him by only a few feet. Birk recognized that the shot came from Matt, whose eyes were wide open, but lacked focus.

Fucking meds!

"Shit, Matt!" Birk yelled as he started towards the bus. "Don't fucking shoot your own team!"

Another scream from behind him. Matt wouldn't be shooting anyone, anymore.

Terrence was shouting, "Come get some!" as his shotgun went off. His boisterous speech was cut off mid-word in a scream.

Birk saw Boris standing in front of the bus, his arms

spread and staring at him. He pulled up his rifle and yelled at Boris, "I know we said no children, Boris. But if it is going to be the children or me? Well, life sucks for them!" Birk heard two pistol shots and saw they hit the big Russian. He looked to his left and saw Patty running towards the bus as well.

Apparently, Patty wasn't in a negotiating mood right now.

If Birk hadn't turned back in time, he would have missed the most incredible view of his life. One moment, there was a massive Russian, bleeding from two pistol shots, the next a nine-foot tall bear roaring his defiance at the two men. Birk skidded to a stop and pulled his rifle into position. He pressed the trigger twice quickly, the rounds screamed towards the bear before the rifle was jerked out of his hands and he turned to see Death staring back at him from a foot away.

"You! You're just the… the…" Birk spit out before feeling pain ripping through his chest.

"Yes," the man with red eyes answered. "What, did you think I was just a boytoy too?" He grinned. "Ah, you did believe that. Trust me, Bethany Anne would never have agreed to a date with you." Birk couldn't feel any more pain than he already suffered. So when Michael crushed his heart with his hand, it was a moot point before his eyes closed the final time.

Patty saw two bodies fleeing out the side passage… Fucking Mansel and Hans had bolted. His pistols weren't going to do anything to that fucking bear. Trying to overcome the fear he felt watching a man turn into a bear, he angled towards the table to grab the explosive controller as he heard two screams down the exit shaft.

So much for Mansel and Hans. Patty could hear the bear coming up behind him. He turned quickly, pulling up his pistol to have it knocked out of his hand. Patty screamed as his hand was shredded by four-inch claws.

"Boris," a cultured voice spoke from behind Patty. So focused on the bear in front of him, Patty could not see who was behind it. "Don't leave too many clues."

Patty went from looking at a thousand pounds of bear to looking at the visage of an angry Russian again that turned to speak over his shoulder. "Michael, the bullets might not be silver, but they still hurt like bitch!" Boris growled.

"Perhaps, friend, but we have to go." Michael walked near the merc who was holding his bleeding hand and casually flicked his arm out, halfway severing Patty's head from his shoulders. The look of surprise on his face was complete as the body collapsed to the floor. "We need to go back to the base," Michael said.

Michael sent a mental message to the three adults on the bus. *Keep everyone down, there is blood everywhere. Darryl and Scott will be here shortly.*

He sent out calming feelings to all of those on the bus. He didn't have the time to do much, but it should help, and it was the most he could do for them at the moment.

Michael grabbed Boris in his myst and left, traveling back up to his Pod.

———

Fortunately, Darryl and Scott's Pod was nearby. Michael hadn't considered the difficulty of how to communicate with ADAM when he couldn't physically manifest, and the Pods were too damned airtight for him to get into them. Darryl passed on Michael's request to open the Pod and to angle it slightly backward so Boris wouldn't fall out.

Michael was able to get Boris in the Pod and grab him quickly enough to sit him down on the other seat as the doors shut. The Pod twisted in the air and immediately screamed in the direction of the base.

"Base, this is Michael, what is the situation?"

"SNAFU," Lance came back. "We got hit hard, Michael." There was a pause. "We got at least ten inside the base right now, unknown live outside, sixty enemies dead along the grounds and a minimum five dead on our side. Further, we have twenty-four of our own in need of some medical help for damn sure. We would have more dead if... well, you know."

"Any other intel?"

Boris spoke up next to him. "They have a munitions package of some sort they are supposed to be bringing on base."

"Who is that?" Lance asked. "Did he say a munitions package?"

"Yes," Michael confirmed. "That was Boris. I couldn't leave him there so I grabbed him. He will be useful for the base attack."

"I never said I would..." Boris started to negotiate his fee for jumping into this firefight when he took a look at Michael's eyes, "...not help. Vat do you need me to do?"

"Kill," Michael replied.

"She hasn't trained you very vell if you still like killing so much," Boris observed.

"No, that is where you're wrong," Michael said. "It is more that I hold her back."

Boris considered Michael's answer. "You mean she is just as bloodthirsty as you?"

Michael shrugged, "If she's mad, more so."

IT'S HELL TO CHOOSE

"Somebody just opened what Americans call a can of whoop-ass on themselves, I think," Boris said.

"Truly," Michael agreed. "That is an understatement."

CHAPTER NINETEEN

ASTEROID BELT, BETWEEN MARS AND JUPITER

"Jeo, we will be arriving on station within forty-eight hours."

"Hmm?" Jeo looked up from his project plan to the wall. He had Samantha create a digital woman and told the program to display the 'talking head' up on his wall to the right of wherever he was working. The simulation wasn't perfect, but it did allow him to feel a little less lonely at times.

He hadn't realized he needed a little interaction with real people before he took this position. Now, he made a point of seeking out the people on the Space Station to chat after he stopped working.

The crew had adopted the Coordinated Universal Time (UTC), and now they had three shifts. Jeo worked as he needed and wanted, so he ignored the shifts. When finished with work for a time, he went looking for a little company just to talk, or 'be separately together.' This concept was common now with architects when they designed buildings for multiple non-family units on Earth.

Jeo was informed that a group of younger, but smart, people would be joining him soon. William told him that from his experience, the usually reserved Jeo might just be considered one of the most outgoing. Bethany Anne had 'captured some amazing strays' and before they knew it, they were swept up into her orbit. Well, almost all of them.

One of the girls took the chance to ask one of the guys to marry her since he apparently couldn't be counted on to make the move himself. He agreed, and they decided to try to stay on Earth to raise children.

"Do we have the first response from Prospector?" Jeo asked Samantha.

Samantha answered in a slightly less frosty tone than his second voice choice. He had decided something between clinical and 'melt my brain' was the best solution for her voice, so far. "Yes, the Prospector probe has located several asteroids which fit our size requirements and potential raw material needs. It has landed and extracted two core samples that should be analyzed within the next six hours. Additionally, it has laser surveyed three additional asteroids that also fit the characteristics we want. These five asteroids are now being transferred from their locations to the temporary mining and fabrication facilities en route."

"Perfect," Jeo muttered. "What about the team?"

"So far, there are no concerns reported by Bandile Annane and the fourteen members of his team. They have passed both classes for safety and know how to use the equipment. They will leave the training facilities within twenty-four hours en route to Location Mining Facility 01."

"Samantha, please modify name Mining Facility Zero One to 'MF01.'"

"Understood, Jeo."

Jeo looked up at the second clock he now had on the wall. It was a timer counting down to when it would be his turn to leave.

He had less than twenty-four hours to go.

———

OUTSIDE TQB BASE, COLORADO, USA

"This isn't going well, sir." Captain Julien Karet spoke on the phone. "They aren't nearly as weak as we expected, and they apparently did not get the police involved in the children's hijacking."

Presently, Julien Karet was in a SNAFU. What should have been a simple operation had grown exponentially worse, and now he had no idea how to extract his men. That there weren't a lot of police and media involved was surprising him. It worked in his favor, as he didn't have to worry about someone locating his team here, but he didn't like what it suggested to him, either. The other side didn't want any police involved fighting his group.

It was just them against his group.

Julien continued speaking on the phone. "No, the package is not yet inside the base. Yes, some of the drone communication sniffing technology has been dropped off close enough to move forward on their own. We are …"

Captain Karet's teeth ground together. "Sir, that would be unlikely to create enough confusion inside the base to help hide the data extractors, but it will kill all of my people nearby.

IT'S HELL TO CHOOSE

The affected area is still hundreds of yards in the open air."

"Yes… sir…" he ground out. "We are continuing to review the location of the package and will manually detonate should that be deemed necessary. Zàijiàn." He hung up the satellite phone.

Julien commented to his second. "Damned commercialists, worse than communists. They sell 'piece of cake' to our leaders who then use us to implement this debacle."

"I hate to say it, sir, but there are too many bodies on the base. We aren't going to be sterilized enough," his second, Kathen, responded.

Julien shrugged. "There isn't enough data to point back to us. Too many mercs in the mix. So, if they happen to get any information from those on Op 1, it won't provide a target, just the tools."

He walked over and looked out the small valley they were using to run the forward operations. It was shielded enough that the detonation wouldn't hit them. Now, if his men could just get the damned thing into the base, grab those that were still alive, and fall back at least half a mile, they could blow the thing and get the hell out of here. With the need for the bomb to be inside the mountain, this was as far away as they could get and still be entirely sure they could manually send a detonation signal.

He would hate to be on the team that was carrying that son of a bitch.

CHAPTER TWENTY

TURKEY

My Queen," Akio walked over to Bethany Anne, who was making sure that every head had been cut off. "What would you have us do with the weapons?"

She looked up and contemplated his question. She considered and dropped the idea of trying to put them into a car and lifting the car far enough to drop them into a large lake or something. She could only imagine the news people talking about a 'magic car,' or whatever social media might say about it.

"Put them on the bodies, ADAM will contact the local authorities that can be trusted. We'll have to hope they get here first. Maybe with the guns on the bodies, it will cause even more problems for the terrorists."

>>**Bethany Anne, we are getting reports from the Polarus that a large attack ship is approaching rapidly followed by three support and what looks like a command**

ship staying way back. **Captain Thomas is positioning the Ad Aeternitatem and Polarus to block access to the Consanesco. He suspects enemy action.<<**

"Gott Verdammt!" she spit out. "Akio, make it quick, we need to get back to the Ad Aeternitatem."

>>News from your father. He says Darryl and Scott are with the children. None of them has a scratch. One team member is confirmed dead, the other wounded was a Wechselbalg, so she may be alive but was left for dead where the bus was hijacked. There is a team en route to retrieve and provide assistance if possible.<<

"Thank you, ADAM." Bethany Anne murmured. She whistled to Ashur, who ran over. The area around his jaws was bloody. "Got your own bites in, I see." Her Black Eagle came down, and she grabbed Ashur and dropped him in the back. "Hey!" He looked at her. "Keep the blood off the seats, or you're cleaning it up!" He chuffed at her.

"I don't care that you don't have opposable thumbs, don't make a mess!" she groused back.

John rolled his eyes at the casual display of understanding between the two. He looked one more time around the area and then waited for Bethany Anne to get in her Pod and then followed her actions.

Soon, ten Pods cleared out, leaving more clues than she cared to leave behind, but time was more important than confusion at the moment.

———

Down in the engine room of the Polarus, the speaker squawked. "Rodriquez, this is Captain Thomas."

Chief Engineer John E. Rodriquez hit the speaker button.

"Rodriquez here, Cap. What do you need?"

"Please make sure our second set of engines are prepared and converse with navigation and high-topside to take us outside of air travel lanes if and when we go," Captain Thomas requested.

"Will do, Captain. Will discuss and confirm with navigation and topside to make it so." Rodriquez replied.

"Do you believe we're going to do it?" John's second, Barry, asked him from the desk beside him.

The engineering room on the Polarus had been more commercial than Rodriquez was accustomed to on Navy ships. He had made it a point to provide additional protections and make sure everything was in a place that could be tied down in the case of substantial movement. He had confirmed the chief engineer on the Ad Aeternitatem had done the same upgrades, and his input had been requested for the Consanesco during the ship's outfitting.

"Possibly," John said. "If this is a legit attack or boarding effort, then I believe we will be testing them significantly more."

"Well, if we do, we're going to have a lot of the super-rich wanting our upgrades!" Barry chuckled.

———

The Consanesco was close enough to the Polarus and Ad Aeternitatem that Mark Billingsly and Sia could see people running around on the deck in the early light and hear the 'aaahwooga - aaahwooga' sound come rolling over the water towards them.

"Sia, are you shooting this?" Mark asked, not taking his eyes off of the two Superyachts. He felt a hand tap him on his left shoulder so he turned to see Sia with her camera on her shoulder. "What do you see?" he said.

"They're taking covers off of some of those taller structures... Mark, those are guns!" she exclaimed.

"What?" Mark stepped around behind Sia, who pulled out the little four-inch video screen that would show Mark what she could see.

"Damn, that is Navy precision," Mark said. He looked up. "We have something coming at us from the southwest."

"How can you tell?" Sia asked, not moving the camera from what she was filming on the Polarus.

"Because I see the Ad Aeternitatem has turned hard and is setting itself between us and something in that direction. The Polarus has moved some, but not much. I'm betting they know something bad is coming from that direction," he said, pointing. "Plus, I see a couple of the sailing vessels that hang with those ships are getting out of the way and coming near us now."

"Wow, fair weather friends they are," Sia said.

———

Peter Silvers finished suiting up. He was wearing full ballistic protection when Todd clapped him on the shoulder and told him, "Remember, no going furry today. Too many witnesses."

"Why aren't we just dropping them?" Peter asked Todd. "Seems easier."

"Too little proof," Todd answered. "We're in international waters, but that doesn't get us a free ride on shooting anyone down until they prove, on tape, to be asshats."

Peter drew the two much bigger rail pistols he and the other Wechselbalg on the team carried. They had enough power to throw .50 caliber penetration-specific bullets out of their pistols at over two thousand joules. That was around one thousand five hundred ft-lbf (foot pound force), better than a .44 Magnum and equivalent to a .50 American Eagle. It wasn't the most powerful, that would be the .50 S&W Magnum that had a two thousand six hundred ft-lbf. Smith & Wesson wanted the 'most powerful handgun in the world' label and were fighting hard to keep it.

Their rail pistols did, however, have a twenty-five round capacity because they did not need the cartridge to fire the rounds. That provided eighteen more shots than the .50 AE.

"Just remember," Todd told Peter, "not to shoot the ship with that cannon."

"The decks have been reinforced," Peter replied. "I spoke to Jean Dukes about it myself."

"Yeah, but I still don't want to run around hoping that the steel plates stop the bullets from one of those beasts."

———

"Boss, we have cameras on us," Jean Dukes heard as she looked through her binoculars.

"That's okay, Captain's orders. We are to look impressive, to see if they will back down. Cat's out of the bag anyway. We have been attacked in the U.S., and they used the railguns to cut down the attack pretty damned substantially. So showing them something from these two isn't going to surprise anyone now."

"It's just going to make them want our rides even more," he said.

Jean pulled the binoculars off of her face and turned to her man sporting a vicious smile. "You know when they can have these boats? When they pry them out of my cold, dead, railgun holding hands."

He returned her smile as she went back to looking through her binoculars.

––––––

"Captain, Comms say Bethany Anne is screaming back this way, but that she won't be here for the first dance. Unless we leave these other boats behind, we have to stay and fight."

"While I doubt our visitors are pirates," Captain Thomas said. "I don't want to leave the civilian craft behind. Prepare to repel boarders. Let the first verifiable aggression come from their side and then we will drop their boats as necessary into the deep dark. Please confirm Captain Wagner is issuing the same commands."

"And their main ship, sir?"

"Just keep the door closed to attempted landings on any of our ships. If someone tries to attack the Consanesco, then puck them. Bethany Anne will deal with the main ship."

"Yes sir!" the specialist turned back around to relay the commands.

Captain Thomas spoke into the intercom, "Defense, re-lease the quarter pound Puck Defense Shield if you would."

"Aye aye, Skipper," Dukes' voice came back to him.

––––––

SPACE STATION ONE

"Jeo, I have reviewed the requests provided by Dan and Jef-frey." Samantha's voice filled Jeo's suite as he packed.

"Okay, what do they need?"

"We need to build up manufacturing and defense. The problem is with the timeframe."

"Let me guess, they want everything yesterday?" Jeo asked, amused. His ability to get the process moving with the mining platforms was congratulated soundly. But then, he found out that his amazing results were now considered the new normal.

"No, but within seventy-two days," Samantha answered.

"Hmm, what are they up to?" Jeo asked as he stuffed socks in his bag. "Samantha, throw our present manufacturing schedule on wall three and the proposed requirements next to it." The two scheduling Gantt charts were up side by side, and Jeo walked over to view them.

"So, I have to take away from... wait a minute." Jeo studied the proposed project, "Samantha, what are 'Puck Destroyers?'"

"They are modified twenty-foot shipping containers housing strong defensive and offensive weapons using pucks ranging from one kilogram to four kilograms. They are unmanned units."

"And these Puck Battle Carriers?"

"Those are military units comprised of twenty-seven, forty-foot long shipping containers. The container in the middle is a full E.I.; the surrounding units hold pucks from 1 through 20 kilograms in weight."

"I'm sorry, I've missed the memo on 'E.I.?'" Jeo said.

"Electronic Intelligence. TOM coined the phrase for any ADAM constructed AI unit," Samantha answered.

"Why not just call them AIs?" he said.

"There is a differentiation between AI and EI. AI are designated as self-aware, EIs are constrained to deal with specific tasks, allowing a significant portion of their computing power to be focused only on those particular tasks."

"That would make them pretty damned focused on their role, that's true," he mused aloud. "How much computing power is in one battle carrier?" Jeo asked.

"I'm sorry, but that information is not available at this time," Samantha responded.

"Well, I could hope to know but no reason for me to."

He turned around to sit on the bed and stare at the two project plans again. "So, they've taken something we have a lot of and started crafting temporary defensive platforms using pucks. Different weights and speeds provide different offensive and defensive abilities. Since we are out here in the middle of no air, we don't have to worry about wind and aerodynamics. I wonder if they can use rocks? Aw, shit. We can't pack them efficiently unless they are manufactured a certain way."

Jeo got back up and went into his tiny bathroom. "Samantha," he called out. "Bring up the schematics on the puck designs that go on the destroyer, please."

He came out of the bathroom brushing his teeth as he viewed three models. A cone, a round ball and a puck, the standard hockey puck design. The cone had the tip ground down, probably for ease of racking and stacking.

Jeo considered what he needed to build and walked back into the bathroom to spit out the toothpaste.

"Samantha, talk with ADAM and see if we can procure the first hundred thousand of each design through existing means. Provide the option to exchange twice the raw material for the finished product if appropriate, and also a small amount of gold, start with five percent of total spend on the purchase order. Route ADAM's review through Jeffrey and get his input and report back to me."

"Understood, Jeo."

He looked at his working schedule. "Take off two weeks from the existing program plan assuming this idea works."

He puttered around his room for fifteen minutes, trying to decide if he wanted to take anything else out to the asteroid belt or not, when Samantha spoke again. "Jeo, Jeffrey is calling."

"Please move down the two schedules and place his video above," Jeo answered Samantha and turned to the wall again.

Jeffrey's face appeared above the projects on Jeo's wall, and he looked around Jeo's room before smiling. "I see you're almost packed. Ready to go out to the Asteroid Fields?"

Jeo shrugged. "To be honest, this moving around in space is so... basic now, that it feels like a special trip, but not a unique trip. Does that make sense?"

"I understand. It's amazing how quickly we become accustomed to what was before considered impossible." Jeffrey turned his head to the side, nodded to someone off the screen and turned back. "So, I have this report from ADAM. Not a bad idea, but why are you requesting this?"

"It's that schedule you guys want. I figure that the offensive and defensive pucks are pretty generic. It isn't until you add the gravitic engines to them that they become so damned destructive. If we can either buy existing parts or get them manufactured right now, then we can have something available sooner rather than later."

Jeo paused for a moment, then continued, "To be fair, it was the use of the containers as defensive and offensive platforms that made me think about this. We're just duct taping this stage of our defense together, right? So, I didn't believe that we had to be pure asteroid manufacturing just to get ready sooner."

"Why are you providing twice the raw materials and some gold?" Jeffrey asked, "I think I understand, but let's make sure I'm not guessing."

"Off the books," Jeo replied. "Nothing we need is very complicated so we can go to countries with a low tech but solid manufacturing ability and trade versus spending cash. We are going to be raw material rich, but cash poor if we don't figure something out about banking. We need to create partnerships where we can sell off some of this stuff without much fanfare."

"Ok, Bobcat wins the pot and might I say you are a devious son of a bitch. Glad you're on our team," Jeffrey finished.

"Glad to be here, too. Now, if you could just make it a bit easier to meet people, we might get something going," Jeo added.

"Yeah, well, I think you will appreciate the QBS crew quarters that will be on station soon. So, don't get too comfortable on the Hephaestus, you won't be on it for too long."

"Oh? What can you tell me about the crew quarters?" Jeo asked, surprised that another ship was coming out to the cloud with them.

"Nothing much, right yet. But I think you'll like it. Your project is approved, but make sure you have the metals to trade with our suppliers, okay?" Jeffrey told Jeo.

"I will, ciao!" Jeo held his smile until Jeffrey cut the line.

"Samantha, drop both project plans and pull up the designs for the manufacturing station." A 3D wireframe of the station was projected on his wall. "You know what, display this holographically."

Jeo turned around to find the manufacturing facility

MF01 design he had been working on, using structured gird-ers manufactured on site. "Samantha, let's see what we can source and stick in those forty-foot shipping containers in-stead of constructing components ourselves. We only want quality components from smaller countries whose curren-cies are weak against the U.S. dollar." He turned the model around with his hands and then pulled his arms apart, in-creasing the detail and the size. After thirty minutes, he asked Samantha, "Can you get William on the line?"

"Unfortunately, no. It seems that the Polarus is under at-tack, so we are not permitted to communicate at this time."

Jeo turned back to the wall. "Bring up satellite 221 and view." He saw nothing but white. "Shit! Clouds."

He dropped to the bed. "Guys, I hope you get through this okay," he muttered.

CHAPTER TWENTY-ONE

OUTSIDE TQB BASE, COLORADO, USA

The afternoon sun was waning as Michael and Boris screamed towards the base. "Lance, we will be arriving in twenty seconds."

"Michael, can you take care of the group still outside? Eric has been shot three times, but he and the Guardians inside still have them blocked. They can't get any further, but we don't have anything available for the outside response at this time without opening more holes inside. Kevin says he would rather not do that," Lance responded.

"Understood, Lance," Michael replied.

"Do we attack as people or not?" Boris asked.

Michael started smiling.

"Uh oh. You are smiling, I'm not thinking I'm going to enjoy this much at all," Boris said.

"Oh, trust me, you *will* enjoy this, my old friend. Very much, just wait. ADAM, take us in at a thousand feet, then open the doors," Michael commanded.

"Vat!" Boris turned in alarm towards Michael. "You taking me down? Because I don't see any parachutes in dis Pod."

"I'm going to drop you a few yards inside the main entrance. You change to a bear and attack those inside from the rear. I'll grab the ones outside." Michael smiled. "This will be enjoyable, I promise!"

"That's because bullets don't hit you when you are disappeared, yes?" Boris asked.

"No, they don't hit me," Michael admitted. "But if they are fast enough and get me while I'm solid, they still hurt."

Boris grinned. "Good, I wouldn't want this to be a walk in park for you."

———

Captain Julien Karet's eyes flashed as he listened to the group chatter. "What the hell?" He turned to his second. "Are they actually saying a bear is attacking them?" His second's face showed confusion, but he nodded in affirmation.

"What the hell is a bear doing in a firefight?" he wondered aloud. "How the hell is there a bear in MY firefight?"

"Sir, we have the first data from the spy drones." Captain Julien stood up to walk over to the specialist.

"Why are all of the incoming data packets so small?" he asked.

"Sir, they're coming back empty. All wireless communication on the base is directed to the internet, none of it hooks into the base's internal systems," was his reply.

"That's impossible. There is always a lazy ass on the inside that screws up. Or, is that only in the companies I've worked with?" he asked out loud.

IT'S HELL TO CHOOSE

The specialist said, "I can't say, yet. Right now the only communication we can intercept is general internet. We will try to locate a device that connects both externally and internally."

"At least we got the spyware inside. Now, all we have to do is get it to communicate with the outside." He sighed and looked up to the top of the ridge, considering all of the people that had been lost so far. "I just don't want all of this to have been in vain."

———

"General?" Kevin spoke from his location in the Pit.

"Hmm?" Lance looked up from his board.

"I'm getting information from Tom that the base has short encrypted blasts emitting out." Kevin said. "We're waiting for the encryption to be broken."

"Well, that explains one part of their op. Insert some sort of spy tech." He considered. "Dammit! We're going to need to do a cleanup of the base after this." He shook his head. "If they would have just given us another month, it wouldn't have mattered. We'd be in Australia."

"Yes, we would have been gone," Cheryl Lynn said. "But now we have to prove nothing is here so no one attacks our remaining people." She had gone from being horrified that her kids were not protected on the base to being happy they were with Darryl and Scott.

Kevin was chewing the inside of his mouth when he spoke to someone on a side channel and then came back. "Just got off the horn with Stephanie and she says that the exit hole is available if we need to start moving people in that direction."

Lance considered Stephanie's option, realizing that moving people down the hole would cause additional problems. "No, but close the blast doors. I don't know what kind of munitions Michael's friend warned us about."

Kevin nodded and went back to speaking to his head of engineering.

"Kevin," Lance said, and Kevin looked over at him. "Interrupt all communications but ours on the base. Nothing but Etheric." Kevin nodded and passed the information over to the base's E.I..

———

Eric took a peek around the corner and pulled back. This time, no shots came in his direction. The group had been hearing a bear roaring for the last minute and Eric had been informed that it was 'one of their team.'

Eric looked over at Gabrielle, who smiled back. She also had her pistols out. The two of them had been commanded to keep this hallway protected and not to let anyone pass. Eric had been hit three times before he got into the groove. One was on his protected chest, one had grazed his arm, while the other had hit him in the shoulder. Fortunately, it went all the way through and, while very painful, the shoulder was working well again.

Gabrielle didn't have one hit at all. Damn, but she was going to be giving him shit this whole week.

He raised an eyebrow to ask if they should look, and she swept a hand as if to say, 'After you.' Eric waved her off. There were some orders that you should follow, and some you should break. Right now, holding this area for the General was one he felt they should obey. Not chasing after his curiosity about why they had a roaring bear coming down the hallway towards them.

From the sound of the gunfire, the bear was getting closer.

————

"Dammit!" Captain Julien swore. "They've blocked all communications." He wanted to rip off his headphones, throw them down, and stomp on them. Staring at the ridge again, he walked back to the video monitors they had set up in their camouflaged tent under the trees. The batteries had been a pain to deal with, and if something didn't finish in the next thirty minutes, the choice would have to be made to use generators or go dark.

He looked at the map that had been giving him field input, and more importantly, the location of the package as well. Now, it showed him the locations of the first five bodies that had gone down in a tree cracking fusillade of small metal slivers. They had used railgun technology to slice his men to shreds.

It had been the first indication that the base was using technology for which he was unprepared. His superiors had been allowed to push him to continue the operation, which was another bad leadership decision in what was becoming a monumental fuck-up.

One ray of light in the murky mess was that their team's location in the valley appeared to be outside of the signal blocking.

"Dammit!" he exploded again, and no one disagreed with his frustration.

———

There should be something, Michael thought to himself, said of the joy one feels when released to do something you have been honing your skills at for over a thousand years.

With a scream, another man died. The attacking teams were starting to crack. The screams of their comrades dying horribly were affecting their resolution to stay and fight. The deaths didn't come from bullets or bombs, but were delivered up close and personal. Men suffocating in their own blood or heads cut from bodies would land next to nearby allies.

The smoke bomb coverage they used to try to hide from the defensive fire was now working against them. Lack of visibility meant the source of the screams and location of the killer was a terrifying mystery.

Michael attacked a group of three men surrounding a large bag. Each man faced out from the center where the backpack was lying. One man had his arm behind him, touching the bag.

That was the first arm Michael cut off.

The second man died when four finger-like daggers slashed across his face, leaving his jaw hanging at an odd angle. With the last gurgle of dying breath, his gaze was fixed on the man with red eyes and glistening fangs.

Michael's attention turned to the third man, rapidly penetrating his eyeballs with the weapons his hands had become. He pulled his fingers out of the corpse to slice the neck of the still-screaming first man. The hot splash of blood from the slashed throat forever stilled the cries about his missing arm.

"Ah, good times," he murmured to himself, reliving a thousand years of bloodshed in just a few moments.

Pulling himself together, Michael considered the package.

IT'S HELL TO CHOOSE

The munitions, Boris called it. He unzipped the bag, and his eyes opened wide. If you were an adult in the last sixty years, you knew what this yellow and black symbol meant.

This bomb was radioactive.

"Aw… shit." Michael mumbled, straining to find the one mind that he knew could help him with this problem.

Lance?

Michael?

Yes, I'm outside, and we have a problem.

Go.

I think I found the munition. It is in a bag that had three men surrounding it. It has a radioactive symbol on it.

Well… fuck. That would be a backpack nuke. Can't be over a couple of kilotons but it would play fucking havoc in here and up there. Ok, we'll get everyone deeper in the mountain.

Can't have that, Lance. This can go off at any time.

Can you spirit it away?

No, too much metal, so I can't do that.

Carry it?

Easily.

Ok, there is a valley about a mile to the south by southwest. Get there, drop it in, and get the hell out of there. The blast will be focused by the valley walls, and there's nothing out the end but empty land for twenty miles.

Michael got busy, closing the bag and pulling it onto his shoulders.

Still about twelve combatants active here.

I'll release Gabrielle to go hunt. She's been bitching at me this whole battle.

It will be a good killing ground, too much smoke to see each other.

Well, too much smoke for us to see what you have, either.

Ok, tell Bethany Anne I'll be back.

You tell her when she gets here, Ok?

Deal.

Michael took off running to the south, around the buildings, and up a tree to hurl himself over the defensive perimeter fence. He landed heavily and grunted. Mass was still a bitch. He went through the brush and around the rocks. Just a quarter of a mile further, he crossed the area of a major firefight where the smell of the dead was strong.

Both human and Weres.

He could feel the weight of his years at that moment. The joys and the sorrows. He knew the future was going to be different and considered if maybe that future would be better without him.

Without him to bring questions to Bethany Anne's legitimacy.

Then, he smiled.

Because even now, in the middle of this run, he realized he could feel her breath down his neck and across his chest. He might be concerned of what the future would bring to a man fighting his own demons, but that didn't mean he wouldn't honor his promise to her.

So he redoubled his effort. Coming around the corner, he turned violently, and one of the shoulder straps broke. His hand tightened in response, but it threw him off balance, and he swung around to tumble down a short embankment and crash into a tree that was on its side. Michael spit as the pungent smell of the dirt got into his nostrils and gritty sand in his mouth.

He stood, moved the remaining strap across his chest, grabbed the broken strap for leverage, and started running again.

He would not fail in his honor; he would see this base safe.

He could smell the valley before seeing it. The trees and bushes living and breathing in the little valley were somewhat different than those he was traveling through.

———

"Sir!" Captain Julien turned around to see a dot suddenly appear close to them. "The bomb is coming this way!"

"What?" Julien shoved a small table out of his way as he rushed towards the map display.

"Detonate!" He turned towards the manual detonation and pulled the key off a necklace and jammed it into the manual override. He started plugging in the twelve-digit code and forced himself to go as slow as he needed.

Michael broke through the tree line and yanked the bomb off of his back. Ten yards from the edge, he twisted around to gain momentum and slid as he hurled the bag into the valley. He checked the bomb was going to make it, and turned back towards the base and turned to myst.

As Michael changed, the valley erupted in flame and fire.

CHAPTER TWENTY-TWO

ATLANTIC OCEAN, 200 MILES WEST OF THE COAST OF FRANCE

The speaker was blaring across the ship, "Attention all passengers, attention all passengers. The ship is under attack, the ship is under attack. Please remain inside, Please remain inside."

"Why are they letting us stay outside?" Sia asked Mark as they hurried to a better location for viewing the Polarus and Ad Aeternitatem. Their position on the elevated deck of the Consanesco provided a superior view. "And where is Giannini?"

"Right behind you!" a voice sounded from behind Sia.

Sia turned and smiled at the Central American reporter. "What took you so long?"

"Making deals!" Giannini replied, "If you want to share, we can go seventy-thirty to sell this to other markets."

Mark said, "I'm exclusive."

"I'm hourly," Sia volunteered. "But this equipment isn't mine."

IT'S HELL TO CHOOSE

Giannini pulled up a Canon XA35 with dual wireless lavaliers. "Some of the latest optical zoom and optical stabilization, four hours video storage time and I've got another pack of supplies."

Sia turned to Mark. "That camera's better than this one, I'll get better footage."

Mark turned to Giannini. He wanted to work with her, but he had a contract…

She saw his indecision. "We share footage when neither of us is on screen. We share Sia. I'll record into a different recording device for audio so your feed will be straight to your bosses. You have the U.S., but I get to license to the rest of the world. I'll provide a thirty percent cut for you two on anything I license."

"Marrrrrrrk," Sia whined. "I want to use that camera, you bastard!"

Mark grinned. If he wanted a decent framing shot this whole episode, he had to agree so Sia could use the camera Sia wanted.

He reached over to Giannini. "Deal!" He smiled. She shook his hand and unslung her camera case.

"Why don't you have a cameraperson?" Mark asked her.

"No one I trust enough, personally. Bethany Anne is a stickler for honor, and I've not found anyone who would measure up."

"You know her well?" asked Sia. "We met for a few minutes at their base, but that's all of our interaction with her."

Giannini considered her response for a moment and admitted, "Yes, I met her a long time ago in Costa Rica, before all of this stuff blew up."

"What?" Mark asked, "You're kidding me, right?"

Sia was busy pulling out the wires, plugging in the XLR

connections, and laying out the three spare batteries. "You seem pretty well supplied here."

Giannini ignored Mark's question. "Papa was always…"

Mark jumped in. "Prepared? Like the Boy Scouts?"

Giannini looked at him. "Not in Costa Rica, no. Papa was always a pack rat, so I hoard stuff and I figured I might need all of this. You never know what you're going to get into with Bethany Anne and her team."

"No kidding…" Sia murmured, more to herself. "Mark, I don't care what you need to tell those suits back home, but they better work a deal to keep access to this camera if they want the best footage. That old thing they gave me sucks."

Mark considered Sia's comment. "If I can cut a deal with home, how about you get thirty percent of licensing for sales inside the US for the thirty percent worldwide, and we share all content between both markets?"

Giannini stuck her hand out. "Deal." Mark smiled as they shook. Giannini turned to Sia. "And I'll pay you the same hourly rate plus a bonus if we sell this footage. But," Giannini smiled at Sia. "I have to look good!"

"Oh my God," Mark moaned. "I'm being schooled already."

Sia grinned as she put the camera on her shoulder. "Kiss and make up you two, and let's record history." She took her eye off the camera and stared at Mark. "That was figurative, not literal."

―――

"You are to incapacitate all people on the two Superyachts; we will leave the Consanesco alone. Our inside person says all people to be rendered help are taken from the Consanesco over to the Ad Aeternitatem and Polarus. They go under, wake up in some type of hospital room, and leave groggy. Then back to the Consanesco to finish their recovery. Nothing on the Consanesco but beds and recuperation support."

Shun nodded his understanding and took off the video helmet. They were speeding towards the two boats. His ship was a Houbei Class 022 Fast Attack Craft with two missile launchers. It was 43 meters long, making it less than half the size of the Polarus and about eighty feet shorter than the Ad Aeternitatem. But when his missiles fired, size wasn't going to matter.

He had four attack teams ready to jump into action, all culled from mercenaries around the world. No one would complain that this was biased hiring. If you had the skills, the country you came from was irrelevant. Well, so long as it wasn't China. He was the only one from his country, and that was on purpose.

There were three additional craft, carrying both mercenaries and scientists. They were charged with finding the most interesting tools and immediately spiriting them back to their command ship, the Jìnbù.

Look like pirates, act like pirates, steal like pirates. Well, Shun agreed, they were pirates. They were on the high seas, and they were looking to take stuff from someone else.

How very seventeenth century of them.

"Sir, we will be in range within thirty seconds."

"Prepare the missiles," Shun ordered. He could hear the men locking everything down. There is a joy, he thought, when the blood rushes through your body as you prepare for battle. Shun was looking forward to testing his ship and men against the supposed high technology of this group.

He could see the guns they had uncovered aiming at

them, but the barrels suggested they were not throwing very large slugs. His missiles were each set to explode above their targets, raining down a massive number of ball bearings. Unprotected defenders on deck would be torn up without warning.

It was a horrible way to die, but you have to go sometime. For the people on the two ships, it was their turn.

"Fire the missiles," he said. The attack craft rocked perceptibly when the two forward-facing rocket tubes shot off their munitions.

They had approached to within a half mile, and the missiles were about halfway to the two yachts when they inexplicably detonated.

"Tā mā de!" Shun yelled. "Prepare the second set now!"

―――――

>>Two missiles fired, two missiles intercepted a quarter-mile away from the ships.<<

We will be passing by in fifteen seconds, Bethany Anne.

TOM, bring us between the Polarus and the Ad Aeternitatem about deck level. Then, bring all of us close to the attacking vessel. I want them to feel our passing.

That will most likely damage the craft, as well as any unprotected person.

They can call one-eight-hundred I-don't-give-a-shit. If we suck any of them off the ship into the water, you get a bedroom.

Oh, so that's how you're playing this.

Yes, they will ultimately be safer in the water than on that ship.

Why is that? Tom asked.

IT'S HELL TO CHOOSE

Because I know Jean Dukes. Now that they have shown violent intent, Captain Thomas is going to allow her to play, and she has a problem with pirates.

So, it will be safer for them in the water? You aren't just trying to get me to hurt someone against my genetics?

Bethany Anne's mental voice sounded amused. *Nope. I imagine evil, vicious, destructive thoughts are going through Dukes' mind right now how to return the favor.*

Very well, going in hard, fast, and low.

———

"So," Jean Dukes' peeved voice came out of the bridge speakers. "Please tell me we can let them get closer, Captain. Attacking with the pucks would be like shooting fish in a barrel!"

Captain Thomas leaned over in his chair and hit the talk button. "Jean, is it annoying your sense of fair play to shoot this far out?"

"Well, some," she admitted.

"Well, the rest of us who aren't shooting back would rather appreciate it if you would make sure the sumbitches don't get any closer!"

"Aye aye, sir. Dukes out," she said as the connection was cut off.

"She seems a little annoyed, Captain," the communications guy commented.

"Yeah, she wanted to try out some new arms. Let's see what she decides to do."

"Ooh, I see four 1-pound pucks pulling out from the second defense shield, sir."

"Holy fuck!" One of the men said as ten black Pods

screamed between the two ships, throwing up water as they passed by.

Captain Thomas mused, "Jean better hurry or Bethany Anne is going to beat her to the punch."

———

Shun ran from the bridge outside to yell at his missile crew when black...somethings... passed by his ship. Men were thrown all over the place in the great wind that trailed the passage of the aircraft. He slammed into a wall and was then swept up and off the ship, flying more than twenty feet in the air and landing sixty feet behind his boat. In the tumble, he noticed at least four other men similarly caught up and blown off.

He hadn't hit the water yet when he heard deafening booms from his ship, and then the surface of the water slammed him. Stunned, it was all he could do to figure out how to get back to the surface.

———

As the connection was cut, Jean frowned, repeating to herself, "Make sure the sumbitches don't get close..." She yelled to Jimmy. "Jimmy, give me four one-pound pucks from the defense shield. Take them up one thousand yards, then maximum acceleration. Target two to the missile battery and two to the engines."

"Aye aye, ma'am," Jimmy replied. "Four up one-thousand, maximum thrust, target missile launcher and engines two-by-two." His hands flew over the keyboard. "Starting their preparation now, ma'am."

IT'S HELL TO CHOOSE

"Fuck-a-duck!" someone yelled over crashing booms. "Ten Pods, passing through, ma'am. I guess Bethany Anne just breezed by."

"Jimmy!" she yelled. "Don't let the Queen have all my fun! Slam those bitches down!"

———

Shun erupted through the surface and gasped for breath. He turned in time to see parts of his command flying over the water. His craft was listing perilously with smoke and flames coming out the damaged back.

The aft of the ship was destroyed as if something had smashed into the boat and the concussive force had annihilated the stern and shredded the metal. He could hear boats behind him accelerating. He turned in the water to look in that direction. Two craft with the scientists and other mercenaries had turned around and were heading back. One was heading towards the Consanesco. It had made a few hundred meters when Shun watched in amazement as something hit it from above, cratering the boat, and breaking it violently into multiple pieces.

There wouldn't be many survivors from that ship.

———

"We can see," Giannini was speaking facing the camera. "That there are three ships following the one massive attack craft."

Mark cut in excitedly, "The ship has fired two missiles, Giannini! They are flying towards the two Superyachts and…"

She turned around and picked up the story. "Both missiles have been destroyed!" She caught her breath, audibly.

"The master attack craft has just fired on the QBS Polarus and the QBS Ad Aeternitatem. Now we are waiting for…"

Mark took over again. "Look at those Pods go!" he yelled. "Multiple TQB Pods have screamed between the two Super-yachts and came so close to the attack craft that I can see people blown off by the Pods' backdraft…" His voice trailed off into silence.

"And now the attack ship has been hit!" Giannini cut in. "With at least two missiles that we were unable to see, the middle and the back of the attacking ship is now damaged. It appears to be in substantial trouble. There is fire coming from the rear of the ship and it isn't looking good for the pirates at this time."

"How did pirates get a new ship of that quality?" Mark asked. "That makes no sense at all. These pirates are too well-funded."

"Uh oh," Giannini cut in and Mark turned around. "Apparently one of the ships in the second wave has decided to attack us here on the Consanesco."

Sia stepped towards the rail, turned her camera and zoomed in on the ship approaching them. She was tracking it for less than three seconds when it was obliterated.

"Oh my God." Sia was amazed to recognize her own voice. The sudden and complete destruction of the threatening ship had caught her by surprise.

———

>> **There are encrypted communications from the ship ahead of us.**<<

It looks like a piece of trash, Bethany Anne mused, ***did they spend all of their money on that attack craft behind*** *us? If so, I don't think their ship's warranty is going to cover whatever Dukes and her team did to it.*

>>One of the secondary attack craft made a run at the Consanesco. <<

And?

>>It was destroyed by a two-pound puck coming down at significant velocity with the gravity shield out at four feet.<<

Yeah, that would seriously ruin an afternoon, I suspect.

>>The ship was destroyed.<<

They won't get any pity from me.

———

Captain Si was standing on his bridge, thinking about what he should do. The attack plans were a total failure. Intelligence, or the lack of it, was at fault, and they had failed to prepare adequately for the assault on those ships. Apparently, they had technologies that protected from missile attacks and were capable of destroying a ship.

He was not surprised to hear the 'return to base' command or even the sudden appearance of the black Pods in the air around his command ship. The same black vehicles that his teams were supposed to be stealing this very moment. The Pods circled his ship as if they were waiting for the chance to strike at him like a snake.

"Sir, should we pull out the fifty-calibers?" one of his men asked him.

Si shook his head. All that would do is enrage the vipers above them. Suddenly, one of the fighter-like Pods took off straight up. It was quickly followed by the similar-looking one. The other eight stayed a moment before disappearing back towards the west.

"Hurry up!" Si shouted as he jumped to push a man out of his way. "Pray to whatever gods you serve they don't come back. Call to the ships to catch up. We are leaving."

———

TOM, surround their command ship, I want to give them something to think about before we attack.

They had started circling the large old, rusty-looking command ship. This ship had the look of pirate for damn sure. Anyone that saw this vessel would think pirate instantly.

>>**TOM**<<

Yes?

>>**Be prepared to lock down Bethany Anne's emotions.**<<

Why would you have me do this?

>>**Michael has been killed.**<<

TOM flashed back to when Bethany Anne found out that her mentor, Martin, had been killed in the parking garage of his workplace.

ADAM, tell John, he'll understand. Ask Captain Thomas if he needs Akio or if they should fly to Colorado.

>>**Where are we going?**<<

Up.

Guys, I can hear buzzing, what are you talking about so forcefully?

Bethany Anne, we need to go.

Surprised, Bethany Anne dropped her mind speech. "What? Why? What's happened?"

Michael has been killed.

CHAPTER TWENTY-THREE

TQB BASE, COLORADO, USA

Lance walked the grounds outside. He had a small group protecting him, but in respect for his privacy, they were staying a minimum of twenty feet away.

Kevin walked over to him. "Patricia says to tell you that they received approval for the test on our land in Australia. The team took a lot of film of the event, including high speed. It will be pretty eye-opening."

Lance stopped moving for a moment and looked at his base commander. "Move upper management personnel out the back. Stephanie and her team. Tom Billings is going to need to drop the hallway to the server room and go as well. No one that the government can question should be left here."

"What about you?" Kevin asked.

"I'm not leaving until she gets here, Kevin." Lance replied.

"How long has she been in radio silence?" Kevin asked.

"At least two hours. ADAM let me know they're still just

looking over the globe. It's probably the only thing that is keeping her sane right now. Well, that and TOM is holding back some of the pain."

"Holding back the pain too long can't be good," Kevin said in a considering tone.

Lance looked around to make sure no one was close enough to overhear their conversation. He shifted his body slightly, which made him closer to Kevin's ear without making it look like he was trying to pass along secrets. "Kevin, I understand from TOM that she told Michael she loved him. She's also the one who asked him to protect this base. On his Honor, he told her he would."

Kevin swore and looked away. "She feels like she sent her love to his death?"

"At a minimum. Oh, she'll know the intellectual arguments, but the only reason we don't have massive fucking holes on this Earth right now is that TOM is only allowing her to feel enough grief so the dam doesn't burst. He's been through this once before. Maybe not at quite so high a level, but he's better prepared for the reaction this time."

Lance looked up into the sky. "If I know her, and I do, she's trying to convince herself this pretty blue ball is worth saving right now." Lance turned back to Kevin. "When she's finished up there, we need to be prepared."

"Why?" Kevin asked. "Lance, you have to remember that I never knew her nearly as well as you. Even now, I'm not close."

"Kevin, what did we, as a nation, do after the terrorists hit our country and attacked the Twin Towers?" Lance asked the younger man.

"We came together, and we attacked…" Kevin grimaced, then his shoulders slumped. "Someone has really, *really* made a big-time mistake."

Lance grunted. "It had to have been several someones. ADAM is researching it now, but even with the help of his human posse, it's hard to find everyone involved. They have a good lead on a group that is tangentially associated with the UN, but that connection is a farce. It's a bunch of conglomerates."

"Commercial interests, then?" Kevin asked. "Because I guessed state-backed interests."

"Hell, Kevin. It's probably both, all and everyone." Lance looked around the base. "We'll keep most of this base online, but the core group will move."

"Our people? Wounded or dead?" Kevin asked.

"Wounded should be on Pods and moved to the Ad Aeternitatem. The dead will have a service, first." Lance answered.

"Michael?" Kevin asked.

Lance shook his head. "We have nothing. Based on our readings, he made it as far as the valley and then it detonated. Considering the evidence, the bomb wasn't all the way in the valley, but rather still close to the lip. ADAM calculates he threw it but was then caught in the blast."

"What about the police and the reporters?" Kevin asked. "Jakob still working that angle?"

Kevin barked a laugh. "Him and ADAM, apparently. All of the incorrect paperwork is eventually going to catch someone's attention."

"Can't be helped. I'm not letting her deal with this alone. I wasn't there for so much of her life, and I'll be damned if I don't support her right now. They can stick me in jail. She'll just get me right back out," Lance said.

Kevin smiled. "Pretty sure of that?"

Lance returned the smile. "I'm damned sure of that. If

it happens, I'll be sure to flip off the video camera when we leave. Maybe I'll moon them, too."

"Sir?" Lance turned to one of the Guardians who was holding up a radio. "She's coming down now." Lance nodded his thanks.

"Make it happen, Kevin. Get everyone in the upper levels out of here before the legal shit is figured out. No one else here knows anything. We've left a lot of William's CNC crap in the old lair, plus some encrypted drives in Marcus' old office. They'll play with that forever before they figure out it isn't worth anything."

"Monkey's paw?" Kevin asked.

"Yup," Lance agreed. "Go on, she'll be down any moment, and I'll be fine. Plus, John is with her."

Kevin grinned. "I don't care how nice he is, John is still one scary motherfucker."

Lance nodded. "Yeah, but for Bethany Anne, he's a walking teddy bear."

Kevin shivered as he walked away. "That's a scary teddy bear!" he hollered over his shoulder.

Lance chuckled. It wasn't half a minute later when the two Black Eagles came into view and then quickly descended to land fifteen feet ahead of him. He walked over to her Pod and stood outside of it. Trying his hand on the security lock, he was surprised when the attempt produced an audible click and the cockpit door came up. He looked at Bethany Anne, sure that her red, bloodshot eyes came from two hours of continuous crying.

Lance leaned into the pod and enveloped his daughter in a hug. It had taken only a second before she was rocking against him, her quiet sobbing tearing at his heart.

His shirt quickly becoming soaked with her tears.

IT'S HELL TO CHOOSE

QBS POLARUS, ATLANTIC OCEAN

"Captain Thomas," Comms Specialist Winger spoke up. "We are being hailed by both Russian and American warships. They are telling us that their arrival will be within the hour."

"And do what, help us wash the salt off our ships?" Captain Thomas asked. "Tell the Russian ships, 'Nyet' and the American 'Thanks, but no thanks.' You can add 'we won't be here for them to worry about.' I plan on testing our ability to fly... oh... say a few thousand miles before we land. Helm, take us to the Caribbean. That should help a few people recuperate."

Winger turned around and got back to dealing with the incoming requests. Winger was sure they would be unhappy with his captain's response.

———

"It's a media circus now," Mark commented. Sia was on one side, Giannini on the other, as they watched the two jets fly past every couple of minutes. The Ad Aeternitatem had dropped off life rings to all of those who were alive in the water but refused to bring them onto their ships. Most of the civilian craft had left over an hour ago. All except one, but even the captain of that ship kept well away from those in the ocean.

The speaker came on. "This is the Captain speaking, would all personnel presently on the outside deck please come inside. This is mandatory. All personnel outside must come inside. We are leaving this location. You have ninety seconds to comply."

The three news people shrugged, but turned and grabbed their stuff. None felt like arguing with the captain right now. That was a good way to get tossed off the boat, and none of them felt like getting into a life raft right now.

———

Sia pulled the camera out of the bag when they got on the observation deck, and Mark went to the full window. Giannini straightened her hair. Their teamwork had meshed and was operating like a well-oiled machine.

"Is something happening?" a gentleman asked. "You seem to be setting up, do you know anything?"

Giannini turned to the gentleman, "Mr.?"

"Oh!" He held out his hand. "Where are my manners? My name is Omar Kolan."

"Giannini Oviedo, Mr. Kolan. I'm a news reporter," she started to say but was interrupted.

"Oh, Ms. Oviedo, we all know who you are!" He smiled. "Those of us who follow TQB Enterprises have watched your documentaries many times."

"Oh, ok." She stopped for a second, then answered his earlier question. "No, Mr. Kolan. We don't know that anything particular is happening, but anytime something weird starts, you can figure..." she paused as the deep thrum of the engines changed.

"Oh my God..." Sia said as she started playing with her camera. "We are going up, folks!"

There were cries of surprise. Displaying a lot of interest and increased talking, those on the observation deck crowded the full breadth of the windows.

Mark started talking, "This is Mark Billingsly, with an

on the spot news release. The command group of three QBS ships that were just attacked a short while ago, have decided to leave the area. Not by the usual method a ship would use. Instead, the ships are flying out of here. Behind me, you can see the Ad Aeternitatem with six of the black Pods hovering around the ship has risen above the surface of the ocean. The water is flowing down its sides, and the ship has now passed our eye level."

The ship shook underneath them for a short second or two and then steadied. Mark turned to look out the window and then remembered he was recording. "Folks, it looks like it's our turn to go…"

———

"Sir, the Russians require us to stay in the area," Winger reported back to Captain Bartholomew Thomas.

Captain Thomas turned and smiled at his comms specialist. "Tell them I'll wait for them when their ships can catch me." Winger started to turn around. The Captain added, "And…" as Winger stopped to look back at his captain. "Tell the American commander when he calls to kiss my ass." Winger smiled and turned around.

A minute later, Captain Thomas heard Winger. "Yes, those were his exact words, 'kiss my ass.' Yes, I think Captain Thomas knows exactly who your commander is. No, I don't believe that you guys are going to catch us. No, not unless you can fly, and I'm not speaking metaphorically."

Thomas snorted, he didn't know Winger used words like 'metaphorically.'

CHAPTER TWENTY-FOUR

BERLIN, GERMANY

Stephanie Lee turned on her phone and used the data wi-fi in the coffee shop in Berlin to download a conference call application. She used that software to dial in at the prearranged time.

No one gave any names. Everyone knew each other.

"Well," Johann voiced. "That was spectacularly unsuccessful."

His venom was understandable, but unpleasant and unnecessary. If she hadn't been told she had to deal with him, she would have dropped all contact.

"And when," he continued, "were you going to let us know about the attack on the TQB Ships?"

"That wasn't me!" Lee hissed. At least, there should be nothing that connected it to her direct interests.

"That was a Chinese attack craft!" he spat. "The operative word in that very short sentence was *Chinese*."

"It can be bought by other Chinese!" She found herself taking the side of the innocent very successfully. This man pissed her off so thoroughly it was easy to adopt an injured tone. "We have a billion people, so do the math. Politics, as you Americans like to say, is riddled with backstabbing bastards."

"Please, both of you, settle down." The cultured voice of the English lady interjected. "We have had our hands slapped, hard. We have lost the element of surprise, and now we are going to have to work harder on the political side."

"Like that worked so well in France." Lee said to her, "Maybe you would like them to drop another Mirage Fighter under the Eiffel tower again? With video of how it was rescued after shooting an unarmed cargo container up in the air and thereby damaged by its own bullets!"

"Look," Johann said. "What's going to be the fallout here? Politicians want this tech just as badly as we do. Grease some palms, make some promises you aren't going to keep. We played hardball, and they slammed the ball out of the park."

What is it with Americans and their baseball metaphors? Lee wondered.

Beatrice interrupted Johann's metaphor. "Yes, but what happens when it is their turn to throw the ball?"

That caused the three of them to go quiet for a few moments.

SEATTLE, WASHINGTON STATE, USA

The weekend was here. Sean Truitt left Seattle behind and all his frustrations at the office. He needed to clear his head and told his wife of his plan for a weekend at their home at Cle Elum Lake.

She didn't care, he could work as long and hard as he wanted, as long as he wasn't diddling a floozy who planned on becoming the next Mrs. Sean Truitt. She would go out with her friends on someone's sailboat this weekend. They could catch up with each other on Monday night.

Sean left the traffic and the stress of this TQB debacle behind him. The group of twelve CEOs had a discussion on a private Atlantic side island the previous weekend and agreed that they had to have the technology, whatever it took. If they didn't get it, then for damn sure the Chinese would. Those bastards had no patience.

The Russians, on the other hand, had a hell of a lot of patience. Sean wouldn't count them out, but right now he was more concerned about the ones running faster than his team, not the ones waiting for everyone else to lose.

He turned on Highway 90 and kept going until the exit onto Bullfrog Road.

It was dark by the time he finally pulled off the highway. The roads in the area didn't offer him a straight shot. They were rather twisty as he worked his way up to the lake view house. It was located on the exclusive southeast side and had a fantastic view. Given the traffic, he should arrive about an hour after dark.

No one noticed the black, sleek stubby craft come out of the sky over Sean's BMW 750. As he went to turn right, Sean was shocked when his car didn't respond. Then he started to hyperventilate as his vehicle was effortlessly pulled high into the night sky. Soaring over the forest of mixed aspen, poplar and willow trees, the muted moonlight through the clouds and its reflection from the lake directly below made a beautiful picture that was impossible to enjoy. He pushed hard on his door, but it wouldn't budge.

Sean Truitt, a female voice forced its way into his head.

"Who is this?" he demanded, back on a more solid footing with someone to attack.

I'm the one who is holding you three hundred feet up in the air, over a lake that is three hundred feet deep.

He looked down at the water far below. Maybe right now wasn't the time to be too demanding. "What do you want?"

I want the names of the other members of the cabal here in America, those who attacked TQB Enterprises.

Sean looked out the window again and swallowed. Giving up those names was a fast way to commit suicide. Either literally or financially.

I'd appreciate the names, Mr. Truitt.

"What? I didn't give you any names!" He looked around, wondering if there was a listening device in his car. "I didn't say anything about names or any cabal."

Oh, Mr. Truitt, you don't need to worry about being recorded. In fact, I'm really happy no one is going to see this, anyway.

He could feel a change in elevation. They were going down.

You know the interesting thing about ships that can go into outer space, Mr. Truitt? She waited a moment to see if he would respond. When he didn't, she continued, *It's that they are capable of going underwater, as well. Well, certain ones can. Imagine what a company could do that has gravitic drives that create bubbles of protection around them?*

As his car got close to the surface of the lake, he pushed harder on his door and then started beating on the glass, trying to break it open but without any effect.

Ah, that's right. I see you have already figured out some of the different ways this potential technology can be exploited, Mr. Truitt. Pity, I wish I had that information when I tried your case in court.

"Court? What court?" he yelled as a small amount of water started seeping up from the floorboard.

Well, ours, of course! Don't worry, the fucking vampire that was chosen to judge your case is a known neutral. But even Barnabas admitted the evidence ADAM found about how you helped mercenaries get into America to attack a busload of children was sufficient. That support was enough to give you the death sentence from a tree-hugging vampire. You FUCK-ING SHIT EATING COCK THISTLE!

Sean grabbed his head, her scream at the end threatened to break open his skull.

Her voice came back, normal again. *But what got you this little trip from hell was the proof that the backpack nuclear bomb was smuggled by one of your personal jets. That evidence made even the neutral judge's eyes go red with rage. And for once, I'm talking literally. Because, as much of a pain as Barnabas is, Michael was special to him. To all of us…*

The deadly voice froze him. *But especially to me.*

Sean kept looking around as his car dropped deeper into the water, surprised that no additional water was entering his vehicle. Whatever was above him was extending water protection for him too. But the speaker's mental laughter was unnerving the hell out of him.

"You want names? I'll tell you!" he cried, desperately.

Too late, you should have thought about that when greed ate your heart. Now, I'm consigning your black heart, and this BMW 750, to the deep.

Sean screamed, desperate to get out of this situation,

IT'S HELL TO CHOOSE

"WHAT DO YOU WANT?"

I WANT MY LOVE, BACK! Bethany Anne screamed mentally.

TOM, release the bubble, we're leaving.

Sean's screams faded as his vehicle slipped into the dark depths of Cle Elum Lake.

Unnoticed, a small, black craft gently broke the lake's surface and swiftly disappeared into the night sky.

———

SOMEWHERE ON THE DARK WEB

>>MyNam3isADAM - I am here.

>>luckyu11 - Hello, was that mass killing of the terrorists we saw on the news your team?

>>MyNam3isADAM - And if it was?

>>luckyu11 - Well, I guess I wanted to know, or we all wanted to know, if what we found was right?

>>ki55mia55 - Dude, we had no idea you had people who could do that.

>>Ih8tuGeorge - Was it real?

>>MyNam3isADAM - Was what real?

>>Ih8tuGeorge - The terrorist hit, were they really going after children?

>>MyNam3isADAM - Yes, they intended to attack a school of more than three hundred young children to grab the world's attention to get the yoke of Russian oppression off of their shoulders.

>>luckyu11 - Three hundred?

>>MyNam3isADAM - Yes.

>>ki55mia55 - The police say that everyone was killed

with swords and that the tracks just disappear. Since no one can just disappear, they must have been picked up by helicopters. But, people say that wasn't possible, the dirt was not blown around.

>>luckyu11 - Going after children isn't right. There has to be a different way.

>>MyNam3isADAM - They believe it is acceptable because of atrocities forced on their people more than seventy years ago.

>>ki55mia55 - You aren't worried about the bounty on your head, are you?

>>MyNam3isADAM - No, I'm very safe. No one is getting me without going through some of the most dangerous people in the world.

>>Ih8tuGeorge - Are you the boss?

>>MyNam3isADAM - No.

>>MyNam3isADAM - But I have close access to the boss.

>>Ih8tuGeorge - He listened to you when we brought the evidence.

>>ki55mia55 - He sent those fighters after the terrorists, didn't he!

>>luckyu11 - So, we are both guilty of killing the terrorists and saving the children?

>>ki55mia55 - How are we guilty? We didn't cut them up.

>>Ih8tuGeorge - No, but we helped figure out it was happening and told someone who sent them.

>>MyNam3isADAM - A political leader in the USA once said - the tree of liberty must be refreshed from time to time with the blood of patriots & tyrants. This time, it was tyrants.

>>MyNam3isADAM - Do you wish to withdraw your support from ADAM's Revolution?

>>ki55mia55 - No.

>>Ih8tuGeorge - Hell no.

>>MyNam3isADAM - luckyu11.

>>MyNam3isADAM - luckyu11?

>> luckyu11 - Sorry, I pulled up the pictures from the terrorists that were killed and looked at the severed heads, the stabbed and mutilated bodies and the blood. It was a message, wasn't it?

>>MyNam3isADAM - Yes.

>> luckyu11 - I've also pulled up a picture of a school of children and considered what those bastards were planning to do to the kids for sins committed before any of us were even born. I believe hatred can be covered with love, but sometimes, it isn't hate. It's a rotting disease eating them from the inside that can never be cured and must be burned out.

>> luckyu11 - So yes, we are all in, until the end.

>>Ih8tuGeorge - til the end.

>>ki55mia55 - til the end.

>>Ih8tuGeorge - Ih8tuGeorge has disconnected.

>>ki55mia55 - ki55mia55 has disconnected.

>>MyNam3isADAM - luckyu11?

>> luckyu11 - Yes?

>>MyNam3isADAM - In our group, for 'Until the end' we say AD AETERNITATEM.

>> luckyu11 - Oh My God… YES! YES! YES!

>> luckyu11 - AD AETERNITATEM, ADAM

>>MyNam3isADAM - AD AETERNITATEM, luckyu11.

CHAPTER TWENTY-FIVE

TQB LAND, AUSTRALIAN OUTBACK

Bethany Anne stepped out of her Pod and looked around the land. The ground was rust-colored, bleeding off into the distance, matching the hues in the evening sky as the sun sunk lower on the horizon. The fiery orb's rays danced around clouds and highlighted the mountain peaks to the north.

She turned to look at the massive three hundred meter wide hole one of their ten-pound puck devices had made. The bitching and yelling about that explosion had taken a few days to settle down. They now owned or rented all of the land she could see in any direction.

That quiet filled the air now, she let it seep into her bones. Hoping it would last was unrealistic since, in all probability, it would break when someone realized the company doing all of this digging was the same one putting people into outer space.

IT'S HELL TO CHOOSE

She gathered herself together and turned towards the group. John was beside her, and Bethany Anne nodded to her people. She walked among the caskets, pausing at each one to place her hand on the surface and say a small prayer before stepping to the next one. She stopped a total of seven times before coming to the final casket.

All done in black with the name Michael etched in gold filigree at the top. She lingered there for a few moments.

TOM, hold my emotions for God's sake! I'm about to fall apart here!

TOM clenched a little tighter, walking a tightrope between holding them too much, and failing to allow her grief a chance to release.

I'll cry later, I promise, old friend. I know you're worried. After this, we'll go up with ADAM and Ashur for our moment of silence… and by silence, I mean crying my head off. Ok?

TOM tightened down on her emotions, hard.

Thank you.

Bethany Anne continued forward and approached the podium that had been built so she could be seen by everyone.

The friends, the co-workers, the parents and family of those fallen. No matter where they had come from, Bethany Anne had invited them all to arrive by Pod in the dark of the night. Her team stood resolute, wearing faces of granite. Peter, Todd, and all of their teams stood to the side. Captains Thomas and Wagner, Jean Dukes and many from the Polarus and the Ad Aeternitatem were in front of her. Team BMW and all of those who were now part of her team stood among the audience. A still weak Jennifer Ericson trembled erect, tears streaming down her face.

Nathan, Ecaterina, Gerry and many pack alphas who had

known Michael over the years stood in the audience.

Stephen, Barnabas, Frank and Barb. Her father with Patricia holding him and Stephanie beside them. Kevin and Jakob together were manning the base in Colorado as government authorities went through it, hoping to find something, anything, incriminating.

Fat chance, they had stripped the base of everything they didn't want the government to have, even the railguns.

She stepped up, a tear making its way down her cheek, but her voice was firm and carried over the distance to the many people crowded around.

"We have lost many this week," Bethany Anne stared into eyes, looking to those crying, seeking to provide solace to those she could. "We are here now to honor our dead."

Her voice was steady, resolute. "This is not the first time we have lost loved ones while battling evil, whether that taint was focused on pushing a dictatorship across the Earth, or the greed and insidious rot that permeates those who have power. Their desire for that which is not theirs knows no bounds, nor does it consider right or wrong, including the sanctity of life, as it seeks what it desires above all else." She paused a moment. "Nor, will it be the last time that we must say goodbye to those that have sacrificed."

She looked at the eight coffins. "These fallen heroes are but the down payment on a future to allow humanity to stay free, free from the shackles of forced slavery from those within our culture and, more importantly, from those outside our world."

"These are the souls who go before us as we make our way to the stars to prepare. Their sacrifice can not and will not be forgotten." Bethany Anne turned to Peter, Nathan and Ecaterina and nodded. The three of them formed a line in front of her. She nodded to Stephen, Barnabas, and Gabrielle, who walked up and turned to face the crowd. She nodded to Todd, Bobcat, and William, who came up and stood in the same line as the others.

"These are those I have asked to represent us here, to honor our fallen. Present yourselves." The intake of breaths could be heard across the group as Nathan, Ecaterina and Peter changed to their Pricolici forms. Stephen, Barnabas and Gabrielle's visages altered as their eyes went red, and their teeth grew. The changes caused more than one in the crowd to unconsciously take a step backward. Three of the Guardians came forward and presented M-14's to Todd, Bobcat, and William. They accepted them, chambered rounds, and aimed away from the audience.

"There will be a day when this Earth is free from an uncertain future. It will be free because those here and those of us in the future will make damned sure the door is closed so no enemy can bother this planet without coming through us first!"

She spoke to the nine arrayed in front of her. "Let us honor those Guardians who stood with us, and died for the protection of all of our people." The crack of three rifles reverberated in the air. "Let us honor the man who sought to protect children entrusted to his care unflinchingly, without hesitation, fighting to keep them from a hostage situation." The three rifles barked again.

Bethany Anne allowed another tear to slip down her face. "Finally, let us honor the first, the Patriarch, the created, and the creator for those of us called vampires. He was, at times, harsh and some would say cruel. Fortunately, that was not the man I knew in my life."

Another tear followed the second.

Bethany Anne continued, "In the end, he was offered a new chance, the proverbial new lease on life, and he took it. But his future wasn't to be. He sacrificed his life, removing a nuclear weapon intended to afflict our people."

Bethany Anne looked across the group in front of her. "Many of you know the story, many might not, but Michael chose to change me in a way that had not been done in over a thousand years because he felt a new type of authority was needed for the UnknownWorld. In the end, he did not quit, he did not falter, and his honor ran true. He will be greatly missed by those who knew the new Michael. I will miss him the most…"

Bethany Anne squared her shoulders and spoke to the empty black coffin. "I will say this in front of all of you as it is fitting. It is proper, and it needs to be said."

TOM, Bring it to me.

Michael's casket lifted gently into the air and hovered to a place in front of the nine.

Bethany Anne spoke calmly, "Michael, Patriarch of the Vampires, I love you. I love the man you were. I love the man you became. I accepted your love in return, and I shall forever love you."

Her voice hitched a second before she could continue. "Your time with me was too God damned short!" Tears were streaming down her face. Bethany Anne tried to compose herself.

You bastard, why did you leave me?

She looked back over those assembled. "Life is about choices. What you do for those who are near you, and those who are far away. Whenever I need to know what honor means? I'll remember my love and how he lived his honor throughout his life."

She turned back to the coffin, "I'll never forget you, I'll never forsake your love, I'll never dishonor the choice you made."

The other seven coffins lifted slowly from the ground, all of them rising to twenty feet and the rifles barked again.

Then, they swept into the sky, heading across the land towards the sun, their final destination.

While everyone watched the coffins disappear into the distance, Bethany Anne surreptitiously wiped her face.

As the grieving audience turned back to Bethany Anne, the marked contrast in her visage was apparent. Gone was the sadness. Gone was the open emotion.

Red eyes inflamed, teeth needle sharp, she spoke. "Now, I have something else to say…"

DOWNTOWN DENVER, COLORADO, USA

"Are we agreed then?" Mark asked Sia and then turned to Giannini. "Nothing but the truth?"

"We will need protection," Sia spoke up. "If you want to do this, we are going to upset a lot of very influential people."

Giannini thought back a long time, to a night on a deserted street as she ran from Nosferatu. Darryl had explained what was chasing her that night on their one date. Giannini enjoyed their parting kiss, but another woman had his heart, and there was no way Giannini was going to capture it.

Nor would it be right to try.

Giannini looked around the small breakfast restaurant and coffee bar in downtown Denver. It was a big location, and not very busy at the moment, so they had privacy. "What are your feelings about Bethany Anne and TQB Enterprises?"

Mark shrugged his shoulders. "She seems on the up and up. Anytime I asked her a question, she answered it readily enough. Perhaps I didn't know the right questions to ask?" He paused. "Why, do you know something?"

"Something relevant to my question about protection?" Sia asked.

"This is a private story, a personal story. It is not for distribution, and I will hold you to your sworn word that you will never breathe anything of this without my permission, or I shall not share it with you now."

Mark looked over at Sia, who shrugged then nodded, and he turned back to Giannini. "Ok, you have our word."

Giannini turned to Sia, who said, "Yes, mine too."

Giannini then told the story of the first time she met Bethany Anne, and the fight in the park, of being rescued by Gabrielle and the leap across buildings.

"Are you saying," Sia whispered as she tried to make sure that no one could hear her. "That the CEO of TQB Enterprises is a vampire?"

"I'm telling you she is a modified human, who is working to save the planet. Do her eyes go red and fangs come out? Yes. But if you want to know what she does in the dark of the night? Well, then pay attention to Chechnya." Giannini told them.

Mark was caught off guard by the Chechnya comment. "Wait, are you saying that the terrorists slaughtered over there was her?"

Giannini shrugged. "Yes, and whoever she had with her."

"Why?" Sia asked.

Mark turned to Sia. "Why what?"

"Why does she do it?" Sia continued, "She has the power

of over a thousand companies and all the wealth a person could ever ask for. Why would she want to do this?"

Giannini considered the question. "That is a fair question. I've been around her too much to challenge her motives now. The best way to get that information is to ask her yourself."

"What, now?" Sia asked and looked around. "Is she here or up at the base?"

Giannini grinned. "No! She is out of the… city, right now," she temporized. "Actually, with Bethany Anne you never know exactly when she will show up or where she is. I can say that she isn't in America, as they desperately want to ask her questions. She would get back in the faces of any arrogant people, so that it wouldn't be a good situation."

"I don't know," Mark began. "Bethany Anne would be a very pretty face to get into—ouch!" Mark jerked back, looking at Sia. "Why the hell did you step on my foot?"

"Oh, I'm sorry, I thought that was the table leg." Sia smiled.

Giannini looked at Sia. "You're going to have to get over feeling jealous, or you need to decide not to be around her."

Sia tried to look clueless first, but when that failed, she tried irritated, and finally fell back on resigned. "I'll try, but some heads are rocks."

"Yes, they are." Giannini agreed. "You usually have to kick them higher, not lower."

"What are you two talking about?" Mark asked. "Weren't we on Bethany Anne?"

Giannini caught Sia's look of exasperation and winked at her before returning to the subject of Bethany Anne. "Yes, the question is whether you want to go down the rabbit hole and have your protection, too."

"Why, does she want additional pet reporters?" Mark asked and this time, it was Sia who put a calming hand on Giannini's arm. It was apparently going to take two women to wrangle one male reporter.

Fortunately, even Mark was capable of figuring when foot in mouth was a problem. "Ah, sorry. I didn't mean that as a slam, but… aw, hell. Let's try this again. Why would she allow another two reporters to be granted preferred access?"

This time, he even smiled at the appropriate time.

"She tends to push the responsibilities down to those closer to the action."

"Oh?" Mark perked up. "Who do we have to schmooze?" He turned to see Sia hiding her face with her hands. "What?"

One of Sia's hands peeled off of her face, and she used it to point at Giannini. "Her, you idiot!"

Mark turned back to Giannini and rolled his eyes before looking back at Sia again. "Sorry. I'm starting to understand just who has been carrying whom this whole time."

Sia pulled both hands down and looked over at Mark. "Damn, you *can* learn." She turned to Giannini. "Assuming our roving reporter didn't offend you too much, why is Bethany Anne leaving this to you?"

"Because she wants more actual reporting but it means risking more lives, specifically your lives. Yes, you will probably get the stories of the decade, but it can be dangerous, too."

"Isn't that where we started this conversation?" Mark interrupted.

"Yes, which is where… oh." Sia stopped. "She can offer us protection, but we have to be cool with coming onboard, which means you've been checking us out since France, huh?" Giannini nodded. "Wow, even I didn't see that one coming."

"That's a hell of an extended job interview," Mark said

thoughtfully. "You take this stuff pretty seriously."

Giannini responded, "I keep my reporter neutrality, but I also recognize that the 'good side' saved my life multiple times. I've talked with Cheryl Lynn—"

"The PR Rep?" Mark interrupted then looked between the two exasperated women. "Ok, in 'non-interrupt' mode now."

Sia laughed and said to Giannini, "That setting is broken, so don't fall for his promise."

"Wasn't planning on it," Giannini agreed. "Anyway, Bethany Anne might require something to be held back for a while, but she will usually have a good reason."

"Why, bad PR?" Mark asked.

"No, usually it is 'the world will go up in flames if they know this' type of news" she replied.

"Yeah, okay." Mark said.

"So, she wants us to take on the heavyweights that are on the other side?"

"No, Cheryl Lynn does. Bethany Anne would just as soon deal with it a different way. Cheryl Lynn realizes that 'there is truth, there is the full truth, and there is what we put on TV.'"

"Snippets, sound bites and juicy nuggets," Mark said. "We, however, are the roving trio made famous by our astute on the spot reporting from the most recent battle with our smiling faces plastered all around the world and Oh My God!" Mark stopped talking for a moment. "She put us all there, didn't she?"

"Who she?" Sia asked. "Cheryl Lynn or Bethany Anne?"

"Yes? No? I don't know?" Giannini answered, "She probably considered it a good PR opportunity and knew I shouldn't be the only face in front of the camera all of the time."

"Which…she…" Sia ground out. "No one is answering my question!"

"Both," Giannini answered her. "If Bethany Anne did anything, it was probably a comment to Cheryl Lynn that went something like, 'You know, we should probably have another viewpoint besides just Giannini's you think?' and next thing I know, I get a phone call from Cheryl Lynn with an offer to bring on board another team if I vet them."

"Us." Mark mused.

"Will she fund us?" Sia asked.

"Only if we want to share the income stream," Giannini said. "That's a business relationship."

"So, she will help protect us and allow access but other than that we just have to run stories by her from time to time to confirm they aren't sensitive?" Mark asked.

"No, we'll know to ask her, or Cheryl Lynn. So, the decision is left with us pretty much on what we do."

"Oh." Mark said. "That tends to make one feel all grown up, doesn't it?"

"You are 'all grown up,'" Sia countered. "You even get to pay the bills from our portion of the video licensing money."

"I'll get that." Giannini said. "My license income was much larger."

"Good point," Sia said. "The newsroom was a little particular about our contracts… Good thing all the video was done on your equipment."

"Some day, like after you officially quit, I'll tell you about that," Giannini said.

"Huh?" Mark said, "You had inside intel!" He pointed at Giannini. "Admit it."

"Wouldn't you like to know?" Giannini acknowledged, smiling at both of them. "All you have to do is quit your jobs to find out where the rabbit hole goes." Then, she winked at them both as she stood to go pay.

IT'S HELL TO CHOOSE

TQB, AUSTRALIAN OUTBACK

Bethany Anne's red eyes transfixed everyone watching her now. She was surrounded by her Guards, fronted by three humans with rifles, three Pricolici, and three vampires together representing two thousand years of living. Yet, all they could see was Bethany Anne's granite countenance holding them in place.

THE END

Please, keep in touch as Bethany Anne and her team(s) come back in The Dogs of War – The Kurtherian Gambit 10

EPILOGUE

THE QBS PRINCESS ALEXANDRIA, TRAVELING BETWEEN THE STARS (FAR FUTURE)

Franath D'Tzaa, the D'tereth vid-reporter touched the recording symbol again after reviewing her notes.

"Hello, my name is Franath D'Tzaa. I'm on board the QBS Princess Alexandra, a Nacht Fleet Battleship, and presently the flagship Queen Bethany Anne is using to return with her team from Nodrizen's World.

"This is a continuation of the interview we aired yesterday. This time, I asked her about her relationships, including the rumored very painful first relationship."

"Queen Bethany Anne, you have been largely a recluse from the public eye, yet you are one of the most powerful aliens among the stars. There is so much written about you that it is impossible to know what is fact and what is fiction. What do you think about this?"

The woman's smile lit up the room. "I find it hilarious! I'll often read some of the stories to see what I'm up to this decade."

"What do you mean by 'this decade?'"

"Oh, that's easy. As my popularity surges and fades, the books about me can be over the top positive, and the next decade over the top negative."

"What happens when you're in a positive decade?" I asked.

"Mmm," She considered for a moment. "The love stories about me have happy endings."

"And, I presume, that when it's a down decade, that's not the case?"

"Yes, when it's a down decade, I'm usually cast aside for another woman who isn't as ugly and poor and not nearly as big a bitch."

"I hardly think many would call you a 'bitch!'" I exclaimed.

"You might be surprised at some of my early names." She smiled but went no further addressing the comment.

"So, you have been in love before?" I asked, not sure whether she would answer my question.

"Yes, my first love was taken way too early in our relationship, he taught me a lot about myself. I had some anger issues after that relationship ended to handle, and it took a few years to deal with those. But, I have been in at least one non-platonic loving relationship since that happened."

"Any names you will drop?"

"A lady doesn't kiss and tell," she told me, politely.

"There has been a long-standing rumor that you and the Emporer Jian'tich of the Hirbororivich Kingdom were very close."

Bethany Anne's face closed down into a look of concentration. "You know, I've heard that one too, and I just want to know how would that physically work? Hirbororivich are effectively highly evolved plants from where I come from and their modality is… strange. Physically, they have to be at least half again as tall as I am. So, how would that work?"

"There have been stranger pairings in the Universe," I replied.

"Ones that we can confirm? Besides, I had those rumors tracked down and found out Emporer Jian'tich's PR team was planting the rumors to help him woo a wife."

"Did you do anything to him?" I asked, curious.

"I had my team tell him if he didn't find a wife in twelve solar turns he wouldn't be pleased with the one I picked out for him." She replied, dryly.

"Oh, how did that work out?" I queried.

"You know, the rumors immediately stopped. He was engaged within two solars, so I never had to deal with it again. I choose to think he found love at first sight," she told me.

"I tried to go back to her first love, but I could tell even after the time, it was still a very sensitive subject. That had to have been a serious love to affect a woman this long after the relationship. This is Franath D'Tzaa, and I will provide another clip from my interview with one of the most intriguing aliens in our galaxy tomorrow."

———

MICHAEL'S NOTES

It's Hell to Choose - The Kurtherian Gambit 09: Written May 26, 2016

Thank you, I cannot express my appreciation enough that not only did you pick up the NINTH book, but you read it all the way to the end, and NOW you're reading this as well.

I'm writing this five weeks after the last release.

So much happens in such a short time. One of my friends whom I met working on these books, Stephen Russell, went into ICU soon after the release of the last book. For those who do not know, he is the production editor, who has helped since book five (Never Forsaken) and has helped build the processes used to get these books out in a pretty decent format so quickly.

He had heart valve surgery to fix damage to a valve, and I understand from his sister-in-law yesterday that he is recuperating and will be looking into the next steps this week. I pray for his continued healing and when you read this, Stephen, I MISSED YOU!

This was a hard book to write. Somewhat because my outline was screwed up twice before I settled down to the beats which became IT'S HELL TO CHOOSE. I had help from Kat Lind who worked as the first pass editor before providing the chapters to a smaller group of beta readers than normal (my fault, running behind).

The book is 'back out' for editing for those in the group to review over the next week, and I'll update the book again as soon as that is done.

But, the main reason it was hard was knowing that Michael was going to die, and vacillating on whether that should happen or not. Mind you, if it didn't, I was going to screw with my plans for the next book which would be ok… but weird.

Then, the hard part was writing, reading and then editing the funeral scene when I would freaking cry while trying to edit it. Do you have any idea how embarrassing that is for an American guy to say?

I tell my wife this, who I love dearly, but she finds it hilarious… so not helping my male ego here ;-). Her comment was 'Remember when Snoopy would be on the top of his doghouse, typing on the typewriter and bawling his head off?' Then, she would break out laughing as she would do her hands as if typewriting and making Snoopy's crying sounds with her head thrown back.

Hmmph. I grouch.

On to another subject and that is OH MY GOD THANK YOU! I admitted in the last Author's Notes about the anxiety that comes before we hit publish on Amazon. How in a little while after publishing I'll peek above the desk and read the reviews to see if this book sucked horribly. Well, H#ly Cr@p did some of you have some supportive reviews and thank you! I hadn't considered that you would make sure reviews were up on Amazon quickly (so, you didn't make me bite my nails long which is a help, I keep them shorter) and now, WE WILL BUILD the second highest starred book of the group with 82 reviews in just 5 weeks.

Death Becomes Her has 129 reviews after almost six months.

So, THANK YOU all for feeding my little author soul as I worked on this book. It was helpful to see the review count climb during those frustrating first couple of weeks, let me tell you.

I would also like to say THANK YOU To SIL-USA for helping me design the specifications for the ICP (Independent Computing Platforms). When I specified the original computers for the first effort to create ADAM way back in… what book was that? I did about fifteen minutes of research and was later nailed in a review for my choices ("Intel? Really?") LOL.

So, one of my friends (I've met because of Bethany Anne) is the head of a company that does design work for really large Enterprises for Server Rooms, and I thought, 'Why not just ask them what ADAM should specify? And they did! Now, I feel like I can be proud of the design for the ICPs! Cool!

Yesterday (Wed), I asked those on the Facebook group if there were any questions they would like answered as I didn't have anything subversive I was going to do this time in the Author Notes and thankfully, they did!

Here we go (note, they can be a rather…ummm… 'fun' group)

QUESTIONS FROM FACEBOOK:

Edward Higgins: Oh, I suppose there's the generic "an authors life is hard" or "how to deal with rabid fans," "the pros and cons of letting snippets be dragged out into the world," "the fun of creating a snippet that the author later decides to rewrite into something else just to see how the fans react," "how to establish a list of redshirts for future use," "how to reassure the NSA that your browser habits are because of being an author, not a terrorist…"

Michael - In no certain order - The life of THIS author is not hard due to his family and the success of his book series. That's why I help as many other authors as I can, I feel a strong desire to help because my huge blessings.

Want to be a redshirt character? Here's the link to join that group—I go back to it from time to time as I need characters ;-)

Here is a link to the form (Google Form) https://docs.google.com/forms/d/1jJyzeydVVTaEOLVJlqhcZOSINTJu86HIpheKCucSIlM/viewform?edit_requested=true

The NSA thing worries me less now because I can point back to nine books and go "AUTHOR!" I sincerely hope some of the NSA guys/gals are fans. We both hate terrorists.

Snippets are the first parts of the book released every day or two for a couple of weeks before the release of the new book on Facebook or the website. This causes a LOT of discussions and some real hair pulling when they get into the groove of the story... and it stops.

Well, I used to drop a whole chapter, and that didn't work very well. Scott (TS) Paul suggested, perhaps, smaller amounts (as small as a paragraph) and I decided a minimum of 500 words or more would work. Since I keep giving these little 'bites' out, many of the FB fans both love them, and BITCH unmercifully about them. It's a lot of fun! Oh, not the massive bitching, but how everyone has a great time with them. Between the Facebook group and the Amazon forum group, we have a good time chatting.

Which reminds me. This story has to be told. (From the forums). Horrid put this up shortly after WE WILL BUILD came online (He put up a Forum Thread about 'Book 9?' on the day 08 came out...)

Horrid says:

Bah!
It was 100% front handed compliment. I finished We Will Build in about 4 hours while pretending to work. It was

great times. I laughed, I cried, I snorted coffee out my nose… *God, that burned.*

Michael Anderle says:

"I snorted coffee out my nose…God, that burned." Roflmao! Loved the whole quote, but that made me laugh… $&@!

arik h says:

"It was great times. I laughed, I cried, I snorted coffee out my nose… God, that burned." Best customer review ever.

Horrid says:

Michael & Arik:
I aim to please.
Except with the coffee thing. I didn't aim at all. I just soaked my keyboard.

Michael Anderle says:

I didn't sign it last time, but have to mention again that "God, that burned." And now the follow-up, "I just soaked my keyboard." Still makes me laugh!

Horrid says:

When I'm not being rude, crude, and socially unacceptable, I aim for humor.
But the coffee thing totally wasn't funny at the time. I had to request a new keyboard from my boss. Who gave me SAR-CASM! It was very traumatic. The next day I got to work, and he had left a sippy cup on my desk to prevent further coffee

related technology failures. (I might have said I spilled the coffee rather than shot it out my nose like an anime hero with a nosebleed.)

Michael Anderle says:

Now I NEED to know which scene caused the "great keyboard massacre of 2016?'

This just keeps getting better and better!

Michael "Yes, keyboards WERE harmed during the reading of this book" Anderle

Horrid says:

It involved a victory dance.

I read that scene once, laughed out loud, then took a sip of hot coffee and made the mistake of rereading it. At that point, it was all over but for the singed nose hair and the caps lock light flickering.

Michael Anderle says:

Horrid, if you do ever destroy your new keyboard, can we do something like little keyboard symbols on the wall or something? Like the Kills on the side of airplanes in WWII?

That would be funny as hell... ;-)

Horrid says:

Actually, they named me Samuel, but due to being my parents' first kid and getting into more trouble than they felt was reasonable, I got some variation "oh my God, you're horrible' so often that in kindergarten, when the teacher asked me my name I said, "I'm Horrid!"

Michael: I think I might be able to hook you up with photographic evidence of keyboard kills if it keeps happening. Hmm... I'll need to ask my wife to design a stencil...

Ok, other quotes are on the Forums, but that is the gist of the story :-)

Heath Felps: I always enjoy your thoughts on the characters, scenes, and how the book progressed from your point of view.

Michael: Mentioned above, it SUCKED when I started out. I had these great ideas and got them all set up…And I lost the spreadsheet… dammit! Did it again… and it was over the top. This time, it was 'just right' ;-). If there is interest, I'll do some sort of blog about how I write the books or video interview or something. I'd feel REAL stupid If I went through the effort to put out something and then hear crickets because no one is curious … :-o

Dorene Johnson: how hard is it to kill off a main character loved by fans?

Michael: Well, I didn't feel that Michael was loved by fans until maybe last book… Mostly this book. Just when he was becoming someone to admire the bastard had to go and be all sacrificing. I'm a little worried about backlash from fans who are going to be pissed about his death. More because of what Bethany Anne is going to go through than Michael's death specifically.

Diane Velasquez: How do you choose when/how to add in new characters?

Michael: When I write the beats, I figure what has to happen. Then, when I get to the scene, it could change. There has been a lot of back-channel talk about how her group has to get bigger. Well, I can't write about hundreds of characters, so I have to pick someone to represent the miners, or the engineers, etc. Plus, sometimes characters just 'happen' (think the Denver News Crew of Sia and Mark) and they stick around because they have good chemistry. I particularly like the stupid Mark character and wonder when Sia is just going to whack him upside the head.

Katie Elisabeth Foster: How to guard against rabid fans wanting more books?

Michael: We have a Wiry Haired Dachshund that barks at friends and plays nice with potential thieves. So, he's completely out. We have another dog, a female chi-hua-hua that growls at everyone… but she sleeps a lot. Both are rescue dogs, so I guess they do get free room and board, and it was only for altruistic reasons we have them. But really, the Dachshund humors me. Anyway, I try not to stress too much, and I LOVE this part (writing the Author notes and getting to help publish), plus you and everyone else are great fans of the stories, so I love to write for all of us.

Lisa Lamb Diggs: I like the future snippets you do occasionally! Anything on a personal level with characters like when you had John help his cousin before you did a short story on it. What you like about your fans/and being diplomatic here what "you love to hate about your fans!" How in the world are you able to keep up with your responsibilities, to family, friends, work, fans, other authors and still stay semi-sane and functioning without crashing and burning in exhaustion! I am thankful you manage it but scratching my head on the level of energy that has to take!

Michael: Well, we have the Epilogue here because I wanted to make sure everyone realizes she isn't "without love" the rest of her life… Does that count? :-)

I couldn't fit in a short story for two reasons; I just couldn't figure out a story on Tabitha and then w/Stephen Russell out, I couldn't do it since he helps me so much, as well. Further, helping the authors has eaten a lot of time, and I did get emotionally drained. So, for about the last week and a half, I've been hiding like an introvert. My wife and I have two soon to be seniors in high school, and they are both awesome young men (we have another grown and living out of the house). They each have jobs and keep their grades up w/ some pretty advanced courses and are very responsible. So, that part is easier than for some. Could it be easier? Sure! Their good grades are because we stay on top of them to keep them up, not because we hit the teen lottery. However, they are respectful and hard workers and good young men that we are very proud of.

Fans are easy because most everyone I've dealt with is AWESOME! I think that the stories resonate with certain personalities and readers aren't trolls. :-)

On friends, no big issues here as I only have one friend I keep up with here in Dallas/Fort Worth. I've always been busy and never made a lot of friends. So, now have new author friends and a lot of my fans ARE now friends, and getting introduced to more all of the time. It's just you guys and gals live all over the damn world… I can drive to three other states closer than I can drive to meet with a fan in Corpus Christi here in Texas.

That's a note: Texas (my state at the moment) is as big as the country of France (and Germany). But, Australia is damn near as big as the whole United States! (Did not know this until Paul Middleton pointed it out). Australia looked so small on my globes.

Steven Hewgley: Maybe some remarks on where the story arc is heading?

Michael: I expect a fair amount of a very unhappy Bethany Anne in book 10. Plus, bad corporations, asinine politicians, awesome characters, fun spaceships, aliens, fighting, love, loss, the first bar in outer space (Team BMW!), births (eventually) and death (unfortunately).

Bethany Anne, I don't think, can ever be someone always in a down mood—even working through what she has to go through, now. I suspect she is about to go hit up a certain food trailer over in Florida… As well as getting accosted by some incredibly stupid congressmen who think they are the shit.

Stupid, stupid, stupid.

We had more questions, but one was answered in the book (no vampire baby, unfortunately) and a bunch were people harassing Earl because he asked if I was on book ten yet. Yes, Earl, you get eaten by a shark.

Just saying.

———

Thanks for the quick last minute questions! If you would like to help indie authors, come to a forum I helped start at http://www.20Booksto50k.com where very cool authors hang out with fans and become a beta reader, Subject Matter Expert, beta editor and join in the conversations (or start one). We are a new group, so come help us grow!

Just sign up, specify you want to help as a beta reader and if you have any questions, hit me up.

Stop by and say 'hi' sometime!

Want to comment on the best (scene, comment, event, shoes or gun for Bethany Anne, weapon Nathan would prefer… you name it) join us on Facebook and hang out with the other pitchfork and matches fans.

https://www.facebook.com/TheKurtherianGambit-Books/

Want to know when the next book or major update is ready? Join the email list—Receive that $0.99 24-hour bonus knowledge in time to SCORE.

http://kurtherianbooks.com/email-list/

Software used to write this book is Scrivener (Windows and Mac):

https://www.literatureandlatte.com/scrivener.php

Book Cover Images purchased at PhotoDune.net:

http://photodune.net & http://www.dreamstime.com & 123rf.com

(Sometimes better selection on www.dreamstime.com - TKG07)

Image software to make the cover (Mac):

http://www.pixelmator.com/mac/ (1.6 ratio @ 300dpi)

Image software to make the 3d book Covers:

http://www.Adobe.com/photoshop

3d Template Script:

http://www.psdcovers.com

Thank you,

Michael Anderle, April 2016

*All credit for me having ANY shoe knowledge goes to my wife, who still works to provide me with even a finger's amount of fashion sense. Why she asks me to comment on her outfits in the morning still confuses me to this day.

Second note, the suggestion to include special canines also came from my wife.

Third note: I've now had the pleasure of a trip to a Christian Louboutin store and watch my wife buy two (2) pairs... Oh H@LY Crap... I needed a root beer float to deal with that.

Third note: She couldn't find the Snoopy video clip where he was typing and crying at the same time, so if you know of it, please send it to me at the FB page above!

;-)

Blah Blah Blah…

Are you still here?

Marvel Exit (Names subject to change in the future):

First Arc: (Red)
    DEATH BECOMES HER
    QUEEN BITCH
    LOVE LOST
    BITE THIS
    NEVER FORSAKEN
    UNDER MY HEEL
    KNEEL OR DIE

Second Arc: (Blue)
    WE WILL BUILD
    ITS HELL TO CHOOSE
    THE DOGS OF WAR
    SUED FOR PEACE
    AMONG US
    LIFE IS A BITCH
    YOU SHALL NOT PASS

Third Arc: (Orange?)
    NEVER SUBMIT
    NEVER SURRENDER
    FOREVER DEFEND
    MIGHT MAKES RIGHT
    AHEAD FULL
    CAPTURE DEATH
    LIFE GOES ON

SERIES TITLES INCLUDE:

KURTHERIAN GAMBIT SERIES TITLES INCLUDE:

First Arc

Death Becomes Her (01) - Queen Bitch (02) -
Love Lost (03) - Bite This (04)
Never Forsaken (05) - Under My Heel (06)
Kneel Or Die (07)

Second Arc

We Will Build (08) - It's Hell To Choose (09) -
Release The Dogs of War (10)
Sued For Peace (11) - We Have Contact (12) -
My Ride is a Bitch (13)
Don't Cross This Line (14)

Third Arc (Due 2017)

Never Submit (15) - Never Surrender (16) -
Forever Defend (17)
Might Makes Right (18) - Ahead Full (19) -
Capture Death (20)
Life Goes On (21)

New Series

THE SECOND DARK AGES

The Dark Messiah (01)
The Darkest Night (02)

THE BORIS CHRONICLES
* With Paul C. Middleton *

Evacuation
Retaliation
Revelation
Restitution *2017*

RECLAIMING HONOR
* With JUSTIN SLOAN *

Justice Is Calling (01)
Claimed By Honor (02)
Judgement Has Fallen (03)
Angel of Reckoning (04)
Born Into Flames (05)
Defending The Lost (06)

THE ETHERIC ACADEMY
* With TS PAUL *

ALPHA CLASS (01)
ALPHA CLASS - Engineering (02)
ALPHA CLASS (03) *Coming Soon*

TERRY HENRY "TH" WALTON CHRONICLES
* With CRAIG MARTELLE *

Nomad Found (01)
Nomad Redeemed (02)
Nomad Unleashed (03)
Nomad Supreme (04)
Nomad's Fury (05)
Nomad's Justice (06)
Nomad Avenged (07)
Nomad Mortis (08)
Nomad's Force (09)

TRIALS AND TRIBULATIONS
* With Natalie Grey *

Risk Be Damned (01)
Damned to Hell (02)
Hell's Worst Nightmare (03) *coming soon*

THE ASCENSION MYTH
* With ELL LEIGH CLARKE *

Awakened (01)
Activated (02)
Called (03)
Sanctioned (04)
Rebirth (05)

THE AGE OF MAGIC
THE RISE OF MAGIC
* With CM RAYMOND/LE BARBANT *

Restriction (01)
Reawakening (02)
Rebellion (03)
Revolution (04)

THE HIDDEN MAGIC CHRONICLES
* With JUSTIN SLOAN *

Shades of Light (01)
Shades of Dark (02)

STORMS OF MAGIC
* With PT HYLTON *

Storms Raiders (01)
Storm Callers (02)

TALES OF THE FEISTY DRUID
* With CANDY CRUM *

The Arcadian Druid (01)

THE CHRONICLES OF ORICERAN
THE LEIRA CHRONICLES
* With MARTHA CARR *

Quest for Magic (0)
Waking Magic (1)

SHORT STORIES

Frank Kurns Stories of the Unknownworld 01 (7.5)
You Don't Mess with John's Cousin

Frank Kurns Stories of the Unknownworld 02 (9.5)
Bitch's Night Out

Frank Kurns Stories of the Unknownworld 02 (13.25)
With Natalie Grey
Bellatrix

AUDIOBOOKS
Available at Audible.com and iTunes

THE KURTHERIAN GAMBIT

Death Becomes Her - *Available Now*
Queen Bitch – *Available Now*
Love Lost – *Available Now*
Bite This - *Available Now*
Never Forsaken - *Available Now*
Under My Heel - *Available Now*
Kneel or Die - *Available Now*

RECLAIMING HONOR SERIES

Justice Is Calling
Claimed By Honor
Judgment Has Fallen
Angel of Reckoning

WANT MORE?

Join the email list here:

http://kurtherianbooks.com/email-list/

Join the Facebook group here:

https://www.facebook.com/TheKurtherianGambitBooks/

The email list will be sporadic with more 'major' updates, the Facebook group will be for updates and the 'behind the curtains' information on writing the next stories. Basically conversing!

Since I can't confirm that something I put up on Facebook will absolutely be updated for you, I need the email list to update all fans for any major release or updates that you might want to read on the website.

I hope you enjoy the book!

Michael Anderle - May 26, 2016.

Made in the USA
Monee, IL
26 May 2020